B 2.64

H. Me/K

D1319893

GREEN ROSE OF FURLEY

Books by Helen Corse Barney

FRUIT IN HIS SEASON

GREEN ROSE OF FURLEY

GREEN ROSE
OF FURLEY

❧ ❧ ❧

BY HELEN CORSE BARNEY

❧

Crown Publishers, Inc. New York

PRINTED IN THE UNITED STATES OF AMERICA
BY THE HADDON CRAFTSMEN, SCRANTON, PA.

TO MY FATHER

FRANK ELLIS CORSE

FOREWORD

For the benefit of the curious, may I whisper the fact that there really existed a Furley Hall, which in its heyday was surrounded by broad acres of flourishing gardens. Although this delightful Quaker home was selected as a background for my story, the narrative is entirely fictional, and does not relate to any persons living or dead. In fact, the characters were named much as a parent labels a child in honor of some beloved connection.

In the gardens of Furley there once bloomed a green rose, the Rosa Chinensis Viridiflora. The bush lived for a phenomenally long time, but I presume that it perished some fifty years ago from the flames that destroyed the venerable mansion.

My historical data were gleaned from many sources, principally from Scharf's *History of Maryland,* Volume Three, published by John Piet in 1879. For the stories of escaping Negroes, I relied largely upon reports from older members of the Friends Meeting, especially upon those of my Cousin Alice. This dear Quaker lady left with me rich childhood memories: fragrant strawberries served with pastry which I ate while I listened round-eyed to her anecdotes of the Underground Railroad. With slight modifications I pass these stories on to you.

CHAPTER
ONE

The soft darkness of a summer night crept gently into the valleys of Maryland bringing with it a temporary sense of peace and security, although the year was 1862 and the nation rocked with restlessness and apprehension.

Through the valley the waters of a lazy creek bubbled and purred contentedly, cows slept in the lush grass of the pasture land, and on a slight rise above the stream, the brick chimneys of a massive Georgian mansion pointed skyward.

So stood Furley Hall, like a mother hen with wings outstretched to shelter its sleeping brood. Between the wings rose the main body of the house, two stories high, with a spacious attic tucked beneath the roof. Surrounding the Hall, landscaped gardens lay wrapped in the whispering harmony of the night, a sleepy symphony, warm and mysterious. Here and there in the garden, the darkened branches of giant lindens and maples offered hospitality to cheery robin and quarrelsome jay.

From an upper window of the Hall, a dim light made a tiny patch of brightness and silhouetted the figure of a young woman who appeared cautiously at the window and rested her round arms for a moment upon the sill.

Her wide blue eyes strained into the dark tunnel of the tree-bordered driveway as she bent her head and listened attentively. To her alert hearing came the incessant murmur of the creek, the chorus of frogs along its bank and the chirp of crickets in the pasture land. The night breeze toyed with her brown curls and brought with it a suggestion of roses and boxwood from the garden below.

A sleepy voice sounded from the poster-bed in the lighted room. "Sister Susan, what's thee doing?"

"Hush, Hetty," came the quick reply. "I thought I heard Pa coming along the road, although it's much too soon. I'm so anxious about him."

"La, Susan, come on to bed. Pa can always get himself out of a tight spot. Thee'll catch thy death of night air."

Susan did not answer. Her quick ears had detected the brisk tread of approaching horses, and she was listening for the reassuring noise of heavy wheels upon the graveled drive.

After a moment she turned from the window and snuffed the candle. "Someone's coming," she said nervously. "I can hear two horses but no wagon. Spies may be out to watch or even search our house. Thee'd better get dressed again and come downstairs. If we have trouble visiting us, we've got to dispose of it before Pa arrives with the packages."

Life was exciting to Hetty, and she would be heartbroken to miss the thrill of two horsemen arriving unannounced. Scorning the bed-steps, she leaped with agility to the floor, and began pulling on her clothes.

Without waiting for her sister, Susan left the room and stood for a moment at her mother's bedroom door. There was no sound, so she crept on down the hall past the room where her two younger brothers, Billy and Frank, were fast asleep, past the room where she had tucked her sister, Myra, away for the night, and finally she reached the wide stairway. It was still dark except for the dim pattern of light outlined by a fan window above the massive entrance in the hall below.

With her hand lightly on the stair rail, she hurried downstairs. She reached the front door just as the horses clattered up to the house. There was a moment of intense expectancy while Susan lighted an oil lamp on the table by the door. She heard the laughing voices of two men out by the hitching post, then their heavy steps on the drive and across the porch.

In this Quaker home, where Negroes fleeing from slavery were given shelter and assistance, the cruel slave-catcher was always an imminent threat.

Susan was braced for just such an emergency, and without waiting for the vigorous banging of the knocker which would surely have alarmed her mother, she slipped the bolt and hospitably swung open the door.

Instead of the sheriff, she was amazed to see the happy face of her Cousin James, the only child of her Aunt Cassandra.

"James," cried Susan. She embraced him warmly. "Come inside, dear James. I'm so very glad to see thee."

In her joy and relief, she had not noticed the tall young soldier who stood modestly in the shadow. Now James stepped aside and said to his friend, "Come on in, Calvin. This is my cousin, Susan Coale, Calvin Pancoast."

Susan greeted the stranger falteringly. In the darkness of the porch, she had not noticed his attire. Now, by the light of the lamp, she saw that both young men were wearing the dark blue uniform of the Union army.

She was aghast. Fighting was prohibited in the Quaker Book of Discipline. To disobey the rules meant that the culprit must become an outcast from the Meeting. The Society of Friends was inexorable in that respect. James would be found guilty of a willingness to engage in "human butchery" and he would be forever disgraced. She stared at him with unbelief.

The joy faded from his face. "I know," he said softly. "It hurts thee to see me like this, but remember that I, too, have been brought up on the Discipline. It instructs us to obey the dictates of conscience, and I feel I must join in the defense of our Union. But come, can't thee give two weary officers a smile and a bite of food? We are as hungry as bears."

Immediately Susan was her usual self. "Of course. Forgive me. I was startled and a bit shocked, but I'm sure thee always does what thee feels is right. Come with me and I'll see what Aunt Henny can produce on short notice."

Thus reassured, James carried the lighted lamp to the dining room and set it on the table, where it cast a warm glow on polished mahogany and gleaming silver.

"Sit down, please," said Susan. "I'll tell Aunt Henny to bring some refreshment."

At this moment Hetty opened the door, peeped in anxiously, and then, with a surprised and delighted cry, hurried into James' arms.

"Hetty," he exclaimed admiringly, "I declare thee's quite grown up since I last saw thee—and pretty, too."

"A little less surprise in thy voice, and I'd take the remark for a compliment," she said, and laughed. "Thee must have expected a fright."

"Dear Cousin," he chided, "thee knows I meant it in the right way. Now may I present Calvin Pancoast, who is my friend, neighbor and lieutenant."

She welcomed Calvin with all of the prettiness she had practiced before her mirror.

Susan, watching her with amusement, became suddenly conscious of the fact that she herself had been rather awkward in her greeting. She also noticed that this tall young soldier who had appeared so unexpectedly out of the night was extremely personable. His dark hair waved above a broad sunburned forehead and his eyes, deep-set and kindly, held a yearning sadness. He might be interesting. But now she must attend to his physical hunger.

"If you will excuse me for moment," she said, "I'll see about something to eat."

She descended three steps and crossed a hall leading to the kitchen.

"Is dat you, Miss Susan?" a voice greeted her from the darkness. "You comes a creepin' in yere jest like a speerit."

"I'm a very healthy spirit, Aunt Henny. Has thee anything cooked? Cousin James is here with a young man, and they are hungry."

"Where's dem udder folks? I got victuals cook a plenty jist a waitin' fer Mister Willum ter bring 'em in."

"Pa hasn't come yet. He won't be here for some time."

"Yassum." The old woman waddled to the pantry, and brought out a baked ham which she sliced and arranged on a platter. To this she added some cold chicken, a salad of eggs and potatoes and a bowl heaped with fresh strawberries. By the time she had finished, the rolls were heated in the oven, and Susan helped her carry the feast to the dining room.

James was standing at the mantel. With obvious pleasure, he watched Hetty's efforts to entertain his friend. She was a vivacious creature, he thought. Really an amusing little piece, and so improved. She was rounding out in the right places and might still be a beauty like her two older sisters, Cornelia and Susan. But neither Cornelia nor Hetty could compare with Susan, so capable and so understanding. He adored her, but then, so did all her family.

Susan entered the room carrying a heavy tray, and he sprang to take it from her. Calvin, however, reached her first.

"Please allow me," he begged.

She released the tray, and smiled her thanks. As he stood holding it awkwardly, his eyes caught hers and held her gaze compellingly. Her heart throbbed faster. Consternation seized her, and she turned away from him to lead the way to the table.

"Bless my soul, Aunt Henny," cried James to the aged

Negress, "if thee isn't healthier than ever. Is thee glad to see me?"

"Yassuh, I sure is," said Aunt Henny. "But don't you go making fun of my fatness. I reckon I gotta taste stuff afore I feeds it to my white folks. It's dat tastin' what stick to my ribs."

"It's not all on thy ribs," he teased. "But what do I see? Ham? Chicken? Let me at it. I haven't had a good meal since I left home a week ago."

They sat at the table for a happy half-hour. James told about various experiences he and Calvin had shared, and of their final decision to join the army. From among their friends they had raised a company of a hundred men, and it was agreed that James should be their captain and Calvin his first lieutenant.

"How did you decide?" asked Hetty.

Calvin grinned. "That was easy. He enlisted more men than I did."

"And now," said James, groaning, "I'm unable to swallow another morsel. That dish of strawberries with so much rich cream would have stalled a less starved animal. I am too full to move, but I must see my favorite aunt. Dare you rouse Aunt Deborah from her slumber?"

Susan hesitated. "Mother will want to see thee," she said, "but she will be surprised and grieved."

He nodded. "Perhaps thee had better go ahead of me and warn her," he suggested.

She rose at once. "We'd better go right away before Father gets home. He is away—on business." Her voice assumed an anxious tone. "Hetty, thee entertain our guest and we will be down directly."

Hetty did not need a second invitation. She led Calvin to a porch which overlooked the rose garden, and there she engaged him in an animated though one-sided conversation.

It was there that James and Susan found them some minutes later.

Poor Deborah had been shocked indeed to learn that her sister's only child had enlisted in the army, but she readily forgave him.

"And now," announced James, "we must be on our way. By sunrise I hope to be through Baltimore and well along toward Washington. Our men will be impatient, Calvin. Let's get started."

"Thee knows," warned Susan, "that Baltimore, while still in Federal hands, is a very hot-bed of Southern sympathizers?"

"Yes," agreed Calvin, "but we understand that the situation is under control."

She answered gravely, "It was very bad when the Pennsylvania troops transferred from the Northern Central to the B. and O. railroad. There was some bloodshed. Now the people are more accustomed to the sight of troops, and it's not likely you'll have any trouble."

He looked very serious, and said in a quiet, convincing tone, "We are here to bring order and we would not want to create confusion or be a cause of violence."

Susan felt a growing respect for and confidence in Calvin. Glancing up, her eyes met his frankly and understandingly. He smiled and she felt the quick color flood her face.

Hetty cast a sidelong glance at Calvin. "Thee'll come soon again, won't thee? Oh, please say thee will." The little minx is trying to get herself a beau, Susan thought.

The lieutenant bowed, and turning to Susan, said, "Thank you very much for such delightful hospitality, Miss Susan. I hope to see you soon again."

When they had gone, Susan turned down the wick in the oil lamp and watched the flame flicker into a thin column of smoke. Then she followed Hetty upstairs. Something was wrong with her. For no explainable reason, she felt out of patience with Hetty.

When she reached her room, she found Hetty already out of her petticoats.

"Oh, Susan," Hetty whispered rapturously, "isn't Calvin just too divine to be human? Does thee think he really likes me?"

"Very likely," answered Susan. "How could he help himself? Don't thee think it's a bit indecent to go after a man so obviously? And, Hetty, what's the use of falling in love with him? Pa would never let thee marry a soldier. Thee'd be read out of Meeting like poor Sister Cornelia when she married her Episcopalian."

Hetty buttoned her stiffly starched nightgown. "As to that," she said impudently, "I'm not so sure that I'd care."

"Hetty," begged Susan, "thee doesn't know what thee's saying. Think of the disgrace to the family."

Hetty made a face. "My family could live it down," she suggested. "Besides, I don't think that anyone should accuse Calvin of doing wrong. He is fighting merely to uphold a principle and he believes he is doing right. It's all in the way we look at it."

Very dramatically she seized the sheet and draped it into a toga about her thin body. Mounting the steps to the bed, she struck an attitude and cried, " 'The fault, dear Brutus, lies within ourselves.' "

The bed swayed beneath her, and she fell in an ignominious heap among the pillows.

In spite of herself, Susan was forced to laugh. Without undressing, she curled up beside Hetty to wait for her father's return from his dangerous errand.

CHAPTER

TWO

❧ ──────────────────────────────

Susan tossed restlessly. Her thoughts were torn between her father's mission and wonder about the two Union officers.

It was after midnight when she roused with a start. Distinctly now, she heard the clomping of hooves on the pebbles and the crunch of heavy iron-rimmed wheels.

She sprang from the bed and noiselessly crept downstairs to the kitchen where she found Aunt Henny dozing before the empty fireplace.

"Dat you, Miss Susan?" whispered the old woman.

"Yes, Aunt Henny. Pa's coming. Thee can get ready, for I hear the wagon in the drive."

Aunt Henny waddled to the door, dropped the wooden bar and drew the chain. As the door swung open, a heavy wagon drawn by two stout horses came around the house and stopped. In the faint light it could be seen that a small forest of maple and evergreen trees stood upright in the wagon, for the owner of Furley Hall was a Quaker nurseryman, and the wagon was of the uncovered kind used for hauling trees and shrubbery.

As the sweating horses came to a stop, a rich cheerful voice issued from the darkness. "Daughter Susan, is all in order?"

"Yes, Pa. Did thee get thy packages?" Susan asked anxiously.

"I did indeed," he replied, "one large bundle and seven little ones." At that, he whistled softly.

Immediately there was a stirring of leaves and branches on the wagon, and a colored woman with an infant in her arms scrambled stiffly from her hiding place among the trees. Six small children climbed after her to the rear of the wagon and she lifted them down.

Susan and Henny herded them quickly into the welcoming shelter of the kitchen, and as the door closed behind them, the wagon rumbled its way to the barn.

"My land sakes," exclaimed Aunt Henny, "how she ever run away wif all dem young uns hangin' on her? She jest like a possum."

The poor slave was too frightened to answer, and Susan said kindly, "I dare not make a light here, but thee bring thy children and follow me to the attic. What is thy name?"

A trembling voice replied, "Keziah, ma'am."

"Very well, Keziah. Come now."

A small child whimpered, and Aunt Henny lifted him in her comforting arms and carried him to the top of the attic stairs. "Dere now, honey," she said. "Don't you cry no more. See, Miss Susan makin' a light."

Susan lighted an oil lamp and Keziah gazed about her fearfully. The window was covered by a quilt.

"See, Keziah," Susan said cheerfully, "nobody will find you here. Aunt Henny will bring you some cornbread and milk, and then you must get some rest. Don't be afraid. We'll take good care of you."

The Negro woman, her eyes streaming with grateful tears, said impulsively, "Missy, may God bless you fer all you done fer my pore chillen." She leaned against a cupboard and sobbed. "Oh, missy, I so skeered count of my ole man Jasper. Dey'll sho' beat him daid."

"Perhaps not, Keziah," comforted Susan. "Stop crying and tell me what happened."

The woman wiped her face against her sleeve and in a broken voice told her story. "Massa, he need money powerful bad. Fust off, he done sold our two big boys, fourteen an' fifteen. It near bust mah heart seein' dem carried off ter slave market. Dey was cryin' dey eyes out." She twisted her hands together in an agony of remembrance.

"That was very hard, Keziah," said Susan softly. "Perhaps we can get them back again. I can't promise, but we will surely try."

"Yassum? Dat good and I sholy thanks you." Somewhat heartened, she continued her story. "Last night, man come to see massa. Jasper, he in pantry an' he hear what dey talks. He powerful skeered. De man go home an' massa done tole Jasper ter git four mo' chillen ready for a new home come mawnin'. Pore ole Jasper, he cry an' beg, but it warn't no use." She rocked from one foot to the other and little rasping sounds came from her throat.

"There now," comforted Susan. "My father will help thee, but why didn't Jasper come away with thee?"

"He stay back so he kin throw dem slave-ketchers off our scent. He wait twill things gits quiet in de big house. Den he gits a wagon from Quaker man name Mistah Moore, an' he fetches us to Mistah Moore's house. Dat way, can't no hounds foller us."

"What did Friend Moore do with you?"

"He done lift us down to Norfolk, an' a man hid us on boat an' spread big sail all ober us. Us sail all night an' all today, an' den your pappy git us from boat an' fetch us here."

"What will thy master do when he finds you're missing?" asked Susan.

"Dat I dunno. Jasper, he'll ack like he supprise. He gonna

say I want him to hide dem chillen in a cornfield, but he'll say he love he massa too much fer dat."

Susan was skeptical. "Does thee think thy master will believe such a story?"

Keziah shook her head sadly. "First off, he believe. Den he gits all de folks out ter hunt fer us. Dey don't find us in no cornfield, and I skeered what he do wid Jasper."

Old Henny reappeared with a pitcher of milk and a trencher of cornbread, and proceeded to dispense hospitality to the hungry little ones.

"Come now, Aunt Henny," said Susan. "Father will want to have the house quiet. Good night, Keziah, and have no fear. God has helped many good colored people on their way to freedom, and God will not fail thee either. Get thy rest now, and I'll come to thee in the morning."

She led the way downstairs and saw Aunt Henny safely to the loft over the kitchen. William Coale had come from stabling the horses and was waiting for her in the sitting room. She kissed him fondly.

He was a man of medium height and handsome appearance. Good living and temperate habits consistent with the Quaker tradition had tended to enlarge his waist, but William was a man of indefatigable energy and his many activities had kept his figure from becoming overportly. He had a firm handsome jaw, a straight nose and remarkably blue eyes that twinkled with kindly humor. His one vanity was a brown wig that drooped across his broad forehead and hid the tops of his ears. He wore the clothes of a country Quaker of some means, their plain cut and drab color relieved only by the whiteness of the hand-sewn linen shirt and stock.

From William, Susan had inherited firm features, clean healthy skin and twinkling eyes as blue as the larkspur in her flower garden. And it was from him that she had developed a fine appreciation of the gentler qualities of the spirit, a kindliness and a protective nature.

Now she addressed him with quiet eagerness. "I wish I had been with thee, Pa. Was it very exciting?"

William smiled at her enthusiasm. "No more than usual, although there is always added risk when we are carrying little children and have to keep them quiet. However, I arrived at the wharf after dark and the captain helped me transfer his dangerous cargo to my wagon. Then I came home by back lanes to avoid search officers. Word has not yet got around about Keziah, but by tomorrow or the next day, there will be handbills posted, and it will be impossible to move a woman with seven little children. Everyone suspected of harboring runaway slaves will be closely watched. I think Keziah will have to stay right here until I can get a letter to the Central Committee in Philadelphia. They will send a boat down from Elkton, but it may take several days."

He spoke calmly, but there was a hint of anxiety in his voice which did not escape his daughter. "Now thee get to bed, my Susan. I'm going to Baltimore in the morning and thought thee might like to ride along. Henny can look after our charges while we're away. Now I must go to Mother. She won't sleep until she knows I am safely home."

"But, Pa, before thee goes, let me tell thee what happened this evening. Cousin James arrived from Germantown. He has raised a company of fighting men with himself as captain. He brought another officer with him, a wonderful fellow, and, Pa, thee'd never guess."

William's eyes twinkled. "I can, too. Hetty fell in love with the officer."

Her eyes widened. "How did thee know?"

"I know Hetty. She's probably in love as usual, but did thee consider whether she was in love with the officer or with his uniform? Don't let it worry thee. The thing that distresses me is the news that James has so far deviated from the way of Truth as to abandon the instructions of the Friends Discipline. I must go to thy mother at once."

With his arm about her, father and daughter proceeded quietly up the broad staircase.

Susan set the lamp on her dresser and removed her frock and linen petticoats one by one and hung them in her wardrobe. Having buttoned herself into a long-sleeved high-necked gown, she combed out her curls, plaited her hair in two pigtails and extinguished the light.

Before joining her sister in the high poster-bed, Susan peered anxiously from the window into the peaceful garden. Across the darkness of its flower-bordered walks, the deeper shadows of the linden branches swayed gently, making grotesque shadows among the shrubbery.

An owl hooted in a tree close by the window, and there was a slight rustling as a mouse scampered to shelter.

God, who was mindful of all his creatures, would protect his black children. Susan breathed a little sigh as she joined Hetty in the security of the poster-bed.

CHAPTER
THREE

A mockingbird's repetitious call wakened Susan. She lifted her head and thoughtfully observed her younger sister who was still asleep, one thin arm hugging the pillow. Susan saw that Hetty's face was beginning to round out and lose its impish expression. Long dark lashes lay against her cheek and hid the mischievous blue eyes. She was almost beautiful.

Very softly Susan crept from the bed, dressed and went to her mother. By this time William would be up and perhaps a mile or two away, riding his saddlehorse about the nursery while he issued instructions to his hired Negroes.

Deborah, frail and beautiful, was waiting for Susan, who, as she entered the room, made her mother smile with pleasure. "A good morning to thee, my dear. Father tells me that his errand was successful, and I'm so concerned about the little refugees. Thee leave me be for the moment, Susan, while thee runs up to the attic and brings me word of them, that's my good girl."

Susan obeyed eagerly. Aunt Henny was in the attic ahead of her, and was about to administer a sticky-looking mess to a little boy who cowered wild-eyed against his mother.

"What's the matter, Aunt Henny?" inquired Susan anxiously.

"Dis yere li'l Jerry, he spittin' up he gizzard," explained the old woman. "I'se givin' him a yarb tea."

"He scared sick, ma'am," added Keziah.

Susan was troubled. "It's much too hot up here," she observed. "Suppose thee carries Jerry down to thy room, Aunt Henny, and cares for him there. I'll speak to Pa about fixing a cooler hiding place, perhaps in the cellar."

"It ain't too hot, miss," said Keziah apologetically, "and don't you go to no bother. Ef I kin jest keep my pore chillen away from them slave-ketchers, us kin stand a li'l heat."

"We'll see," promised Susan absently. With so many children, Keziah would be a problem to move from one hiding-place to the next. This was only June and the attic would get hotter as the summer progressed. It seemed obvious that the refugees must be passed along on their journey northward as quickly as proved feasible. Meanwhile Keziah would have her hands full keeping so many little mouths closed, for if spies came on the premises, it would not do to have a hive of little bees buzzing under the roof.

Leaving instructions with Aunt Henny to see that the children were properly cared for, Susan returned to her mother. If she felt troubled, Deborah must not know of it.

"They are all in good spirits," she reported, laughing. "Pa is going to take me into town this morning, and we'll stop at Cousin Thomas Scott's and pick up some clothing for them. Cousin Sarah tells me that she has a big chest full of things for all ages and ready to distribute as needed. Then, when the children are bathed and dressed presentably, I'll bring them down to thy room for an exhibition. Thee never saw anything cuter than the little ones. They're as black as ink and have evidently been well fed."

Deborah smiled contentedly. "I shan't worry about them," she promised. "With thee and Father to plan for them, I know everything will be satisfactory."

Susan settled her on the porch and left her to the care of the other daughters, Hetty and little Myra.

"Now thee run along, and get thyself ready for town, my dear," commanded Deborah.

"I will, Ma," promised Susan. She ate a hasty breakfast while Aunt Henny scolded.

"You better had take your time and eat your breakfast," she grumbled. "Pushin' in victuals so fast make you skinny and ugly like a ole weasel."

"Never mind about the future, Aunt Henny. Is my dress ready?"

"Yas, miss. I got it laid out all press nice."

"Thank thee, Aunt Henny."

Susan ran upstairs and hastily changed into her second-best. It was none too soon, for promptly at eight o'clock, William was ready with the carriage. Promptly at eight, Susan came from the house, and Aunt Henny's yoke mate, Uncle Toy, assisted her to the seat beside her father. The drab gray of her shawl and bonnet set off the color and sparkle of a face glowing with youthful anticipation. William rattled the whip in its socket, and at the sound, the two horses set off at a brisk canter down the maple-bordered drive. Now that they were alone and safe from prying ears, they could discuss their problems.

"Has thee any plan for moving thy packages, Pa?" she asked anxiously. "It's pretty hot up there under the roof and I wish we could contrive a safe hiding place in the cellar."

"I've been considering something of the sort," answered William thoughtfully. "As for moving them northward, the way has not been revealed to me. God will take care of them all in due season. This morning we will stop to see Thomas Scott, and while thee selects suitable clothing for them, I'll arrange with Thomas for transportation."

"I wish we could help Keziah's husband, Pa. Can't we?"

William nodded. "We not only can, we will. I got up early this morning and wrote a letter to Friend Moore who helped

Jasper get his family out of Virginia. I have asked him to superintend the man's escape and also try to locate the two boys who were sold in the slave market at Richmond."

"How could he ever find them?" asked Susan.

"There will be a record of the sale and he will go to the purchaser disguised as a peddler. That is the way he operates. After showing his pins, needles and other wares, he will get permission to sleep in some outbuilding on the place. When night comes, he will visit the slave quarters and talk with the two boys. By morning, he will have them miles away."

For a while she was silent, revolving these matters in her mind. Suddenly she remembered something. "Pa, on our way home, does thee mind stopping at Clifton, please? Cousin Johns Hopkins offered to give Myra a puppy, and I'd like her to have it."

"How did he happen to offer the dog?"

Susan smiled. "The last time he was at Furley he was amused by the way her white duck follows Myra around, and he laughed when she told him she had named it for fat old Uncle Oscar. Then Cousin Johns told her he would give her a puppy."

"We won't stop at Clifton," William said, smiling, "but I expect to see Johns Hopkins at his store, and I'll remind him about the dog. I'd like Myra to have it. She seems inclined to a heaviness that is unlike my high-spirited daughters. I'm minded to buy some kind of spinet for her. What does thee think of it?"

"Pa!" Susan's blue eyes grew wide with unbelief. "What would the Friends say to having music in our home? They might appoint a committee to visit us and tell us it's wrong. Then we would be disowned."

William frowned. "I've considered that possibility. In Myra's case, I'm buying the instrument to help her retain her poise, and I believe the Friends will be broad-minded."

"Well, Pa," she said slowly, "if thee is very sure in thy mind, let's brave the Meeting and get it today."

Accordingly, they drove first to Stieff's piano store and arranged for the purchase. That very afternoon, the instrument would be delivered.

Now that the deed was done, Susan was very happy. As they left the store, she said, "Oh, Pa, did thee notice the beautiful satiny wood, and the little wreath of flowers painted on the cover? Myra will love it."

"I trust it will meet her need," answered William. "But now I want to visit Hopkins' store and stop at another shop, so suppose we drive down Broadway."

The horses went slowly over the cobbled street, avoiding country wagons, for as they approached the market, they found the way cluttered with vehicles.

"This is market day,'" observed William, "and I suppose the fruits and vegetables have the right of way. Suppose we stop here under this big catalpa tree, and thee hold the horses until I return from my errand. I'll not be gone long and thee can look across the market place and watch the activities there." He passed the reins to Susan, climbed over the wheel and disappeared among the marketers.

Glad for a rest in the shade, the horses stood quietly, and Susan looked about her with interest. People were passing to and fro busily. Ladies, followed by slaves carrying market baskets, went from stall to stall buying vegetables and meats. Right before her was a flowerstand, bright with color and sweet with the odor of roses, and there across the street, an aged man walked about selling sweet lavender and musk. Against this colorful background, a pair of Mendicant Sisters from a nearby convent were going solemnly on some errand of mercy. It was a fine, lively scene.

The peaceful sounds of the market place were suddenly interrupted by the sharp rat-a-tat of a drum and a squad of blue-clad soldiers swung into view. As they came to a halt near Susan, people rushed from every side and soon a small crowd had collected. Farmers leaned across their stalls to listen, and a lean hound hurried from a nearby alley to push his way among the spectators.

Finally, the drums were still, the crowd quieted down and the officer in charge made a vigorous appeal for recruits. A great buzz of conversation and excited shouts followed. A man stepped forward. Immediately two others joined him. At this display of patriotism, the crowd broke into wild cheering. Flags were waved and excited voices sang "Yankee Doodle."

Suddenly a woman's shriek sounded from the market stalls, and a moment later a goose egg, somewhat the worse for age, came hurtling toward the three recruits. It missed them but smashed against the wall over their heads and spattered them and the bystanders. There was wild cheering again.

A police officer arrested a market woman and led her, protesting, to jail. As soon as quiet had been restored, the squad shouldered arms and marched down the street and out of sight.

Susan sighed with relief. She had watched the little drama with excitement. Now she wondered what was keeping her father, and she looked eagerly in the direction he had taken.

Less than a block from where she sat, Susan noticed a group of men collecting around a platform. They put their heads together, apparently to hear a coarse story, which caused loud guffaws.

A moment later a bell rang and an auctioneer, whip in hand, mounted the platform. From a door behind him, an enormous Negro, naked except for a pair of short britches, was shoved forward to the slave block. He was ordered to stoop and stand, to lift heavy weights and flex his muscles. The buyers crowded about him to examine his condition. The bidding started and the coarse voice of the auctioneer urged it on until, finally, he yelled, "Gone for fifteen hundred dollars."

The new master led the unresisting Negro to a wagon and they drove away.

That was over. Susan looked about for her father, but he was nowhere in sight.

A young mulatto girl, grinning and apparently pleased, was sold to a farmer. There was more coarse laughter as he lifted her before him on the horse and disappeared in the crowd.

The door of the slave pen opened again and a man in shackles, a woman and two young children were brought to the platform. The woman clutched her husband and children, frantically trying to hold all three at once. She reminded Susan of a hen shielding her chicks from a threatening hawk.

The auctioneer shouted something to her and cracked his cruel whip. The man tried to receive the blow, but he was too late and the whip snapped across her shoulders, so that she leaped back and released her hold on her husband and children.

With a gasp of indignation, Susan dropped the reins and climbed over the carriage wheel. Her cheeks were flaming and her jaw set firm in anger as she bore down upon the group about the platform. So intent were the buyers on the business at hand that they did not see Susan until she had snatched the whip from the astonished auctioneer and thrown it on the ground.

"Don't thee dare strike that poor mother again," said Susan quietly.

The man grinned. Noting her Quaker garb, he raised his hat. "No, ma'am," he said. "I jest wanted her to loosen her grip on the man so the gents could get a look at him, ma'am. No harm intended."

Susan did not answer. She looked about her hoping to discover a sympathetic face. She realized that she was encircled by grinning, derisive men hardened to cruelty of this nature. Instinctively she stepped back.

Recovering his brazen manner, the auctioneer continued. "We'll sell this lot together! Jake, Celey and two offspring, both male. These are fine healthy niggers of Colonel Worthington's stock, all in prime condition. Step up, folks, and look 'em over."

Nobody came forward. There was a pause and then further exhortation. Finally a man spoke. "Mister Arnold, I'd like to bid on the woman and children," he said.

Arnold glanced sideways at Susan and said sullenly, "All right, if nobody won't bid on the group, we'll take them separate. Sorry, miss. This business ain't pleasant for me neither and I advise you to be on your way. Don't try to mess in what ain't no concern of yourn."

Then, determined to ignore Susan and go forward with his business, he picked up the whip, cracked it suggestively and cried, "We'll take the buck first. Step out lively, Jake, and let the gents get a good look at you."

Susan clenched her hands at her side. What could she do? She had no money and the buyers were coming forward now, pinching the legs and arms of the cowering Negro, examining his teeth and the condition of his feet. Sweat streamed from the Negro's body and he rolled his eyes beseechingly toward Susan who felt utterly helpless. Where was her father?

She covered her face with her hands and tried to clear her thoughts. There was a way. There was always a way. God was her Father and He was always present. "Behold, God is mighty and despiseth not any—if they be bound in fetters and be holden in cords of affliction. Ye can of your own self do nothing. Stand ye still and see the salvation of the Lord."

As in a bad dream, she heard the voice of the auctioneer: "Come now, what am I offered for this fine strong buck?"

CHAPTER

FOUR

After leaving Susan in the carriage, William had proceeded on foot to the wholesale grocery house of Hopkins and Brothers.

An obsequious clerk hastened to welcome him. "Good morning to you, Mr. Coale. Can we be of service?"

"Thank thee," answered William. "I've come on business with Johns Hopkins. Is he about?"

The clerk bowed. "He is always glad to see you, Mr. Coale. Go right in."

William knocked once at the private sanctum of the merchant. Then he opened the door and laughingly called, "What, Johns, thee's not sitting down this early in the day, is thee?"

Johns Hopkins rose from his desk and extended a cordial hand. He was a small man with dark hair, a prominent nose, wide mouth and shrewd kindly eyes. At the age of eighteen he had left his father's farm and entered his uncle's business. Now, at sixty-seven, he owned not only the wholesale house, but a comfortable Saratoga Street home and a fine estate of three hundred thirty acres in the country. For all his great wealth, he lived simply, dressed plainly and ate moderately, living his life in a manner consistent with his Quaker upbringing, consistent, that is, in all but one respect: the shelves of his warehouses were well stocked with boxes and barrels of groceries, but not content, he had added bottles and demijohns whose contents were more spiritous than spiritual. Because of this worldliness, the Friends had first warned and finally disowned Johns from membership in their Society. For reasons best known to himself, Johns had never married. He was a lonely man, and his pleasure at seeing William was genuine.

"Sit thee down, William, my good friend and neighbor. Thee did such a good job at landscaping my grounds at Clifton, that its beauty has me practically shackled. It's all I can do to leave it these bright June mornings. Besides, we're having our difficulties here. Our business relations have been largely in the Valley of Virginia and adjacent territory. This war is creating problems which make me prefer to stay at home and enjoy my gardens. But now, what can I do for thee?"

"My needs are few," answered William. "A barrel of molasses to sweeten old Henny's cornbread and a barrel of oil to feed the lamps of Furley. Can thee oblige me?"

"Gladly." Johns called to his clerk, "Ferguson, when William Coale's wagon calls, see that he gets a barrel of oil and one of molasses and bill him at the usual wholesale rates."

He turned again to William. "A man with a family the size of thine deserves wholesale supplies. But thee didn't come all the way to town for that, did thee? Despatch thy wagon at any time with a note and I'll be glad to honor thy request."

"Thank thee, Johns," said William gratefully. "No, I had other business on my mind." He paused.

"Yes, yes, go on!"

William leaned forward and spoke slowly. "Johns, I have made a purchase."

Johns considered his friend gravely. "What in tarnation did thee get—an elephant?"

"Johns," confided William, "I have bought—a piano."

The old merchant tilted back in his chair and regarded his neighbor with amazement. "William, what madness is this? Is thee trying to join me in getting thyself spewed forth from the Meeting?"

"Not at all. I have no desire to share thy shame. My little Myra is given to despondency and I do not like it. I thought some kind of instrument would furnish her with an outlet for this condition. What does thee think of it?"

Johns laid a sympathetic hand on William's shoulder. "Very sound, my friend. I like the idea. Moses Sheppard has left money so that distressed persons can be treated sensibly. Enoch Pratt tells me he will add some of his earnings to the fund and make the project a sizable one." He thrust his hand into the desk drawer, and took out a tin box which he opened. "But come, I have some fruits that should interest thee. The sea captain who brought them here called them love-apples. I believe he said the natives called them to-mato or some such jabber. I'll give thee one to carry home, and I believe they aren't poisonous, although I wouldn't trust the captain's word."

He put the round red fruit in his friend's hand, and smiled at William's obvious pleasure.

"I'll take it home and plant the seeds," promised William. "But speaking of home reminds me of Susan. I left her sitting in the carriage under a catalpa tree near the market. I must get back to her."

"I'll walk that far with thee," offered Johns. "I'd like to see her. I'm very partial to thy Susan. She's a lovely girl, and if I'd been blest with a daughter—" He paused.

"She'll do," William said, and smiled.

And so the two friends started back to the carriage, stopping only once to make a purchase at a bookstore. As they came into the market place, William looked toward the catalpa. "There's the carriage," he exclaimed, "with the horses unattended. Where's my Susan?"

"I think I see her," answered Johns shortly. "Thee go and take care of thy team before they take fright and bolt for the country. I'll get Susan."

As he approached the slave block, Johns saw Susan standing quietly, her face covered with her hands.

The young Negro man had been brought forward, and stood with streaming eyes waiting for the fall of the gavel that would separate him forever from his little family.

"What am I offered?" cried the auctioneer, who had somewhat recovered his usual brazen manner. "This is a husky nigger, young and in good condition. Come now, what do you bid?"

"I'll pay thee two thousand for the family and not a cent more," came a quiet voice.

The auctioneer peered over the heads of the buyers. A look of amazement crossed his face.

"Thank you, Mister Hopkins," he said. "And who else will bid? Come now, this gentleman knows a good bargain, don't you, Mister Hopkins?"

"Thee knows I'm buying them to be manumitted and I care nothing for their services," answered Johns drily.

"Any other bids?" asked the man sullenly.

"I'd like to have the woman and children, Mister Arnold," suggested one man, glancing nervously at Susan who had dropped her hands from her face and now turned upon him indignantly. "But if the gentleman wants the whole passel I reckon there's no use of me interferin'."

Susan's face became suddenly radiant. "Thank thee, my friend," she said gratefully.

Johns Hopkins spoke to the auctioneer. "In about an hour, I'll send a wagon for my Negroes," he said, "and I'll attend to the purchase price."

Arnold was extremely polite. "Thank you, Mister Hopkins. I'll take good care of them until you get them."

"Thee'd better."

Arnold's eyes narrowed shrewdly. "And who is the young lady who is to own them?"

"That," said Friend Hopkins, "is none of thy business!"

To Susan he said shortly, "Come, I'll take thee to thy father."

Gratefully she took his arm and they crossed the market place to the carriage. "Oh, Pa," she cried, "Cousin Johns did the kindest thing. He bought a mother, father and two children to keep them from being separated. He was so good, Pa."

"No such thing," barked Johns. "I bought them to save a very lovely Susan from distress, and I warmly recommend, William, that hereafter thee keep her away from the slave market. It's no fit place for a tender young woman reared in the Quaker faith."

William looked from Susan's flaming face to the more serious one of his friend. "I'm afraid my daughters are a trifle impulsive," he said. "I hope Susan has not caused any inconvenience."

"Under the circumstances, no, but I'd not answer for what might happen to her if she interferes again. Good day, Susan. Thee keep away from slave markets. And good day to thee, William. I'll be riding over to Furley soon to bring the puppy to Myra. In the meanwhile if thee is disowned by the Friends because of that music-box, we can organize our own Meeting and call it the Society of Outcasts." He cackled gleefully and watched while the carriage went on its way toward Thomas Scott's.

CHAPTER

FIVE

Susan was glad when they left the cobbled streets of the city. Once on the dirt road, the horses trotted briskly. The highway, overarched by tulip and maple trees, was flanked with fields of ripening wheat or lush green corn, and along the sides bright daisies made a lacy edging.

Her thoughts, however, were of her recent experience. "I'm sorry, Pa, that I forgot myself and left the horses. I'm afraid I lost my temper."

William regarded her gravely. "Never mind now. That's not the important thing. Thy real consideration must be to protect Keziah. Handbills will be posted and spies put on the alert, and we do not want to do anything to excite suspicion."

Susan knew this was true. Friends were not averse to helping distressed slaves across the Canadian border. Many of them maintained regular hiding places, moving the Negroes forward from station to station during the night, and because these passengers were never seen, the system was known as the Underground Railroad, and the passengers were referred to as packages.

Susan was sorry to think that she might have directed suspicion to her father's house.

Seeing her distress, William said kindly, "Thee did not ask me what I have in this paper. Where's thy curiosity? See, I bought a gift for Hetty. Thee may give it to her."

He handed her a small package, and she held it carefully

but asked no questions. The plight of the slave Celey was a poignant reminder of the complete dependence of Keziah on William's resourcefulness.

She was still considering the matter when they reached Kenilworth, the comfortable stone home of Thomas and Sarah Scott.

On the wide verandah, Thomas sat reading the day's issue of the *Advertiser*. The hounds at his feet suddenly pricked up their ears and barked a brief warning. Thomas laid aside his paper and went to the porch steps to receive his guests.

"Well, well, I'm happy to see thee, William, and thee, too, Susan. Come right in. You're just in time for a bite of dinner." Then he called, "Ikky! Where's that Ichabod? Ikky, take this carriage to the stable and care for the horses."

"Now, Thomas," remonstrated William, "that is kind of thee, but we must attend to business and leave immediately for home."

"I'll take no excuse," said Thomas.

William said in confidence, "I'm storing some dangerous cargo, and I should get back to it."

"Nonsense," snorted Thomas. "The Almighty will care for His own and thee can go home when thee's nowhere else to go. I've matters of prime importance to discuss with thee, and Sarah would like a word with thy charming Susan."

Sarah appeared in the doorway. "I thought I heard welcome voices," she called cheerfully. "Come right in and share our meal. I've the greatest plenty and it will be a joy to have you."

Susan hesitated. "We really should go home," she objected. "Mother was a bit upset last evening over my Cousin James' enlistment, and when I'm away, poor Hetty has all of the responsibility."

" 'Twill do her good," said Sarah heartily. "She's a big girl now and will soon be taking over a home of her own. Stay to dinner and we'll not try to keep you longer."

Accordingly, William gave the reins to the Negro, assisted Susan from the carriage and followed her into the house.

Sarah embraced Susan heartily. "Thee run upstairs to the front room where thee'll find water and towels at the washstand. I'll be with thee just as soon as I have two more places set."

Susan, who was a frequent visitor at Kenilworth, was immediately at home. As she tidied herself, she took a careful look at the front bedroom with its two huge canopied beds, wardrobe, chest of drawers, oaken chest and washstand. White curtains swayed gently at the windows, revealing pots of red geraniums on the wide stone sills. It was a beautiful room, Susan thought.

In a moment Cousin Sarah rustled starchily up the stairs and into the room.

"Did thee find clean towels?" she asked. "Now I'll just take a look around and be sure we're alone." She peeped under the bed curtains, and having satisfied herself that all was well, she beckoned Susan to the chest of oak.

"Here," she said, "I have a quantity of clothing ready for distribution. William suggested that you have visitors. Take what thee needs for them."

"We have a tall, thin mother and seven children," answered Susan. "I'd like one change for each of them."

Susan selected what she needed from the generous store provided by various Friends, and packed the clothing in a muslin bag which the two women carried to the hall below.

Immediately a gong sounded from the dining room, the men appeared from the library and the four Friends went in to dinner. Although frugal in most matters, Quakers believed in good living, especially here where food was both varied and plentiful. Meats, vegetables, fruits and jellies were in abundance, and while they feasted, there was a lively discussion of the political situation.

Many of the neighbors had enlisted in either the Northern or Southern armies, and feeling ran high. The Friends kept their opinions to themselves and had no arguments with the hotheads.

Now President Lincoln had announced to Seward that he felt it a military necessity to free the slaves, since they were providing the Confederacy with trenches and food.

To this many Northerners did not agree. Horace Greeley published an article addressed to the President which stated, "We complain that the Union cause has suffered and is now suffering immensely from your mistaken deference to rebel slavery."

Lincoln's reply to this was eagerly awaited by the nation.

When these matters had been thoroughly discussed by Thomas and William, Sarah suggested, "Suppose you men sit on the porch to sip your coffee while I take Susan to the garden. I'd like to send a bouquet of my pink roses to Deborah."

While the men arranged for the future of Keziah and her family, Sarah led Susan along the garden paths where a light breeze brought odors of pinks and roses, mint and sweet marjoram.

"I'm so distressed to hear about James' joining a military company," confided Sarah. "Poor Cassandra. I feel for her."

"Yes," said Susan, "Aunt Cassy will blame it on the influence of a neighbor's son, Calvin Pancoast."

Sarah laughed. "To Cassandra, James can do no wrong," she said. "It's bound to be somebody else's fault. I imagine James is just as much to blame as the other fellow. They tell me all a man has to do is raise a company of a hundred men and place himself at the head as its captain. The whole business is a madness."

From the porch came William's voice. "Come, daughter, we must tear ourselves away from this good company. Mother will be anxious and we both have serious work awaiting us."

To Thomas he said, "This morning I went to see Johns Hopkins on a matter of groceries, and while I was away from Susan, my impetuous girl visited the slave market. Fortunately we arrived in time to save her from undue distress, but as a result Johns has several Negroes to manumit."

"Don't feel too badly about it," said Thomas. "Johns won't miss the money. Let me assure thee that I will forward the news about thy packages by special messenger on the train this afternoon. The Committee in Philadelphia will send a boat down from Elkton. By the day after tomorrow at the latest, help should arrive. However, by that time the slave-catchers will be in full cry. There is need for watchfulness."

According to the Fugitive Slave Law, any person hindering the arrest or attempting the rescue of such a fugitive was liable to a fine of one thousand dollars, imprisonment not to exceed six months and the payment of one thousand dollars to the owner for each slave lost. That was the law, and William knew only too well that if caught in the act of breaking it, he would pay the full penalty.

Now as they drove briskly home, William silently considered these matters and Susan thought joyously of the success of her outing. In the muslin bag at her feet she had a new dress and chemise for Keziah, dresses and petticoats for each of the little girls and pants with shirts for the boys. She thought of the long hours spent by the Friends in preparing these garments and a warm little feeling of gratitude came into her heart.

In her lap she held the bouquet of pink cabbage roses to take to her mother and a plate full of peppermints Cousin Sarah had sent to the children. Best of all, she carried the assurance that Friends would continue the rescue of the Negro refugees.

As soon as they reached Furley, Susan arranged the roses in a bowl and carried them to her mother's room.

"Is thee napping, Ma?"

"No, dear, just resting." Deborah smiled. "Tell me all that you did. The roses came from Cousin Sarah, I know."

"Yes, Ma. Cousin Sarah sent her love and made us stay to dinner."

The other children gathered around their mother and listened to the story of Susan's adventures. As the report progressed, the four pairs of blue eyes grew wide with interest.

"I'd have told that Arnold something if I'd been there," boasted Billy.

"It's a good thing thee wasn't," retorted Hetty.

Susan produced the package. "Here is a gift for thee from Pa, Hetty. Open it, please."

"I hope it's candy," said Frankie.

Hetty quickly unwrapped the package. "Oh, Ma, look," she cried, "it's 'Poems by John Greenleaf Whittier' all my own. Isn't it beautiful?"

Frankie was disappointed. "Wisht it was candy," he whispered.

"Then here's thy wish," said Susan, "a dish of peppermints from Cousin Sarah. Ma will divide them among you." She handed the dish to her mother and left the room.

While the family attention centered upon the mints, Susan sped away to the attic where Keziah was busily engaged in making corncob dolls for her children's amusement.

"Keziah, I have clean new clothes for all of you," she announced joyously. "If thee can keep the children quiet for another day or two, we'll take you on a boat to a place where some very kind people will care for you. How is little Jerry?"

"He ain't feelin' too good, Miss Susan."

Susan was worried. If Jerry was unable to proceed with the rest of his kin, he would have to stay at Furley and become another burden.

CHAPTER

SIX

For two days Susan busied herself with the refugees. Now the old clock in the hall pointed to noon, and Susan went to the kitchen to speed Aunt Henny's preparations for the midday meal.

"Comin' right on," announced the old woman. "And say, Miss Susan, dat li'l Jerry, he sho' cute." She rolled her eyes at Susan. "Be mighty nice if us could keep him."

"How is he?"

"Still a spittin' up some but he better. Come mornin', I gonna carry him outside an let him set in de sunshine. Dat'll fix him. He been shet up too much and skeered. He need sunshine."

Aunt Henny was stirring a kettle on the stove, and now having produced a satisfactory concoction, she used a copper ladle to transfer the savory contents to an immense tureen. This she carried from the kitchen and set it at William's end of the dining room table. It contained a stew of young chickens and fresh mushrooms, enriched with good Jersey cream and seasoned to suit the most exacting taste.

She lifted the lid for a moment and sniffed approvingly. Then she waddled to the open window and seized the frayed end of a rope. Immediately a mellow clang came from the copper bell and echoed throughout house and garden.

Along the hall came the quick swish of petticoats, and from porches and garden, the heavier sound of booted feet, as William and Deborah with five of their eight children assembled as promptly as their legs would propel them.

The young people stood, each behind his chair, until the mother was seated. Then they took their places and bowed their heads for a silent blessing.

In appearance, they were much alike. All but the youngest had inherited their father's remarkable blue eyes and his sense of humor. The three older children had left the nest: Ezra and Cornelia were married; George was away at medical school. The remaining five, now gathered at dinner, were Susan, aged twenty; Hetty, seventeen; Billy, fourteen; Frank, twelve; and Myra, eight.

Of the three daughters at home, it was easy to see that Susan was nearest her father's heart. As she sat beside him at the table, her brown hair curled becomingly above a face which was serene and beautiful. She was neither thin like Hetty, nor plump like her married sister, Cornelia.

While William ladled out the chicken, Deborah poured tea or milk for her children, and there was a ripple of happy conversation around the table.

"Myra," said William, "I'm going to get a piano teacher for thee from town. What's the matter, Mother? Is thee still troubled?"

Deborah sighed. "The Friends won't like it. I'm afraid we'll all be read out of Meeting for having music in our home."

"Tut, tut, Mother. Thee let me worry about that. I'll fix it."

She smiled bravely. "Very well, William. I'm sure thee knows best."

At this point, there came a loud insistent knocking at the front door and the grumbling of Uncle Toy as he shuffled across the marble tiles. "Yas, yas, I'se a comin'."

"I'd better investigate," said William. "Excuse me, Mother, this may be a stray package."

Or, thought Susan, the sheriff with a search warrant.

An immediate hush fell upon the family as William walked to the front hall. There was the clank of a great key in the lock, the creak of an opening door, and then after a silence a halting and apologetic masculine voice.

"What's the matter with thee, Uncle William? I'm not a ghost. This is my brother officer, Calvin Pancoast."

"It's Cousin James," Frankie whispered.

The entire family flocked from the table to the hall where the two young men confronted William.

"Well, James, I'm surprised and delighted to see thee," said William. "I was under the impression that thy company would be in Washington by now."

"That was our expectation, Uncle William, but at Baltimore we were ordered to proceed only as far as Fort McHenry and remain there for further orders. It seems that a party of rebel recruits is reported to be passing somewhere near there. Tomorrow we will be covering the road south. We can only stay for a few minutes."

The family returned to the dining room. James sat beside his aunt and Susan placed Calvin beside a willing Hetty.

"Thee has known James for a long while?" she asked.

"Yes," answered Calvin, "we lived in adjoining houses and attended the same school. He often spoke of his cousins. His mother has Susan's daguerreotype on the parlor table. Susan is a wonderful girl, isn't she? Do tell me about the things you do together."

"We're quite busy," answered Hetty. "Susan does most of the housekeeping and Pa has set up a little schoolhouse in one of our outbuildings where I teach the children, Myra and Frankie. Billy goes to school now. He got to be a little too much for me."

"I can imagine that you had your troubles," said Calvin and laughed. "How about the two younger ones?"

"Oh, they're all right. I can still spank them."

"She can't either," muttered Frank. "She tried it once and does thee know what I did? I just ducked under her petticoats and held on to her legs and she couldn't get at me."

Calvin suppressed his amusement and quickly changed the subject. "I don't suppose you dance?" he ventured.

"Well, not exactly, but Pa doesn't mind the Virginia Reel. We just say we're going to play the Virginia Reel, just like playing croquet or playing grace hoops, and in place of music, we clap our hands."

"What a wonderful family you are," he said. "I was an only child, and when I lost my parents, your Aunt Cassandra was kind to me. James and I are like brothers."

"I'm sure of it," responded Hetty. "After supper let's take a walk. Would thee like to?"

His eyes wandered across the table to Susan. "Will your sister come with us?"

Hetty frowned. "No, she has to put Ma and the children to bed, but she won't be long about it."

Indeed! Susan was amused and a bit indignant. She took Myra to her room, and was about to leave when the child said, "Dear Susan, I think maybe somebody is hiding in our attic. I hear the strangest noises up there. Does thee think we had better look?"

"No, Myra. Thee go to sleep and I'll be back as soon as the company leaves. And don't thee go up to the attic. There are always mice and bats up there. Thee wouldn't want a dirty old bat to get tangled in thy hair."

Susan hastened downstairs but Hetty and the lieutenant were nowhere to be seen, and an hour had passed before they returned from their stroll. The young man was listening with rapt attention to Hetty's chatter.

When the guests had gone, William conferred with Susan. "By this time," he said, "the messenger from Thomas Scott will be in Philadelphia and the packet boat should be on its way. I can't afford to wait until I hear that it's arrived. To-morrow night I'll carry the packages to the wharf at Joppa, and only hope that the boat will be awaiting us. Thee have everything ready, Susan. We'll leave at nine tomorrow evening."

"All right, Pa," answered Susan. She was not quite sure that all was right, but she would do her best to make it so.

CHAPTER

SEVEN

The sun had barely clipped the horizon when Susan awoke to the sound of a woodpecker drumming against the edge of the roof. She was immediately reminded that she had a busy day ahead of her.

Early though it was, she could hear the soft patter of bare feet across the attic floor, and she thought with both anxiety and relief that in a few more hours Keziah and her offspring would be on their way to the abandoned bayport of Joppa.

Quickly she bathed her sleepy eyes at the washstand and dressed in plain gray linen. Then she ran upstairs to the attic.

Keziah, who was patiently amusing the children, was happy to have an early visitor.

Susan said, "Keziah, I have good news for thee."

"Yes, ma'am," whispered the poor slave. "You done hear from my Jasper?"

Susan was touched. "No, Keziah. That will come later when Jasper can follow you. Right now, my father thinks it will be best to take you on your way tonight."

Keziah nodded. "Wisht Jasper could have got yere so's he could go 'long wid me. But I doan want you in no trouble my count, dat's foah sho'."

Susan said quickly, "We aren't afraid. Is thee?"

"Yas'm," came the decided answer.

"Then let's stop worrying, for we've got lots to do. The children have to be bathed and dressed in their new clothes.

Then I want to take you all downstairs to see my mother. You will need food for your journey, but Aunt Henny will attend to that."

They went to work in earnest and by late afternoon were ready. Uncle Toy was set to watch the drive for intruders and Aunt Henny kept an eye on him to see that he didn't go to sleep.

Then Susan took the refugees to her mother's room.

"How clean and neat they are," exclaimed Deborah. "Sit down, all of you, while I read to you from the Bible."

Obediently they sat at her feet while she read and explained. "Thee knows, Keziah, how a hen gathers her chickens under her wings away from the storm? It makes no difference whether they are black or white. Is this true?"

"Yassum. Dat I unnerstan, dat biddy-hen." Keziah nodded. "I try not to be skeer no mo', but talk 'bout dem slabe-grabbers give me de shakes."

"That is understandable," said Deborah kindly, "but thee try to remember what I've told thee."

"Yassum, an' I sho' thanks you." Keziah took her children and crept back among the chests in the attic.

Aunt Henny packed a basket with provisions, and toward dark, the wagon, filled with trees and shrubbery, was brought to the back door. William and old Toy prepared themselves for the task ahead.

Billy, coming from the stables where he had been watering the two riding horses, found Susan in the garden. "The moon is getting bigger," he observed. "It should give light enough for Pa to see his way without a lantern. I wish he'd let me drive the wagon tonight. I asked him, and guess what he said."

"What did he say?" asked Susan.

"He said he was afraid I'd find something to distract me

on the way and would forget my errand. That isn't fair, is it, Susan? Thee knows I'd do my duty, doesn't thee?"

"I hope so, Billy." Susan said. "By the way, thee doesn't know who did his duty by one of the two pies that Aunt Henny baked for supper, does thee?"

A guilty look suddenly crossed his face. He could fib to Hetty but not to Susan. "Well," he admitted, "Sammy Heater came over to play with Frank and I couldn't let him go home hungry, could I? Ma wouldn't have liked it."

Susan laughed. "Billy, thee is a scamp," she said. "Just refuse pie at supper time and Frankie and I will say we don't want any either. Pa has his mind on the trip he has to take and thee may not be discovered."

Billy gave her arm an affectionate tug. "Thanks, Suse," he said, "Thank thee for being so kind."

She thought of the way Hetty had appropriated the lieutenant. Her family all adored her, but somehow she always seemed to be the loser. Last night she gave up a beau to Hetty; tonight her dessert went to save Billy.

"Come now, Billy," she said, "call Myra and Frank, please. Pa wants an early supper, and the music teacher is coming this evening to give Myra her first lesson on the piano."

She returned to the house and arranged a bowl of sweet peas for the table. Then she went to her father's study and knocked softly.

"Come in," he said gently.

Opening the door, she crossed the room to where he sat at the window, his Bible open on his knees. She drew up a little stool at his feet and rested her head against him.

"Pa," she said, "thee is worried, isn't thee? Hadn't I better drive along with thee? That little Jerry is still very miserable."

"No, my child. Toy will drive the horses and I trust that folks we meet will think we're making a late delivery of nursery stock. A lady on the wagon seat would only attract attention. And, Susan, I'm not worried. The Heavenly Father watches over all his children. It was not mere chance that secured Keziah her freedom. The way was opened for her escape just as surely as the parting of the Red Sea for the children of Israel. And God never fails. Could thee imagine Divine Love operating a plan so weak that it must needs bog down in midstream?"

"No, Pa. I'm sure that all will go well," she answered. "I went up to see Keziah this morning and we had a long chat. Uncle Toy carried up buckets of hot water, and I had each child take a sponge bath and put on clean clothes. Then Mother talked to them. Aunt Henny washed the soiled things, so they have a clean change to carry with them. They're having their supper now, and by nine o'clock the children will be tired and ready to sleep on the long drive."

He regarded her proudly. "My dear Susan, thee remembers everything."

She was pleased at his praise. "Just now I'm remembering that thee must have thy supper."

"Bring it to me here, please, on a tray. I'll eat in the quiet."

She did as he requested, and left him to his prayers. He did not need her company on his dangerous mission. He walked with love and his faith filled her with a sweet assurance.

The sun set and the family had supper.

Myra asked, "Why do we eat so early tonight, and where's Pa?"

"Pa has a load of trees to deliver," answered Susan quickly, "and thee must be through thy supper and ready for thy music teacher when he comes."

Myra's expression brightened. "Perhaps he'll play something for us."

Hetty was interested. "A handsome dark-eyed Southerner," she observed, "and I hope he falls in love with me."

While they discussed him, the young man arrived, and was escorted to the parlor where the pupil was introduced to him. With an elaborate flourish, he seated himself at the piano, pushed the long hair from his eyes and began an overture.

Hetty, peeping through a half-opened door, breathed a sigh of ecstasy.

For an hour they listened with breathless interest. Then their pleasure was interrupted by a terrific banging at the front door. Susan ran to open it, and was nearly knocked off her feet by young Sammy Heater, who panted from hard running.

"Susan," he gasped, "there's men at our house searching for runaways. Tell thy pa quick. I got out the window and crawled on my belly till I got to the road so's I could warn you."

Susan gasped. For a moment it seemed that all their efforts must end in disaster. Then she ran to Hetty. "Go quick," she said. "Tell Aunt Henny to bring the people down from the attic and get them in the wagon. Tell Uncle Toy to unfasten the horses and be ready. I'll get Pa. And, Hetty, don't forget the food."

She ran to the study. "Pa," she cried, "the slave-catchers are coming. Aunt Henny is loading the wagon. Please hurry."

He was very calm as he bowed his head for a moment and then reached for his hat. "Thee meet them at the front of the house, my dear," he said, "and hold them back as long as possible. And feel no fear. All is well."

"Yes, Pa, I'll do my best," she promised. "I'll run up to Aunt Henny's room and get little Jerry."

She had reached the stairs when the slave-catchers clattered up to the front of the house.

Hearing them, poor Keziah moaned softly. She hustled her offspring before her. "Doan let um git me. Please doan let um," she begged tearfully.

"Shet yo' mouf an' keep a movin'," Aunt Henny advised. "Yo got dem chillen ter git away, and yo' ain't got no time fer yappin'."

"Where my li'l Jerry?" pleaded Keziah.

"Thee get him, Aunt Henny," whispered Susan. "I'll have to go to the front door."

"He too ailin' ter go," said old Henny firmly to Keziah. "He in my baid soun' sleep, an' dat where he gonna stay. When dat Jasper come, he kin fetch him along ter you. You gotta go on an' leave him. I'll make out lak he mah gran'chile. No, you ain't got no time fer good-bye. Jest git."

There came a sound of determined knocking at the front door, and Hetty said, "Thee go, Susan, before the house is knocked down. I'll take care of everything here. I've got a plan."

"All right, Hetty." With a fast-beating heart, Susan went to the front door and slowly unfastened it.

On the doorstep stood Arnold with a sneering slave-catcher.

"Sorry, miss," observed Arnold politely, "but you Quakers are suspected of harboring runaways, and I'd like to search your house."

"Come right in," said Susan cordially. She hoped that Arnold had not recognized her, but she was mistaken.

He gazed at her impudently. "Well, well," he said, "if it ain't my little friend, the champion of liberty. I'm pleased to meet you again, miss. If it hadn't been for Mister Johns Hopkins, you'd 've made a monkey out of me. As it was, no harm done and I trust no feelings hurt."

Susan forced herself to smile. "It seems to me thee might find more pleasant employment," she suggested.

"Right you are, miss, but a man gets hardened to that sort of thing. I'm the sheriff of this section, and on market-day I act as auctioneer. Gives me a chance to meet the gents, and that part I like."

The slave-catcher said, "You got a nice place here, miss. You mind if we look around?"

"Does thee have a warrant?" asked Susan.

"Right here in my pocket." He produced the paper.

Susan said, "The music teacher is entertaining us. Please sit down while I read the warrant."

The musician broke into a fresh assault upon the keyboard. Susan prayed that his strength would last until the wagon had pulled away from the back door. Faintly came the muffled cry of a baby, and an attentive expression appeared on the face of the slave-catcher. Then, as the music came to an end, he tapped his foot impatiently.

"Have you time to listen to just one more?" begged Susan.

The sheriff hesitated, grinning foolishly at her, but the other man was positive. "Let's get on with our business first," he said, "and listen to music playin' later."

"Very well," agreed Susan. "This is the parlor. You can see there's nobody here. By the way, is it a man or a woman you're hunting?" She had paused with an oil lamp in her hand.

"A woman, ma'am, and seven children. They oughten be too hard to find."

Myra started to speak. "I think if you—" But Susan quickly interrupted. "Go on with thy lesson, dear, I'll take care of everything."

The girl returned obediently to the piano and Susan led the way upstairs. Room after room was searched. Finally they reached the little door that led to the attic. Someone was behind that door and coming downstairs. Arnold unfastened the latch and threw the door back, revealing Aunt Henny with a basket on her arm.

"Who is this?" he demanded.

"It's our maid, Aunt Henny," said Susan uneasily.

The sheriff said, "This Keziah is supposed to be skinny. That ain't her."

"No, suh," said the old woman, "mah name Henny and mah bones is well covered. Could you let me pass, please, mistah, and please doan point no gun at me. I ain't no slave."

"Just a moment," said Arnold, "what have you got in your basket?"

"Jest some li'l bitty scraps of victuals I been layin' round up dar foah mah pet squirrels," answered Aunt Henny sullenly.

"You were bringing your scraps of food down. You weren't taking them up. I guess we'll take a look around." He pushed her aside and ran upstairs.

Henny had folded up the pallets and packed them out of sight in a great chest. She believed she was about to remove the last vestiges of recent occupancy. Now she lumbered on down to her bedroom and left the interlopers to reach their own conclusions.

They made a quick survey. Suddenly the slave-catcher pounced on a sodden cloth. "Here's a wet diaper," he announced triumphantly. "Miss, you've had a baby here and that very recent. Come, where is he? You'd better fetch him out."

"Well," said Susan indignantly, "I'm an unmarried woman, and I assure thee, I have no illegitimate offspring. The very idea."

The man was angry. "Come on, Arnold," he said, "let's look over the kitchen and outbuildings. They've got away from here, but they ain't far away."

Leaving Susan, they tramped down to the kitchen and found it deserted.

In the room above, Aunt Henny sat beside her bed and fed broth to little Jerry. "Keep real quiet, honey, ef mens comes in yere. Keep yo' lil mouf shet an' doan say nothin'."

The two men entered by the back stairs, glanced at Aunt Henny and the child, searched the cupboard and looked under the bed.

"Gram'mammy goin' ter sing you ter sleep," crooned the old woman.

Without speaking to her, the men clattered downstairs and returned to the front hall.

"Is dem bad men gonna git me?" whispered the child fearfully. "I wants mah mammy, I does."

"Dere now," soothed Aunt Henny. "De mens all gone now. Yo' mammy she can't come, but soon yo' pappy gonna come an' kerry li'l Jerry home again. You jest go ter sleep, sugahfoot, an' trust Aunt Henny. I gonna tell you story 'bout ole Mistah Bullfrog."

"Tell me," begged the child.

"You lay still a minute, honey. I got business downstair wid a coupla hosses. I come back soon. Shet yo eyes an' mak lak you sleep."

She followed Arnold and his man to the kitchen, and quietly by way of the back door, she slipped out into the night. There was no longer any sound of the wagon, and much relieved, she took the carriage whip from the wall and went about her mission.

Arnold and his man tramped noisily through dining and sitting rooms to the front hall where Susan awaited them. The music teacher had gone; her mother and the children were nowhere about. Perhaps they had gone to bed.

"Everything all right?" she asked pleasantly.

"It is and it ain't," answered Arnold. "We're out to find them niggers, and we intend to get them. When we do, you're going to get what you deserve. Your father will pay his fine and get six months' board at government expense. That's the law."

Susan smiled bravely. "As to that," she said, "sufficient unto the day is the evil thereof."

At this moment there came sounds of squealing horses and galloping hooves.

"Our horses are loose," yelled the slave-catcher.

The two men rushed from the house in time to see their riding horses in full gallop toward the creek.

With angry oaths, they ran across the porch and were about to follow in pursuit when around the corner of the house dashed the Coale family carriage. In the light from her lamp, Susan recognized Billy sitting on the box holding the reins and yelling to the horses. From the rear of the carriage a thin black face gazed fearfully at her, and two small black faces peeped from half-lifted carriage curtains.

Even in the darkness, Susan realized that something seemed amiss. It suddenly came to her that Billy was driving the carriage with Ginger and Firefly hitched to it. They were riding horses and unaccustomed to pulling a vehicle. No wonder they ran so fast. Susan remembered that at this time of night the carriage horses would be in the pasture, and Billy had used the only ones available.

While Susan stood on the porch, listening to the sounds of the retreating carriage, Arnold and his companions ran along the creek whistling and calling to their mounts. When they were out of sight, a dark shape separated itself from the trunk of a nearby sycamore tree and waddled silently into the house.

Susan followed. "Aunt Henny, what happened? Answer me, what is thee doing with that carriage whip?"

The old woman sank down on a chair, laughing and crying all in one breath.

Susan took her firmly by the arm. "Aunt Henny, quiet thyself. What happened?"

"Stop pinchin' mah arm, honey. How I gonna tell you sumpin, you holdin' me lak dat?"

She released the arm. There was no hurrying Aunt Henny. Slowly Susan pieced together the story.

Hetty had waited until Keziah and her children were safely

48 ·

hidden among the trees in the wagon. Then, as the vehicle rolled away into the darkness, she ran to the house and called the children.

"Myra, did the music teacher go?" she asked.

"Yes, he went home."

"Then I want you to help me with a big pretend. Billy, thee go hitch the horses to the carriage and bring it to the side of the house. Aunt Henny, go upstairs first by the back way and see that there are no tell-tale signs of Keziah and her children in the attic. Then just as these men are ready to leave, cut their horses loose and hit them with a whip."

Henny hurried to obey her.

Hetty then drew Myra and Frankie to the fireplace. The fire was out and a few charred pieces of wood lay in the grate.

"See," she said, "we're going to pretend that we're runaway slaves. I'm going to blacken our faces with some charcoal, and I'll wrap a stocking around each of your heads so your hair won't show. I'll wear Aunt Henny's bandanna."

Before the men arrived at the kitchen, all was in order. Billy was ready with his unwilling team, and helping the children, Hetty climbed with them into the back of the carriage. A moment later Aunt Henny came around the house, whip in hand, unfastened the sheriff's two horses and gave them each a vigorous cut. They squealed and bolted.

Then as the front door opened and the men rushed out, Billy shouted to the horses, and the carriage careened around the house, passed in front of the chagrined pursuers and rolled away along the drive.

When she had drawn the story from Aunt Henny, Susan said thoughtfully, "If Billy takes to the York Road he will find it not as smooth as the way Pa took toward Joppa, and the thing that worries me is that Billy's driving Ginger and Firefly and they may get out of control."

"Don't you worry, Miss Susan. Dat Billy got a way wid

hosses. All he got to do is talk to um and dey'll gentle down."

"I hope thee is right," said Susan. "What an evening we have had! I think Pa sensed some trouble brewing, and he prayed for guidance."

Feeling very apprehensive, she went to her father's study. As she expected, his Bible lay on the table, open at the place where he had been reading when the slave-catchers arrived.

"And the children of Israel went into the midst of the sea upon the dry ground; and the waters were a wall unto them on their right hand, and on their left . . . I will sing unto the Lord for he hath triumphed gloriously."

She sat in his chair and bowed her head on her arms. She would wait here until the family returned. Perhaps the waters would roll aside for her, too. She'd wait and see. Finally quiet came to her, and because she was young and very tired, she fell asleep.

CHAPTER

EIGHT

Once away from Furley, William said, "Toy, thee'd better slow the horses down a bit. It's a warm night and we don't want them to give out. Besides, unseemly haste will surely arouse suspicion."

Thus admonished, Toy drew the horses down to an easy trot. As Billy had predicted, the half-moon shed enough light to make progress possible without the use of wagon-lanterns. As they passed through the farm lands, an occasional dog barked at them, and from a roadside pasture, a horse whinnied a soft greeting.

At the railroad crossing, the wagon stopped while a freight train rolled unhurriedly across the road. The watchman, out of idle curiosity, swung his lantern into the back of the wagon. "Looks like ye are movin' your woods," he observed.

William laughed genially. "I'm a nurseryman," he answered, "and I find it safer to deliver my goods by night when there's no withering hot sun to shine into my wagon."

"Right ye are," came the friendly answer. The lantern was withdrawn. Toy clucked to the horses and they proceeded.

As they approached the Chesapeake Bay, houses became more frequent. Built of brick, stone or wood, they stood like sentinels along a maple-bordered street. For Joppa, during the Revolutionary period, had been not only the county seat, but also a thriving port, its harbor busy with shipping, its houses alive with people connected with shipping, or with the business of the court. Later the county seat had been removed, first to Baltimore and later to Towsontown. The port was soon abandoned for the safer one at Baltimore, and most of the houses now stood deserted and empty. It was indeed a ghost town with only a few lazy fishermen to keep alive its seafaring tradition.

"It must be close to midnight," observed William to old Toy. "Fortunately for us, the few people left in this town should be asleep. Thee'd better drive straight ahead to the wharf, for unless I'm mistaken, a boat is coming in now. At this time of night, it's almost certainly the one we're looking for."

If William expected the wharf to be deserted, he was disappointed. A few idle people had already gathered on the shore to watch the landing. Seeing this, William said, "We'll have to change our plans, Toy. Thee pull into this side street, and wait for me. Whatever thee does, don't leave the wagon."

"No, suh. Ah sets right yere an' keeps watch."

William set out to do some reconnoitering. He reached the rickety wharf in time to see the captain toss the mooring-line ashore. Willing hands seized it and made the boat fast to an insecure piling.

William called, "I'd like to have a talk with thee, Captain, if thee's time for me."

"Come aboard, sir," came the quick response.

William stepped into the boat and extended his hand. "I'm William Coale," he said. "Is thee looking for an assignment of goods for Elkton?"

"Aye," replied the captain. "Packages from Thomas Scott. Come into the cabin."

Once inside, William made short work of his business. "There's no time to wait until the crowd melts away," he warned. "You must get off at once. I'll drive along the river road a piece. The folks on the waterfront keep their boats tied up along the bank. I'll borrow one and row out from shore. Thee put off in a few minutes, and thee'll find us not too far upshore."

To this plan the captain agreed, and William returned to the wagon where Toy nodded peacefully and a terrified Keziah peered fearfully from her hiding place.

"Come, Toy," said William kindly. "I know thee's tired, but we have work to do and thee can rest tomorrow."

They made little sound as they drove along the soft dirt road until they came to a tiny wharf with a boat tied securely to its piling. Two oars lay drying on the bank. A short distance away a house stood silent and dark, its occupants apparently asleep.

Keziah and her six children were transferred very quietly to the boat, and while Toy remained with the wagon, William rowed the refugees out into the bay. A few moments later the larger boat picked them up. There were whispered farewells, and the captain said, "I've orders to put them ashore in a lonely spot near Elkton where Quakers keep a hiding place. Barring storms or a raiding party, you got nothin' more to worry about."

He waved his hand and they glided away into the darkness.

When William returned to the shore, he tied the boat, put the oars back where he'd found them and was about to join Toy when a quiet voice beside him said, "Who does thee think thee is, a borrowing my boat without permission?"

William smiled. "By thy speech I believe I am a plain Friend like thyself. I am William Coale and I borrowed thy boat to deliver certain packages for shipment. Thank thee for the use of it."

"I am Eben Hollingsworth," answered the Quaker, "and I'm glad to have been of service. Will thee come to the house for a glass of raspberry?"

"Thank thee, no. I'll be getting on my way. First, however, I'd like to make thee a present of a few young fruit trees from my wagon. I'm out to make a delivery, and I'd be glad to have thee receive them."

Accordingly, the trees were unloaded and Friend Hollingsworth received them gratefully.

William returned to the wagon, and while both he and Toy dozed on the seat, the weary horses took their time and plodded slowly toward Furley.

It was nearing two o'clock when William was startled by the sound of galloping horses. Fences lined the road and there was no immediate place for the wagon to turn aside. A moment later two panting horses came to a halt beside the wagon.

"Where are you going at this hour of the night?" cried the rider. "You had better give me the truth. I'm Sheriff Arnold."

William yawned sleepily. "I'm a nurseryman," he said modestly, "and because of the hot sun, I chose this time to deliver a load of young fruit trees."

Arnold leaned from his horse, and scanned the wagon with attention. "What's your name?" he asked.

"William Coale is my name."

"Aha! I've just come from your place. So you delivered some trees, did you? Just where did you take them?"

"To Eben Hollingsworth at Joppa, just north of the town on the river road. Does thee know Eben? A fine man he is and I hope he'll have luck with his orchard, indeed I do."

"Come," said the sheriff's companion impatiently. "No use wasting time with a stupid countryman. Let's be off."

"He's just as thick-pated as he seems," said Arnold gleefully, "but now I know where the mouse has hidden the cheese. Come on."

Away they went at a sharp gallop.

Old Toy chuckled. "Dey ain't found out much as nuttin,"

he observed to the horses. "Giddap now, you lazy critters. Got ter git mahself to baid."

Another hour passed slowly, and then as the grandfather's clock in William's study struck three times, Susan awoke with a start. Her arm was cramped from the weight of her body and she felt loggy with sleep.

A firm step sounded along the hall, and the door opened, revealing William.

"Pa," she exclaimed joyfully. "I waited up for thee."

He kissed her tenderly. "Thee has much responsibility and needs thy sleep. Is everyone else abed?"

"I don't know. I fell asleep at thy desk and I just woke up. Tell me what happened."

He smiled. "Everything worked serenely. We drove as fast as we dared, attended to our errand and returned without mishap. Now if we can just get Jasper and the two sons who were sold at Richmond, we'll have the family reunited. I feel sure that the way will open for them."

"Somehow it will be managed, Pa. Now let me tell thee what happened here." Susan launched into a glowing account of Hetty's escapade. William chuckled with amusement, but when he heard that the scamps had not returned, he lifted his eyebrows.

"Perhaps I'd better saddle a horse and ride to meet them," he said thoughtfully.

"That thee can't do," answered Susan. "The carriage horses were out at pasture and Billy had no time to go after them. Pa, he's driving the riding horses."

William's eyes dilated. "No," he exploded. "He couldn't even get the harness on Firefly, and as for Ginger, he would bolt the minute he felt the drag of a vehicle. Is thee sure?"

"Quite sure, Pa, but thee knows Billy. As Aunt Henny suggested, he can do anything with horses. Don't let's cross any bridges."

William took a quick turn about the room.

"Let's see," he said. "They have the riding horses. The wagon horses are too tired to start out again, and we have carriage horses in the field but no carriage in the shed. I guess if Providence has cared for my children until now, there is no reason to believe that the protection will not be continued. Thee go to bed, and I'll lie here on the couch and wait for them."

She brought him a pillow, and was about to leave when she heard the distinct sound of steel-rimmed wheels on the graveled drive.

"Pa," she exclaimed with relief, "I think they're coming."

They went to the door and listened for the slowly approaching carriage.

"One horse has gone lame," announced William as he heard the uneven clomp.

In a matter of minutes, Hetty and the children were safe in Susan's waiting arms while William and Billy put the horses and the carriage away.

Hetty had used the borrowed bandanna to remove some of the charcoal from their faces, but their appearance was still so grotesque as to send Susan into peals of suppressed laughter.

"Oh, Susan," cried Frankie, "thee should have been with us. We had such fun. Billy let the horses run until they were tired. Sometimes we went on one wheel and sometimes on four, but it made no difference, we kept right on."

"Did the men catch you?" Susan inquired anxiously.

"Yes," said Hetty, "but not for about an hour. We had the black rubbed off our faces by that time. Thee should have seen how mad they were when they saw we were white!"

"The men told us to stop," said Myra sleepily. "One held the horses' heads and the other ordered us to get out."

Myra imitated her sister's grandest manner.

"Hetty just stepped out with her chin up and said, in that haughty tone she uses when she's play acting, 'Shame on thee, for so distressing a white woman and two helpless children. I'll have the law upon thee for thy low curiosity. Get into the carriage, children. Drive on, Billy.'"

"Yes, and Firefly kicked a shoe and we had to walk all the way home," added Frank.

"Billy said he'd be all right in a day or two," added Hetty hastily. "I'm sorry it had to be thy horse to go lame, Susan, but it wasn't anybody's fault. Did Pa deliver the goods?"

"Yes. I'll get you each a glass of cold milk, and you had better sleep late in the morning."

She kissed them good night, and as soon as William and Billy had returned from the stable, she asked anxiously, "Is Firefly all right, Pa?"

He patted her arm sympathetically. "I think so. His hoof is a little sore and he'll need to rest for a few days. Then we'll see about a new shoe for him. And, Billy, thee amazes me."

Billy looked embarrassed but happy. He was usually in trouble and his various peccadillos had earned him more censure than praise.

Susan took a candle and slowly climbed the stairs. On the landing, she found Aunt Henny sound asleep. As Susan laid her hand on the old woman, she awoke. "My lands, Miss Susan, you done skeer me. Thought dem bad men come back. Is de chillen home yit?"

"Yes," said Susan thankfully. "Everyone is home and all is well."

"All my waitin' an' worryin'," grudged Aunt Henny. "It jest like a fog rollin' ober me. Up above, de sun shinin' all de while." Then she inquired cautiously, "Dem folks got away?"

"Yes, Aunt Henny. God's children are always in their right places." She guided the old woman to the back stairs and listened until she heard the top step creak. Aunt Henny's door was firmly closed and Susan heard a whimper from little Jerry and then silence as he found comfort.

With a grateful sigh, Susan went to her room. She thought of her Cousin James and his handsome friend, and she wondered if they had reached Washington safely.

CHAPTER

NINE

Susan slept peacefully. She had confidence in the Underground and she felt no further worry about Keziah's safety.

Meanwhile, Arnold and his man had continued on the road to Joppa, and within an hour had located the home of Eben Hollingsworth. A violent knocking at the door soon brought Eben to an upper window.

"Who knocks at this hour of the night?" called the Quaker.

"Open for the sheriff," came the angry reply.

There was a moment's silence, and then, "Thee wait there a moment till I get into me pants and slippers."

The sheriff whispered to his man, "Run around and watch the back of the house and I'll wait here."

A few moments later the door opened slowly and Eben appeared. "Now what does thee want?" he inquired pleasantly.

"Surrender the runaways brought here by a Quaker named Coale."

Eben was aggrieved. "My friend, thee does me a gross injustice. I have no fugitives here. Come and see for thyself."

A quick survey of the premises proved the truth of Eben's denial. He lighted a lantern and pointed out the young fruit trees heaped on the lawn.

"Here," he said, "are the fine trees delivered by Friend Coale. See for thyself. This one is an apple and this a quince, and there are peaches and pears besides. Now if thee'll be on thy way and leave a body to get a little sleep I'll be obliged to thee, for I'm planning to rise early and get my orchard planted before the sun gets at the tree roots."

Eben dismissed his unwelcome guests, reentered his house and closed the door.

"There is no doubt that the niggers were here," grumbled Sheriff Arnold. "Let's look in the boats." He walked to the shore and vainly searched the rowboats. Returning, he stumbled over the oars left by William on the grassy bank, and fell sprawling. His face lay for a moment against the wet blade of the oar.

Immediately he cried, "Ah ha! this is the answer. The old rascal must have rowed the slaves out to some larger vessel waiting in the bay. We'll get them yet. Come on, this breeze is freshening, and if the ship carries a good bit of sail, she might make Elkton by morning. We'll telegraph ahead and have a reception committee waiting for her."

Meanwhile, Keziah had put her little family to bed on a blanket spread out on the cabin floor of the boat. In a corner by the door she crouched like a tigress and watched over her helpless young. Gradually the gentle rocking of the boat soothed her, and she felt safe with the kindly captain. No slave-catcher could follow her over this wide expanse of bay. With her head resting against the water cask, she drifted into a dreamlike coma.

She was a child again playing on the shores of her native Congo. The sound of the wind in the sails became the rustle of banana leaves, the slow creak of the boom chafing the mast changed to the raucous cries of parrots and macaws; and the slap, slap of water against the bow translated into easy ripples breaking on the sandy banks of an African river. But the peace of her happy homeland was broken. Slave-traders rounded up her tribe, snapped cruel iron collars about their necks, chained them together and walked them to the shore. It was all she could do to run and keep up with her mother, who carried an infant in her arms. The little one finally died, and was left to the jungle beasts, and still Keziah ran on and on, urged ahead by the whips of her tormentors. On the third day they reached a camp and were branded and put in separate pens. Later they were driven aboard a dirty ship. The men and women were forced to lie down in long rows, each with his or her head resting against the knees of another. The children, in separate compartments, dared not cry. They cowered in terror and at night found some relief in sleep. Each day they were taken, a few at a time, to the deck to be fed. If they refused to eat, the food was forced into them. Those who died were cursed and cast into the sea.

A long month passed and they were put ashore in a strange land. In the slave market, the little girl made a good impression.

"Her father was a Congo chief," said the auctioneer. "She'll likely carry her head high, but once broken in, she'll make a valuable servant."

A wealthy merchant bought the child and gave her to his wife to be trained as a personal maid. She was sweet-tempered and learned quickly, so she was well treated and happy. By the time she had reached the age of fifteen, she had developed into a comely girl, strong-limbed and graceful. Unfortunately her mistress passed away, and Keziah was put up for sale.

A cotton planter recognized her possibilities for improving his slave stock, and bought her as a mate for his houseboy, Jasper.

She accepted her new life without protest and in time learned to love Jasper for his kindness and unfailing humor. Over their lives, however, hung the ever-present threat: "Jasper, step lively or I'll sell your wife and children to the rice swamps. I've no use for laziness." So they had existed, well fed and uncomplaining, until the unhappy day when their two boys were sold away from them.

Suddenly Keziah's dream was broken by a loud voice out of the night. "Pull down your sail, Captain. We're coming aboard."

"Who are you, and what is your business?"

"Federal officers with a search warrant."

The captain argued, but to no avail. He was arrested and Keziah with her children once more became captives.

Completely frustrated, the poor woman flung herself on her knees, and above the terrified screams of her children, she cried, "Please, mistah, where you aimin' to fetch us to?"

The man grinned, showing a row of tobacco-stained teeth. "Back to your master to get me my reward," he barked, "and for yourself, a good flogging which you well deserve for making so much trouble."

CHAPTER

TEN

The birds had ceased their warbling and a portentous silence lay upon the valley. With a troubled face, Susan watched the sky. Storm clouds were rolling in and blocking the sunshine from the gardens. On certain trees the leaves were turning edgewise against the threat of destruction, and along the garden paths, flowers either drooped or closed their petals.

On the porch, Deborah sat in her little rocker and knitted a pair of socks. Beside her, Myra worked on a quilt, carefully fitting the pieces into a pattern, and on the lawn, Hetty taught a young hound to retrieve sticks.

As she waited for the first burst of thunder from the blackening clouds, Susan was conscious of an approaching horseman. She went to the porch rail to listen.

"It's only Billy," called Hetty. "Pa sent him for the mail."

Susan nodded. Billy always walked the horses with provoking slowness until he entered the drive. Then, as he approached the house, he would gallop furiously. It gave him an appearance of importance.

Today he pulled up at the porch so suddenly that Ginger reared and shook his head savagely. "Got two letters," yelled Billy. "Both for Ma. One from Brother George and one from I don't know who."

"Dear, dear George," murmured Deborah. "Get the letters for me, please, Hetty, and be careful of that wicked horse."

Hetty took the letters from Billy and delivered one to her mother. The other she examined before she gave it up. "Who is this from, Ma? Please read it first."

Deborah accepted both letters with maddening deliberation. Then she said, "Please sit down and keep quiet while I read the news. No, no, my dear George's letter first. Just be patient. The other can wait."

Having broken the seal and unfolded the letter, she took her glasses from her pocket and placed them on her nose. Then she read aloud:

Dear Ma: This letter will cause thee some concern, but I am sure thee knows I would never do anything that I did not believe was right. Many of the boys I know have enlisted. Some desire to preserve the Union and some believe in the rights of individual states to secede. We have had some very warm debates here in the medical school and sometimes the hotheads get to fighting. Then I remember that I have been brought up in the Friends Meeting and I keep out of the mess. However, I have been doing a lot of thinking, and I feel I should be of some service. I will complete my studies in a few days and however much I dislike to disappoint thee and Father about having me at home once more, I cannot see my way clear at present. In fact, dear Mother, I have enlisted as a surgeon in the Union Army, and shall go out to do what I can to alleviate the suffering of those wounded in this foolish war. Please forgive me if I cause thee any sorrow. I know I'll be disowned by Friends for entering the conflict, but thee will love me anyway.

Thy devoted son,
George Fox Coale

Deborah closed her eyes and dropped her head against

Susan's arm. The paper fluttered from her delicate hands and fell to the floor.

"Take me to my room," she said quietly, "and send Father to me."

As she drew herself unsteadily to her feet, a sharp flash of lightning zigzagged against the sky. It was followed by a gigantic roar that shook the treetops and sent Aunt Henny scurrying to fasten up her young chickens.

Susan and Hetty took their mother to her room. When she was safely tucked into her bed, Hetty went to find her father, and Susan sat holding her mother's hand.

"It gave me great sorrow," said Deborah, "when my dear daughter Cornelia married that Episcopalian and was dropped from the Friends Meeting for doing it. Frederick is a long way from Baltimore and I am always wondering whether she can be happy among strange people whose ways are so different from ours. It was bad enough to have my big girl leave home," murmured the poor lady. "I just can't allow George to go on a battlefield—he a Friend and named for the founder of our faith."

Susan patted her lovingly. "Never mind, Ma," she said, "we still have Ezra, Billy and little Frank. Just be glad of that. Ezra is such a good preacher, too."

In her heart, Susan was numb with unbelief. George, of all people. George who was always kind and full of life and merriment. Poor Pa would take it hard. He had looked forward with so much happiness to the time when reliable George would be at home again. Pa had planned that George would build up his practice around Furley Hall, and there would be another man in the house with whom he could discuss both business matters and politics.

The door opened and William entered the room. He crossed quickly to the bedside and, kneeling, gathered his wife to his heart.

Dear Pa, thought Susan. He would know what to do. With his own heart breaking, he would find the right words to comfort them all.

Susan went swiftly from the room, and closed the door behind her. She heard the storm break with great fury, sending a torrent of rain against the windows. Hetty had gone to her room to recover from the shock of her brother's enlistment. Billy had not returned from the stable and Frank was with him.

On the porch, Myra still sat as though immovable. She had dropped her needlework and sat staring at the two letters which she had gathered from the floor. When she saw Susan standing at the door, she made a little gesture of sadness.

"Myra," called Susan, "come in out of the storm! Thee'll be soaked."

Myra shook her head. "No," she called. "It's not wet on the porch and I like to hear the rain and the thunder. Besides, I feel very sad about George."

"Thee come into the house this minute, and never mind about George. He will be all right."

"I know," said Myra sadly. She lifted her voice above the din of the storm. "I know he will be all right, but if he goes away, I'll miss him. Ezra is so biggity about being good all of the time. Billy and Frank tease me, but George is good."

A blinding flash and a terrific clap of thunder accompanied by a sharp splintering of timber drowned her last words. Susan seized her sister and drew her quickly into the house.

From the window they looked across the gardens into the grove beyond. Against the side of a giant pine tree, a long white scar gave evidence of the fury of the storm.

Myra still clutched the two letters. "I opened the other letter. Ma won't mind, will she? Read it to me, Susan."

Susan took it in her hand and glanced at the signature. It

was from her Cousin James. With hands that were a bit unsteady, she read:

Dear Aunt Debbie: Thank thee so much for thy gracious hospitality and for thy kindness to my friend. We are stationed for a few days south of Baltimore where we hope to waylay the rebel recruits. In a few days we will be in Washington, and I write to ask a favor. We expect to attend President Lincoln's reception the last evening of next week, and we would like to take Susan and Hetty. The Scotts will be sure to come over for it, and Cousin Sarah will be glad to look after the girls. Because of the war, this will not be such a grand affair as the levee given by Mary Lincoln last spring, but it will be a fine experience for all of us. Please say yes.

Thy loving nephew,
James

Susan's eyes sparkled with eagerness. She would see Calvin again. Before she told Hetty, she must see her father and secure his consent. She explained to Myra about George and the necessity for being brave for their mother's sake.

She heard William coming slowly downstairs and along the hall toward his study. In a moment Susan was at his side. He looked older, but his voice was as calm as ever.

"Mother is asleep," he said. "She is entirely reconciled to the idea of George's noble sacrifice. I suppose we must all look upon this matter in that light and try to be courageous. What is that letter thee carries?"

"It's from James and is addressed to Mother, but I could not wait to read it." She suddenly grew animated. "Look, Pa, James wants Hetty and me to attend the President's reception. We can travel with the Scotts and spend the night with some Friends from the Washington meeting. Oh, please, Pa, say we can go."

She was so eager and radiant that in spite of his very genuine grief over George, William was forced to smile indulgently.

"I'm quite sure it will be all right with Mother," he answered kindly. "I would not care to have you attend a dancing party, but Abraham Lincoln is not likely to give way to unseemly behavior, especially with a war on his hands. I will see the Scotts tomorrow and secure their permission."

"Oh, thank thee, Pa, and I promise to watch Hetty carefully, and see that she doesn't get into mischief."

His blue eyes twinkled. "Thee might keep one eye on thy own behavior," he teased.

"I will, Pa. I truly will. Now I'll run and tell Hetty. She will be so excited."

She found Hetty on her bed, weeping dramatically. "Hetty," she cried, "stop thy wailing. George hasn't gone yet and when he does it will be time enough for play acting. Right now, I have glorious news." She read the letter, which had an immediate effect upon her sister's frame of mind.

Hetty had a sudden bold idea. "Susan, does thee think that just once Ma would let us change from gray to something a little more in keeping with a party—something with ruffles and ribbons and wide hoops?"

"Don't be foolish, Hetty. We're lucky to get permission to go at all. We'll have to wear the usual sober Quaker gray, but maybe we can have new dresses and carry bouquets of roses. I'll ask Pa."

"Ask him now while he's in the mood. In thy hands, Pa is just so much wet clay."

Susan was horrified. "Oh, but he isn't. Pa is a very strong fine character."

Hetty made a little face. "I'll not deny that, but so is thee, and he not only adores thee, he respects thy judgment."

"I hope he'll never be disillusioned." Susan smiled. "Thee wait here and I'll talk to him."

Accordingly, she returned to the study where William was preparing a letter. She came immediately to the point. "Pa, does thee think it would be extravagant if we bought new dresses for the party?"

He regarded her cautiously. "How much will they cost?"

"A dreadful amount, ten dollars each, but going with the Scotts we'd not want to look shabby."

His eyes twinkled, but he spoke seriously. "Beware of outward adornment. I don't want my girls to go strutting about like a pair of peafowl."

"No, Pa," she laughed, "just two little gray doves, cooing contentedly."

He smiled at that. "Very well, my dear, we will buy cloth tomorrow after we talk to Friend Scott. I want to see him anyway to find out if there's news of the goods I shipped by boat."

"Oh, yes, Pa, and do ask if there's a letter from Virginia about the two boys and Jasper."

He looked troubled. "Between agitation over runaways and the presence of two opposing armies in Virginia, I presume it will be some time before anything can be done for them, but don't worry, my Susan, all will come out for the best. Now run along, please, and see that I'm not bothered. I'm writing George to assure him that he must follow the guidance of his Inner Light and do what he feels is right. Tell Hetty to get herself ready in the morning and we'll go to town for the dress material, that is, if the bridges are not all washed out. This was quite a cloudburst."

In the sitting room, Myra sat with her face pressed against the window. The storm had passed and the skies were clearing. Streams of water rushed along the driveway and overflowed the ditches. Susan stood beside the child for a minute. "What's thee looking at?"

"A nest of baby robins in the crepe myrtle under the window. The mother spread her wings over them and made a little roof. See, they're hardly wet."

"Yes," exclaimed Susan, "and there comes Aunt Henny from the poultry house with a basket full of half-drowned chicks to be resuscitated. Let's go help her."

CHAPTER

ELEVEN

In such a large family, new dresses were a real luxury. Susan and Hetty were bonneted and ready when the carriage was brought to the door, and Aunt Henny bustled out to the drive to see them off. She had polished old Toy until his black face gleamed, for he was to drive and care for the horses, while William and his daughters went about their business.

As Susan delivered a few last-minute instructions, Hetty exclaimed, "We're not staying a week, Susan, so stop worrying."

Susan sighed. "I know, Hetty, but I don't like to leave Mother and the children with only Aunt Henny to look after them. She has enough to do in the kitchen."

"St. . . !" chided William. "Thy Heavenly Father has cared for them a good many years, and thee doesn't have to stay at home to watch that He continues in His province. Henny, thee might tell Billy I'd like to have him stay close to the house in case thee needs him."

"Yassuh, dat Billy, he a good boy. Don't you trouble yo'self. Us'll git along fine. Drive careful, Toy, and don't you go to sleep settin'."

Thus admonished, Toy rattled the whip, and the horses trotted forward.

Hetty breathed a sigh of happiness. "We're going to have a gorgeous day, aren't we, Pa?"

"I trust so. After we call at Scott's, I want to see William Whitelock on a matter of business. You girls can buy your materials and I'll meet you later. I want to find out about this new fertilizer called guano that Friend Whitelock is importing from South America. I'd like to buy a small amount for an experiment with my roses." Suddenly he paused. "What's this ahead of us, Toy?"

As they rounded a bend in the road, they came upon a small company of men marching toward them. They carried heavy knapsacks and looked haggard, unshaven and weary, as though they had been marching all night.

At sight of the ladies, they straightened up, stepping with a little more vigor, but it was plain to see they were near exhaustion. Their officer issued a quick command and they stepped aside, leaving the road to the carriage.

As they passed, William acknowledged the courtesy and the young officer removed his hat and bowed politely.

Hetty nudged Susan. "Isn't he handsome?" she whispered.

But Susan was not looking at the officer. Her attention was focused upon a young lad who struggled to keep up with the older men. The rags that bound his shoeless feet were dark with blood and his face was pinched and drawn.

"Oh, poor, poor thing," mourned Susan. "Those men are suffering yet they remembered to be polite."

Hetty asked, "Pa, where are they going? They are obviously soldiers but they aren't in uniform."

"They are undoubtedly recruits trying to get through to the Southern army where they will be furnished guns and uniforms. There are so many Southern sympathizers hereabouts that they will have no difficulty in finding a refuge."

"I think the blue uniforms are better-looking than the gray ones," Hetty observed dreamily.

She has Calvin Pancoast on her mind, thought Susan. There was a softness about her sister's expression that filled Susan with genuine consternation. And it isn't jealousy, she told herself. Pa would never consent to have his daughter married to a fighting man.

So they busied themselves, each with his own thoughts, until they reached Thomas Scott's. The girls remained in the carriage, while William talked with the Friends. The Scotts would be happy indeed to have such bright company on their trip to Washington. They had been invited to travel in the private car of their neighbor, John W. Garrett. They would spend the night in the capital city and return the next day.

To this plan, William readily agreed.

"And now we'll be getting along," said William. "We are going to town to buy material for party dresses. This will be a great occasion."

"Oh, indeed," rejoiced good-natured Cousin Sarah. She followed William to the carriage, and said, "Now, girls, don't buy more than ten yards apiece. Leave some goods for the next one. I wonder if you would get me some skirt braid, and leave it on the way home?" She gave them a dollar and they promised to get the braid.

It was nine o'clock when the carriage stopped in front of the store. William climbed out, carefully avoiding contact with the dusty wheel. He gave some last-minute instructions to Toy and took from his pocket a thin roll of bills which he divided between his daughters. "Here are some of the new greenbacks just issued by the government," he said. "Put the money into your pockets safely and spend it wisely. Think well before you part with it, for I've given you all I can spare."

They lifted their skirts and each deposited her money in a long pocket that hung from a linen band around her waist. Then William helped them to the ground and left them to do as they liked.

There was plenty to see and the girls looked about them with interest. Two little children, accompanied by a colored nurse carrying a basket, passed by on their way to the open square. They were plainly on their way to a picnic. Gentlemen dressed in cool linen suits, with stocks and finely ruffled shirts, passed by them with glances of friendly interest. Ladies in gay street apparel flitted in and out of the shops, and here and there Quakers in somber gray passed quietly about their business, and contrasted sharply with uniformed officers on furlough.

In the distance the harbor sparkled blue and dazzling, and along its edge, white-winged ships rode at anchor.

A haughty lady accompanied by an old Negro passed close to them. She was scowling and scolding at such a great rate that Hetty was moved to laughter.

"Poor old man," murmured Susan, "he must lead a wretched life."

"Yes," observed Hetty. "Does thee know, I'd love to live in the city, and be an Episcopalian and dance and have lovely clothes. Wouldn't thee really, Susan?"

"Goodness, no, Hetty. Whatever gets into thee sometimes? Come on. We don't want to waste any time."

"Let's look around first," begged Hetty. "We'll go into several shops and see the fine dresses, and then we'll go to a goods counter and buy our material. I wish we had enough money for new slippers, too."

"Never mind about slippers. If our dresses are long, our feet won't show anyway," said Susan comfortingly.

"I like to show mine," observed Hetty. "Men don't like big ankles but ours are slim enough to arouse interest."

Susan was amused. Hetty would be eighteen on her next birthday and perhaps she would find a suitable husband.

They entered a shop and walked about admiring the goods on display. People stared at them with interest. Two young Quaker girls modestly clad, with hair combed smoothly beneath their bonnets and white kerchiefs folded concealingly above gently rounded bosoms, provided a sight not unfamiliar in this town. However, these two were so sparkling with animation, and so rosy with health that many an effete beauty looked after them with a sigh of envy.

Finally, when they had bought Cousin Sarah's skirt braid, they went to the dry goods department.

"We want two ten-yard pieces of dove-gray silk," announced Susan.

The clerk was interested. "It's a pity you young ladies are not allowed to wear something pretty," he said. "I have here a lovely piece of pink silk that would become you well, and here is one of blue for your sister." He held up the material, draping it across their shoulders.

"Oh, Susan," breathed Hetty rapturously, "I've never seen anything so absolutely divine. Does thee think that Pa would let us?"

"No, I don't think—I know." Susan hastily threw the gay silk back on the counter. "We'll have the gray, if thee pleases."

Just at this moment there came a loud crash in a nearby aisle. Clerks and customers quickly ran to learn its cause. The girls discovered the aged Negro and his disagreeable mistress in great difficulty. The lady had purchased a large Chinese vase, and had instructed the slave to carry it to her carriage. It was a warm day, the vase was heavy and he had staggered against the counter and fallen headlong. Now he lay prone among the bits of crockery while his mistress whacked at him with her parasol.

"You wicked old scoundrel," she raved. "It's not enough that I feed and clothe you, but you have to show your lack of gratitude by carelessly breaking my vase. I'll take you home and have you thoroughly hided for this and tomorrow you go to the block. That is, if anyone can be found to buy you."

Viciously she struck at him again, and from a scratch on his bony cheek, a thin stream of blood trickled down and fell against a bit of the fragile white china.

Susan's eyes filled with tears. She stepped in front of the

angry mistress. "Stop," she said quietly. "If thee really wants to sell thy man, what does thee want for him?"

The woman suddenly deflated and a look of cunning came into her eyes. The old man was obviously of little further use to anyone. She looked the two girls over appraisingly. One could not tell about Quakers. They looked plain enough, but the narrow-minded creatures always had pockets well lined with cash.

"Abe is a valuable servant," she said shrewdly, "but he has been naughty and I'll sell him for a hundred dollars."

Susan lifted her skirt, and feeling down into the long pocket, she took out her purse and removed ten dollars.

"Susan," remonstrated Hetty.

"This is all I have," said Susan calmly. "I was going to buy material for a dress, but if God can clothe the lilies of the field, He can keep me covered, too. Will thee accept this for the slave?"

The woman looked at it greedily. The purse was hanging empty. She reached out for the money. "Take him," she snapped, "and I hope he's punishment enough to you for your interference."

"I'd like a receipted paper," said Susan with dignity.

Accordingly, the clerk brought a piece of paper and made out a receipt which was signed by the woman. She went away, pleased with having got rid of her nuisance.

Susan and Hetty lifted the old man to his feet, and helped him out to the servants' bench at the entrance to the store.

"He'll be all right for a little while," said Susan sadly. "Come, we'll go back and get thy dress."

Hetty was indignant. "If thee thinks I'm going to the party all dressed up and thee in thy old clothes, thee's demented," she said. "Come with me. I know just what I want to get. We'll buy Abe together and we'll spend our other ten dollars. Really, Susan, it's the only way left. Thee knows I won't be happy unless we share equally. Slippers will cost about four dollars a pair, and we'll have enough to buy each a pair of gloves. Come on."

Knowing Hetty's generous nature, Susan agreed, and when William came for them, he found each of his girls richer by a pair of shining new slippers and gray silk mitts.

"Oh, Pa," said Susan miserably, "thee'll be so tried with me. I've disobeyed the Discipline."

William lifted his eyebrows. Having just completed a good deal with Friend Whitelock, he was in a fine humor. "And what is this crime that my girl has committed?" he inquired.

"Pa, I've bought a slave!"

They stood together looking apprehensively at him from their wide blue eyes.

He was speechless. With eight children, William was accustomed to surprises, but this announcement from Susan took his breath. He drew a spotless square of linen from his pocket and slowly wiped his face.

Hetty pointed to the servants' bench. Upon it sat the old man, holding a shaking hand against the wound on his thin cheek.

William's mouth opened slowly. He cleared his throat and then glanced at his two daughters. "I see," he said. "Suppose you let me help you into the carriage, and then I'll collect your property." He assisted the old man to his feet and let him sit on the floor of the carriage with Toy to support him. William took the reins. "I'll drive," he announced shortly, "and, Toy, thee can hold the old man's head."

Susan wished that her father would speak. She knew that he was turning the matter over in his mind. He would feel that his daughters had obeyed conscience and sacrificed for a worthy purpose, and having made their sacrifice, they would have to abide by it. There would be no new dresses. Well, he had said they might carry bouquets of roses, and Pa's roses were the wonder of all who saw them. The roses would dress up the old gray silks, and in new slippers and mitts they need feel no shame. Her spirits were quite revived by the time they turned again into the Scotts' driveway.

Cousin Sarah was waiting for them, and when she saw the carriage approaching, she laid aside her knitting and bustled down from the porch to the drive. "Do come in," she begged, "I want to see all that you bought. Did you get my braid?"

"Yes, indeed," said Hetty, "and here it is, and here is thy change."

"Very nice, and I thank you both. Mercy on me, William. Where did thee ever get the old Negro? Can't he sit up?"

"He's in a very feeble condition," explained William, "and please don't ask my girls to show off their finery. I'm afraid they've let their hearts rule their judgment. They've bought themselves a slave in place of the dresses they went after."

"Oh, but, Pa," said Hetty hastily, "Abe only cost us ten dollars, and with the other ten we bought lovely new slippers for only four dollars a pair and then we got new mitts. See, Cousin Sarah, aren't they lovely?"

"Yes, dear child," said Cousin Sarah softly, "yes, indeed, they are, and I also see two very lovely girls who've purchased treasure in Heaven. I am going to be very proud of you at the President's reception, and if I know anything about Abraham Lincoln, he would approve your investment. Now do come in and have a bite of lunch. Father and I are all alone, and need some young life to cheer our dinner hour."

"Not this time, Sarah, please," said William. "My son George has enlisted as a surgeon, and I want to be home when he comes to say farewell. I feel a definite urge to get along as quickly as possible. Billy is the only one there to look after Deborah and the children, and that lad has a way of wandering from the straight and narrow path. I wish he thought less of carnal pleasures." He sighed.

"Tut, tut," laughed Sarah, "don't thee be too hard on the lad. He's scarcely fourteen years old and full of the joy of life. He'll settle down some day and be a credit to thee."

"I hope so, indeed."

"And, William," she added in a low tone, "word has just arrived that the goods thee consigned by packet have not arrived in Philadelphia. There has been some miscarriage of our plans."

"How dreadful," murmured Susan.

Cousin Sarah waved her hand to them as they drove sadly away.

Poor Keziah with her six little ones. Susan felt a sickness in the pit of her stomach. She stole a look at William to see how he was affected by the bad news, but she could tell nothing from his expression. He was calm and unperturbed as always.

CHAPTER

TWELVE

It was nearing the noon hour when the carriage approached the last bend in the road. In an adjacent grove, the Confederate recruits had made camp. The men were lying on the mossy ground under the oak and chestnut trees, while one of their number prepared food over a fire. The girls were very hungry, and the odor of roasting fowls reminded them that Henny would be ready with a good dinner.

Filled with pleasant anticipation, they left the carriage at the front of the house. Nobody came out to meet them, and they hastened inside. Myra sat on the hall stairs, weeping sadly. At the sight of her sisters, tears started afresh.

"Oh, me," she cried, "I thought you would never come. Where's Pa?"

"He's here," said Hetty. "What has happened?"

At this moment, William entered the hall. He saw at a glance that all was not well. "Where's Mother?" he asked quickly. "Is she all right?"

"She's in the sitting room," wailed Myra. "She has a poor sick soldier boy and she and Aunt Henny are trying to make him comfortable. Brother George hasn't come. And oh, Pa, my poor, poor little Oscar. He was such a good duck."

"What about him?"

"The soldiers grabbed him up and twisted his little neck. They're eating my Oscar," she sobbed.

Susan and Hetty were indignant. "Never mind, Myra,"

Hetty comforted. "Thee'll soon have the puppy from Cousin Johns."

Susan laid aside her bonnet and hurried to the sitting room where a sheet had been spread over a sofa; upon it lay the young Confederate recruit, weak with exhaustion. His feet dangled over the sofa's edge into a tub of warm water. Deborah sat beside him, while Henny added some healing herbs to the foot bath.

"Is he very sick, Aunt Henny?" asked Susan.

"No, ma'am, he ain't bad. He powerful homesick and he ain't much more'n a baby. Ain't he puny?"

"Has thee fed him?"

"Yas'm, but I so mad at them sojers. They come in yere grabbing chickens and ducks left and right. They gimme a han'ful of money, but missy say it ain't no good. De worstest thing dey done was wringing poor li'l ole Oscar. I done gib em de debbil for it, too."

"Henny!" came gently from Deborah.

"Yas'm," she sulked. "Pore li'l Myra. Her heart busted."

"She'll have a puppy," said Deborah, "and she must learn to be grateful over a few things if she hopes to become worthy of more."

"Yas'm." Henny was unconvinced. She was, to use her own vernacular, "rarin' mad."

Susan knelt beside the sofa and laid a firm hand on the boy's head. "How did thee get here?" she asked.

"Captain done sent me fer more ducks and I reckon I was so tuckered I couldn't make it," he whispered. "I feels turrible. Wisht I wuz home, but Pa went to the army, and then the big boys, and I wuz ashamed not to. A man give me a gun and I figured I could tote it."

"Has thee fired it yet?" she asked.

"Ain't killed nobody," he said regretfully, "but Pa, he's a crack shot at squirrels, and I bet he's brought down a mess of them damyankees. Wisht I could see him or the boys or Ma." Ashamed of his tears, he turned his face to the wall.

William had come into the room to stand at the head of the sofa. Now he spoke. "What's thy name, lad?"

"J."

"J what?"

"J Scudd."

"What's the J for?"

"Nothin', just J. When I born, Ma done show me to Pa, and says she's naming me Josh fer her pappy. Pa says no son of his'n goin' to carry the name of a dad-ratted ole weasel like granpappy. He changed it to Jake and tell Ma he'll likely take a stick to her if he hear her call me Josh. Ma, she's got sperrit. She say ef he call me Jake she'll git the li'l ole axe and lay his haid open. Ma meaned it. She's powerful handy with a axe."

"What happened then?" asked Susan.

"Nothin' done happen. Pa says, 'All right, les call him J, and when he's growed up, he kin decide fer hisse'f.' "

William laughed. "Pretty smart," he observed.

"Yassuh, he ain't too dumb," agreed the boy with some pride.

"Henny," said William, "where is Billy?"

"He's around somewheres," she answered evasively.

"Where was he when the soldiers took the ducks and chickens?"

"Don't rightly know, Mistah Willyum."

"If thee did, thee would not tell, but never mind. If he had been here, there might have been a struggle over little Oscar. As it is, we can better afford to lose the duck than our boy. Susan, thee take charge of this lad, and I'll ride back after lunch and talk to the officer about him. These may be the Southern recruits that James is hoping to intercept."

"There now," said Susan to J Scudd. "Thee heard what my

father said. Go to sleep now and have no worry about the morrow. All will be well with thee."

"Yes'm," came a weary voice, "and I thanks you kindly, ma'am."

Having seen to the immediate needs of the soldier, Susan hurried to the kitchen where she found Aunt Henny in a dither over the unwelcome addition to her problems.

"Dat ole Abe," she scolded, "he powerful weak. Howcum Mister Willyum fetch him here?"

"Pa had nothing to do with it," Susan said gently. "I don't know where he will live, but Hetty and I bought him to keep him from being abused, and he will just have to stay here for a few days."

"Yassum." Whatever Susan did was perfect in Henny's eyes. "Toy," she said briskly, "you go up in dat loft over de meat-house an' fix it up nice fer dat ole man. Fix him a corn-husk bed an' set a chair by it. I'll give him his victuals."

"Thank thee, Aunt Henny," said Susan. "Where is he now?"

"He eatin'. He been eatin' ever since he come. Ack lak he starve."

Susan found Abe on a bench outside the kitchen door. He was just finishing off a bowl of stew and he almost purred with contentment.

"Missy," he said, "I sure thanks you and I gonna work hard. Dat I is."

"What can thee do?"

There was silence for a moment and she repeated the question.

"I jest a stiddyin'," he said. "Reckon I kin take keer dat chicken-house. I powerful handy dat way. I good at huntin' eggs, too, miss. Ain't nary hen kin hide her eggs from ole Abe, miss."

"That's fine," said Susan. "Thee help Aunt Henny all thee

can, and when thee isn't busy in the garden or hen-house, thee might look after little Jerry and keep him out from under her feet."

"Yassum, dat I is. I gonna help everybody an' as de preacher done say, 'De Lord helps dem as helps deirselves.' "

"Dat don't sound good to me," grumbled Aunt Henny shrewdly. "You all gits to helpin' yourself, you gonna git a freewill offerin' from me, and it ain't gonna feel good, neither."

"Miss Susan," called Uncle Toy, "here come a white hoss a hippity hoppin'. Dat sho look lak Mistah John Hotkim."

"So it is," replied Susan quickly. "Thee take his horse and I'll meet him at the porch."

She hurried through the house and was waiting when Johns Hopkins appeared. He had brought a puppy to Myra, carrying it in a basket fastened to his saddle.

Now he came from the horseblock, followed by old Toy, who carried the basket and chuckled with pleasure.

"Ef I sees right, Miss Susan, dey's sumpin' mighty pretty peepin' from undah dis yere basket top, dat a fact."

"Come back to the porch, Cousin Johns," said Susan. "The family are all together, I believe."

After greeting each of the little circle, Johns Hopkins took the basket from Toy and set it down at Myra's feet. "There, my dear," he said, "I've brought thee a little pet that will follow at thy heels all the days of his life, and I trust will be a comfort to thee."

Myra lifted the pup from the basket, and the three sisters exclaimed with delight. It was a soft snugly little creature and very playful. Susan went to fetch a saucer of warm milk, and Hetty brought an old basket and a piece of blanket.

While the girls busied themselves with the pup, Friend Hopkins turned to the two boys who were sitting on the porch step.

"Billy," said Johns Hopkins, "is thee doing well at school?"

The boy squirmed guiltily and glanced sideways at his father. "I guess I could do a little better," he confessed.

"Well, I hope thee'll try," observed the merchant. "For myself, I got my education by studying at odd moments, and so to help along young people like thyself and Frank, I'm leaving my worldly goods to establish a university at Clifton and a hospital downtown. What does thee think of it, William?"

"Excellent," commended William heartily. "Now, Billy, thee work hard and perhaps thee can attend the Johns Hopkins University some day."

"I'll try, Pa," promised the boy.

Johns Hopkins smiled. Thrusting his hand into his coat pocket he produced a copy of the *Advertiser* and observed, "Here is Lincoln's reply to Horace Greeley's attack against what he calls 'the President's mistaken deference to rebel slavery.'

"Lincoln says, 'The paramount object of this struggle is to save the Union. It is not either to save or to destroy slavery. What I do about slavery and the colored race, I do because I believe it helps to save the Union, and what I forebear, I forebear because I do not believe it would help to save the Union.' "

Johns leaned forward and whispered, "I have it directly from a member of the cabinet. On July twenty-second, that was last week, the President read to that body a proclamation of emancipation which he intends to make public very soon. He only waits until the army achieves a forward victory."

William quoted:

" 'O sometimes gleams upon our sight
Through present wrong, the eternal right.
And step by step, since time began
We see the steady gain of man.'

"In my work as conductor of our Underground, I am frequently reminded of those words of Friend Whittier. Especially now, for Deborah's nephew has joined the Northern army in defiance of Quaker teaching, and my dear son George is about to offer his services as a surgeon in the same outfit. As if that were not enough concern, I have three unmarried daughters who must be protected from the fascination of brass buttons and marching feet."

"Thee has my full understanding," said Johns. "And speaking of responsibilities, I have manumitted the two Negroes, Celey and Jake, that I rescued for Susan's sake. My man Nicodemus is keeping them under close observation."

Susan smiled happily. "Thank thee, Cousin Johns," she said softly. "If we can help in any way, please tell us."

CHAPTER

THIRTEEN

In the late afternoon, William rode over to the woods to interview the Confederate officer in charge of the recruits. He found one man on guard while the others, about twenty in all, slept on the ground under the oak trees. The sentry reluctantly roused his officer.

"Captain Carter, sir, a gentleman to see you."

The captain lifted his head, and seeing William, got immediately to his feet.

"I'm sorry to disturb thy rest," apologized William. "I came to report the sad condition of a young lad, J Scudd, who is now a guest in my home."

"Indeed?" said the officer. "I've been worried, not so much for him but for the trouble he might bring upon the rest of us. He joined our recruits against my advice, and I've been wondering about his disappearance. I hoped he had given up and returned to his mountain cabin."

"Not so. He seems determined to remain with you. I am a Quaker, a member of the Society of Friends, and while I do not approve of either slavery or secession, I do not hold any feeling against those who differ with my opinion. Therefore, I am happy to shelter the lad, and have come here to urge that thee dismiss him from service. He is much too young to be able to endure the hardships of war. His feet are badly cut and I can't see how he can proceed farther. How long are you minded to remain here?"

"Only for a few hours. I was escorting these few recruits by night through Towsontown. Unfortunately, we missed the cross-country road we had planned to follow, and ended up here this morning. I am resting my men, and we expect to be on our way before daylight. With the Federal army lying between us and Richmond, we are in a hazardous position, although we find most persons we have met are either in sympathy with our cause, or like yourself, do not oppose us."

"There is much sentiment hereabouts in favor of the Confederacy," answered William. "On the other hand, the Federal government is still in control, and arrests of Southern sympathizers are made every day. I would not want to be responsible for thy presence in my home, and yet I feel thee should see the condition of this lad. Suppose thee comes for supper and thee can judge for thyself."

The officer bowed politely. "That is most gracious of you, Mr. . . . ?"

"William Coale is my name."

"Thank you, sir. I am Captain Randolph Carter of Richmond. I accept your invitation right gladly, sir, and pray your kindness may cause you no embarrassment."

The two men shook hands and William returned to Furley Hall to await the arrival of George. That there would be a meeting of two opposing factions did not immediately occur to him.

At four o'clock, a livery carriage drove up to the Hall. It brought George and one of his classmates.

Susan was deeply affected at this meeting with her brother. Accustomed as she was to the men of her family in the drab unexciting garments of the Quakers, it was something of a shock to see George's handsome figure in the dark-blue uniform of a Union surgeon. Eagerly, she clasped him in her arms.

"Dear George," she managed to whisper, "I think thee is doing a wonderful thing. I only wish I could go along to nurse the poor boys whose lives thee'll save. Pa would never let me, but if Florence Nightingale could do it, so could I."

"Thanks for standing by me, Sue. I'll probably get a good lecturing from Friends, but I know I'm doing right. Susan, this is my friend, Doctor Peter Yarnell. He is another back-sliding Quaker, I'm afraid. His folks live at York, and if it's convenient he'll spend the night with us, and go on his way early in the morning. We have four days to say farewell before leaving for active duty with the army now guarding Washington. With so many Southern troops around Richmond, we'll likely have another major battle soon, and Peter and I will be needed."

Susan extended a cordial hand to the stranger. He was a tall, clean-cut and very shy young man with serious brown eyes and slender nervous hands. Susan liked him at once.

George said, "I brought Peter along for moral support. Where is the family? I might as well have my lecture, and get it over with."

"I don't think they'll be too severe," she said encouragingly. "After all, Pa is always enjoining us to do without fear or hesitancy the thing that we think is right. The sight of that becoming uniform will be a shock, but Cousin James has been here with a brother officer, so although the ice is not completely broken, it has been weakened a bit. Come, I believe they're all on the porch." She tucked her hand in George's arm, and guided the two men through the house to the porch overlooking the garden.

Deborah saw them first and rose, trembling, to her feet. "George, my son," she cried.

She was very tiny, this mother of eight strong children. George fairly lifted her off her feet in a tender embrace, and then turned to receive William's delighted though somewhat serious welcome.

Hetty kissed her brother with dramatic fervor, and then

concentrated her talents upon Peter Yarnell. After fifteen minutes of sparkling chatter, she managed to entice him for a stroll down the garden walk toward the summer-house.

George, looking after them, whistled softly. "It looks as if our Hetty's grown up." He laughed. "Pete's a grand fellow, but so bashful he won't look at a girl."

Susan smiled. "He won't be bashful long with Hetty. Come now, tell us about thyself."

George had a merry disposition, and soon had the family laughing over his adventures at school. In turn, Susan told him of the much anticipated reception at the White House, and George promised to see them there if he could get leave.

"I went over to the camp this afternoon to see the Confederate officer about the lad we are entertaining." William entered the conversation. "I invited him to have supper with us, and I'm afraid I neglected to tell him about George. My guests have always been in agreement, and if not, their differences have been adjusted in the Friendly manner."

"Pa," gasped Susan, "we'll have the Captain and J Scudd from one side; Peter and George from the other. What will happen?"

"Nothing will happen," said William calmly. "They'll just forget their sentiments while they satisfy their hunger. We can't discuss politics, that's all."

As they talked, a roan horse carrying a great broad-shouldered man cantered up the drive. The rider went immediately to the rack, fastened his horse and came toward the porch.

As William and Susan advanced to meet him, his eye passed them and rested upon George and his blue uniform. At once he paused and clapped his hand to his revolver. An angry flush darkened his face. "Is this a trap?" he inquired crisply.

William spoke firmly. "Certainly not, my friend. In this house there are no enemies. Rich, poor and the stranger within our gates all are lovingly welcome. Here in this Quaker home, thee will put all animosity out of thy heart, and find rest and peace for thy spirit."

His manner was so kindly and his voice so filled with tenderness and affection, that the young officer was ashamed. He flushed slightly. "I apologize, sir, but you'll have to admit that I'm placed in an awkward position."

"Not necessarily. This is my daughter Susan. Susan, this is Captain Carter."

Before this dignified mansion and against a background of fragrant boxwood, Susan, in her simple frock, was as colorful and sparkling as a rose from William's own garden.

She welcomed the captain graciously, and turning to the other members of the family, she said, "This is my mother, and this, my doctor brother George who has volunteered as a surgeon."

The captain bowed. George came forward and extended his hand. His eyes were twinkling and there was an unmistakable friendliness in his manner. After an instant of tense silence, Captain Carter cautiously took the extended hand.

Susan said, "We have one of thy boys with us, Captain Carter. I was just about to call Brother George to care for him. Will thee come with us?"

She led the way upstairs to a cool room where J Scudd lay propped in bed. Before him stretched a pair of skinny legs each ending in an enormously bandaged foot.

"J Scudd," said Susan, "here is a doctor to look thee over."

The captain paused in the doorway, watching, while George bent over the boy and took his hand. At the sight of the blue uniform, J cringed and tried to draw away. "Git way from me," he said. "Git out or I'll gut you, you damyankee."

George laughed good-naturedly. "Come now, boy," he said gently. "Thee doesn't want to do anything like that, does thee? It would be a fearful inconvenience to me and a great labor to thyself. How would thee like to get well and go home to thy mother?"

"I ain't going home till I gits my dozen Yankees," announced J.

George felt the boy's head, and said, "He's got spunk anyway. No fever, and I'd suggest that you remove Aunt Henny's poultices and let the feet heal up. In a few days, J will be fit as ever. Can you kill squirrels, J?"

"Ain't fixin' to shoot no squirrels," sulked the boy. "I'm after Yankees."

Captain Carter grinned. "I'm going to send you home, J," he said.

"No, sir, I ain't agoin'," said the boy stubbornly.

"You see," said the officer to Susan, "it's the spirit of the South. You can't beat that."

Tears came to her eyes. "I know," she said, "it's magnificent. I don't agree with the ideas that back that spirit, but I can't help admiring it."

He stood facing her and looked down into her lovely troubled face and the blue eyes clouded with sorrow. Suddenly he reached out and seized her hand. "Miss Susan," he said huskily, "thank you."

From the dining room came the sound of the supper bell, and Susan said gaily, "I'll send thy supper on a tray, J, and tomorrow we'll decide about what thee wants to do."

J pouted but did not answer.

Susan led the way downstairs to the supper table where her father and mother were already waiting with the two younger children. Billy followed and then Hetty with Peter Yarnell.

In this gay and friendly atmosphere the captain soon lost all sense of restraint. Hetty, he decided, was a vivacious child. Susan had everything—charm, beauty, glowing health, vivacity, poise. Every moment he discovered some fresh attraction. They talked about the gardens, the flowers, fruit and trees. He asked about horses and listened with interest to her description of Firefly and Ginger. He told her of his life on a Virginia plantation, his horses, his cotton and tobacco. She was an attentive listener. Finally he spoke of his mother and sisters. He had not realized how starved he was for companionship and for decent food. Aunt Henny's biscuits disappeared at an alarming rate.

After supper, they went to the sitting room.

Peter Yarnell remarked upon the warmth of the July evening, and managed without too much maneuvering to pilot Hetty to the porch. George nudged Susan and whispered, "Peter is really falling in love. He needs just such a chatterbox as Hetty."

Presently the grandfather's clock struck a solemn reminder, and very regretfully, Captain Carter turned to his host. "If you will excuse me, sir, I'm afraid I have been too long absent from my duty. In such delightful company, I have been able to forget the sorrows of the past months, but I will never forget the peace and beauty of your lovely home and family." To Deborah, he said, "Thank you, madam, for your gracious hospitality. I hope we'll be allowed some day to welcome you to Richmond." To Susan, he added, "When this struggle is over, Miss Susan, and I pray that will be soon, may I have the privilege of renewing our too brief acquaintance?"

"Indeed, yes," Susan said, and blushed, "but do remember what Pa said. We don't recognize any as enemies. Thee will always be welcome here."

He pressed her hand, and a moment later the door closed behind him.

"What a decent chap," exclaimed George. "What a pity he takes the wrong side."

"Yes," Susan laughed, "but it's fortunate that Hetty has Peter to amuse her. Otherwise she would be in love with three men at once. She has a tremendously big heart."

CHAPTER

FOURTEEN

In the morning, Peter did not leave Furley. It required very little coaxing from Hetty to change his plans. His Quaker parents would frown upon his enlistment, and why face the ordeal when life was so sweet with Hetty prattling at his side? So he remained for another day to sit with her in the summerhouse and walk with her among the flowers. She told him of the invitation from her Cousin James and of the new slippers and silk mitts.

"If thee and Brother George are near Washington, promise me that we will see you at the reception."

"That is a promise easy to make," he said seriously, "but the fulfillment may be difficult. We will surely come if we are allowed."

When evening came, Susan put her mother to bed and saw Myra and Frank safely on their way upstairs. William was in his study talking to George about his future, and Hetty had disappeared with Peter. The house seemed very quiet and suddenly lonely. Susan strolled out to the porch and stood in the moonlight, drinking in the sweetness of the rose-scented night.

In the distance she heard a clatter of hooves along the highway. At the drive they grew louder, and she walked to the steps in time to greet her Cousin James and his friend, Calvin Pancoast.

"We came to make final plans with you about going to the White House on Saturday," said James. "Then, too, I heard that George was expected home and I wanted to see him."

"As to the reception," answered Susan, "everything is in readiness, as Ma wrote thee. The Scotts are taking us over and we will see you at the White House. If thee wants to see George, thee will find him in the study with Pa."

James excused himself at once and entered the house, leaving Susan alone with the lieutenant.

"At last, Miss Susan," he said, "I can talk with you alone. This time I won't be sidetracked by Miss Hetty. I want to hear all about Firefly and Aunt Henny and your other interests. I mean it, really."

Goodness, thought Susan, why doesn't Hetty come?

But Hetty and Peter were nowhere about, and since she did not wish the tall lieutenant to guess her nervousness, she allowed him to escort her along the scented pathways of the moon-drenched garden. When she had sat beside him at the table on that first occasion of their meeting, she had done most of the talking. Now it was Calvin who must pour out his story of school days with her Cousin James, of Sunday evening tea parties at her Aunt Cassandra's when he and James were growing up.

As they strolled toward the summer-house, he paused to admire the roses that bloomed in fragrant profusion on either side of the garden walk.

"Is it difficult to grow such beauties?" he inquired.

"Not for Pa. He has what is known as a green thumb. He can make almost anything flourish. I said 'almost,' for there is one rose that he can do nothing with."

She walked ahead for a few feet and stopped beside a rosebush. "See," she said, "here is a rose that's unlike all the others. The blossoms are a strange coppery green. Pa has never seen their like and he can't start another bush. He has planted dozens of slips, and he's even tried the seeds of the flowers, but he gets nothing for his trouble."

"How interesting. When will it bloom?" he asked.

"It blooms when it gets ready. As thee can see, there are some tight buds forming now. People come for miles to see it."

Calvin was interested. "Where did it come from in the first place?"

"My grandfather brought it from Europe. He managed to get it here alive and planted it among the other roses. Finally it bloomed, but the flowers did not follow the ways of their kind—to his surprise they were green."

Calvin was impressed. "I had no idea that plants and trees could be so interesting. I guess I've always taken them for granted."

She nodded. "Few people realize how much intelligent labor lies behind the growing of a lovely shade tree or the propagation of a choice fruit or flower. Pa spends hours at experimental work. He lives close to God and is a real friend not only to all mankind but to the little people of the woods."

"Miss Susan," said Calvin suddenly, "I wish I could tell you how happy I am here with you. I felt it at home when I visited James at your Aunt Cassy's. It's a sense of peace and security. I forget a sort of restless yearning after I know not what, and I feel contented and secure. How do you account for it?"

"I suppose it's because thee forgets about fear. Here where everyone is always thy friend, thee knows thee is in thy rightful place in God's world and so finds contentment. Could that be it?" She smiled.

"It is easy for me to believe that I'm in my rightful place when I am at your side, Miss Susan. Do you think your father would let me go to Meeting with you tomorrow? If your brother George goes, there'll be another uniform and they won't throw us out, will they?"

"Goodness, no." She laughed. "They'll undoubtedly try to

change thy way of thinking, and thee'll be prayed over considerably but they'll not bite thee. I'll tell Pa that thee wants to go and I know he'll agree."

They reached the summer-house and stopped abruptly. Voices came from close by, and parting the lilac bushes, Susan looked down upon a somewhat startled Hetty. She was sitting on the lawn in a patch of bright moonlight with Peter kneeling beside her. Both were industriously picking over the grass.

"Sorry to interrupt you." Calvin laughed. "Are you digging for gold or fishing worms?"

Much embarrassed, Peter sprang to his feet and was introduced.

"We were hunting four-leaf clovers," Hetty explained, as she extended both hands to Calvin. He lifted her to her feet and smiled as she took a clover-leaf from her pocket and fastened it on his coat. "There, Calvin, that will bring thee luck." She tucked her arm in his, and in her most possessive tone, said, "Walk with me and tell me what good fortune brings thee back so soon?"

Susan felt a pang of annoyance. She had been so happy, so completely happy. Now she must forget about Calvin. Hetty wanted him, and Susan must not interfere.

With forced gaiety she turned to Peter who was staring indignantly after Hetty and Calvin. "Let's find a clover-leaf for me," she begged. "I'm in need of a little luck."

He looked at her crossly, then at the sweetness of her smile, his pique vanished.

"Gladly," he said, "I've never seen so many four-leafs in one place."

He found the clover and they sat in the summer-house while Susan encouraged him to talk. He found it easy to confide in her. In a short while he was telling about his experiences with her brother George. She tried to listen but her thoughts were with Calvin and Hetty. I could take either of them away from her, she thought, but I won't. She's young and so happy. She shall have the man she wants. So she detained Peter, and gave Hetty an opportunity to be alone with Calvin.

But it was growing late, and James must return to his company. He gave Calvin leave to remain overnight and to attend Meeting.

They stood on the porch and listened until the horse galloped out of hearing.

After George had escorted Peter and Calvin to their room, Hetty confided to Susan, "Peter is a wonderful man, but he's so diffident. I like Calvin better, but he never speaks of love, perhaps because he feels his life to be so uncertain. Anyway, Peter will be gone in the morning, and I'll have the rest of the day to devote to Calvin. Good night, dear Susan."

"Good night," answered Susan dully, "and go to sleep. I'll be upstairs directly."

But Susan did not go to bed. Instead she sat on the porch in the bright moonlight and strove to quiet her thoughts. An owl perched in a maple tree close by and hooted dismally. In spite of her loneliness, she smiled. How stupid I am, she thought. I've been hoping and hoping that Calvin would come, and now that he's here, I'm wretched. Even the owl hoots at me. She closed her eyes and brushed a tear from her face. Then she remembered what her father had taught her. "All things work together for good." She had always believed it; she would believe it now.

She went slowly into the house, closed the door and turned the key. Silently she crept upstairs to her room, hung her frock in the wardrobe and removed her undergarments. Moonlight flooded the room and shone upon her sleeping sister. How sweet and unhurt she was.

Suddenly Susan heard a sound outside her room. Tiptoeing to the door, she laid an ear against it and listened. Someone was creeping along the hall from her father's room.

Stealthily opening the door, Susan saw a dark shape moving slowly along in the moonlight. At J Scudd's little room it vanished from sight and the door closed softly.

What was the boy up to? She wondered. He had been to her father's room, and her father and mother had been in bed and asleep for an hour at least.

She was puzzled as she closed her door and climbed into the poster-bed.

CHAPTER

FIFTEEN

Susan awakened to a realization that Hetty was prodding her in the back.

"Wake up, lazy," she said briskly. "Peter is leaving early for York, and I want to eat breakfast with him and see him off."

Susan roused herself with an effort and inquired sleepily, "Is he really going?"

"Thee knows he is. Quit trying to postpone the ordeal of getting thyself up."

"All right, dear, I'll see that he has something to eat. Did thee tell Aunt Henny?" asked Susan.

"Yes, she knows, and I can smell bacon frying, so I guess it's ready. I don't want Peter to feel neglected, for I do like him. After all, Susan, we're in a war and we should remember that some of the boys may not come through. It's best to keep several lined up, for I don't want to be an old maid, always sorrowing for what might have been."

"Hetty, thee cold-blooded vixen, I'd like to spank thee."

"Don't try it. It's not according to the Discipline," said Hetty, laughing, as with a flounce of her skirts she left the room.

Susan splashed her face with cold water and dressed quickly. She had breakfast with her father, Hetty and Peter, and then they went to the porch to see the young man on his way.

"With your permission, I'll return in a day or so to join forces with George. Then we'll leave for camp together," said Peter.

"That's agreeable to us," answered William heartily. "We'll be rejoiced to see thee. It gives me great comfort to know that George will have a congenial comrade by his side in the coming ordeal. Remember us to thy parents and return when thee has a mind to."

So Peter rode away, and when he was gone, Susan said, "Pa, what's worrying thee? Thee seems bothered and that's not thy usual way. Is it because of the lost packages?"

"No, it's nothing of great moment. I seem to have mislaid my watch. Thee hasn't seen it, has thee? I thought I left it on my dresser last night but it wasn't there this morning. It's of no matter, my dear. God knows where it is, and so it isn't lost. It will come to light again."

Susan stood for a moment, thinking intently. Then without answering she went quickly into the house and upstairs to the door of J Scudd's room. She tapped lightly, and receiving no answer, opened the door and peeped inside. The bed was empty. For a moment, she hesitated. Then, as she heard Billy come from his room, she called him to her.

"Billy," she said, "J Scudd evacuated during the night and Pa's watch has walked off with him. J did not want to be discharged, and I think we'll find him at the camp. Please get Firefly saddled and meet me at the end of the lane—and hurry."

She left by the back door and went quickly to the lane.

A few minutes later, Billy came to her. He was riding Ginger and leading Firefly.

"Thee need not go," Susan said. "I'll be all right."

"No," said Billy firmly. "Pa thinks I'm a scatterbrain, but I'm not. I'm going to take care of thee."

She smiled gratefully. "All right, if thee must, and it's kind of thee."

"Is thee sure that thee ought to do this, Susan?" he asked anxiously.

"Yes, Billy. Come on." She tapped Firefly with her foot

and they loped along the path between fields of tiny growing plants and lanes of trees. The early morning sunshine sparkled on dewy drops that jeweled their path into a fairy carpet. A light breeze tossed the loose curls about Susan's temples, and fanned her cheeks with color.

When they reached the camping place, they found it deserted. Only a thin column of smoke from a recent fire and the trampled condition of the woods were left to tell a tale of recent occupancy.

"They must have left before daybreak," observed Billy. "They haven't got far. I'll ride after them."

"I'm afraid this is a job I'll have to handle myself," answered Susan firmly, "but thee can come along if thee must." At a brisk lope, she followed down the road with Billy close behind her.

Fifteen minutes later, they sighted the recruits. Susan reined in her horse. "Thee wait here," she said. "There are some things I can do better alone."

"Oh, no," insisted Billy. "Thee can't go on without me."

"Don't be silly. Thee let me be, and I'll be all right. Just wait here under this tree."

With that, she cantered forward. In a few minutes, she came up with the soldiers and passed to the head of the column.

Captain Carter was both amazed and delighted. He halted his men and turned to speak to her. "Why, Miss Susan, to what am I indebted for this honor?"

"I'm in trouble," she said simply. "That little rascal, J Scudd, ran away in the night and I want permission to say good-bye to him."

There was a moment's silence while the captain looked deep into her blue eyes. "That little rascal?" he repeated cautiously. "I'm afraid he's been giving you a lot of trouble, Miss Susan. He came out of the hills, and he has his own ideas about the rights of others. My men have had orders to take nothing but necessary food and that is paid for in good Confederate money. We pride ourselves upon our honor. My orders are to have any man shot at once if he disobeys. If the boy has taken anything that does not belong to him, I shall be obliged to carry out the stern orders of war." He looked suddenly very tired and sorrowful. Susan's heart bled for him. He was such a nice person.

She smiled. "I have no complaints to make to thee," she answered quickly, "but I do want to see the lad for a moment alone. I've been nursing him, and I don't want him to run off in this way."

He bowed, and she rode to the rear. In a moment J came to her. He wore an expression of great impudence, but behind it, she detected fear.

"Come on the other side of the horse," she commanded, "where thee can't be seen."

He walked around the horse and stood sullenly.

"Now give me the watch." She leaned forward and held her hand low.

"I ain't got no watch."

"Thee heard what the captain said just now, and if thee doesn't want that bulge on thy chest investigated, thee'd better hand over the watch and be quick about it." Her voice was severe.

The boy spat tobacco against the side of a tree. Then he reached into his shirt, brought out the watch and laid it in Susan's hand. She slipped it into her pocket.

"Thank thee, J." She smiled. "Be a good boy and take care of thy captain."

"Yes, miss, I aims to do that, and I thanks you kindly fer all you done fer me. Only I dassent run home. Ma'd shorely take after me with the little ole axe. Us Scudds don't nary run, miss; us shoots."

She patted his head and returned to the captain. "Thank thee so much," she said, smiling. "J and I made up our differences. It's better this way. Good-bye, my friend. I'll remember thee in my prayers. And—" She hesitated.

"Yes?" Encouragingly, he leaned toward her. There was something in his eyes that made her lower her own.

She glanced nervously about her and then whispered, "Pa insists that we keep ourselves entirely neutral but—"

He nodded. "I understand," he said kindly.

She continued, "The roads south of here may be blocked, for it's more than likely that your presence in the neighborhood has been reported."

"Thank you, dear lady," he said. "We deeply appreciate your interest, and so that you will not feel further concern, I will confide the fact that a wagon will pick us up at the crossroads just beyond here. Near Joppa, a boat will be waiting to take us to Virginia. Good-bye, now, but some day we'll meet again. Of that, I am certain."

She wheeled her horse, and with a wave of the hand, called, "Good-bye, until then."

Billy was relieved to see her safely returned. "Did thee get what thee wanted?" he called anxiously.

"Right in my pocket." She laughed. "Come on, I'll race thee home."

A few minutes later, they clattered up to the Hall with Billy only a length ahead.

Hearing the commotion, the family came from the house to investigate.

George lifted his sister from the horse. "Susan," he exclaimed admiringly, "thee is getting much too pretty. Bright blue eyes, rosy cheeks and a trim waistline; all these charms set off by plain Quaker petticoats. It's no wonder I don't get married. There's no girl quite so charming as my own sister."

She pinched his cheek and kissed him playfully. "No flattery, please. Pa will tell thee, 'Beauty is as Beauty does!'"

She turned to William. "Hold thy hand, Pa, and close thy eyes. I have a present for thee."

William closed his eyes obediently and extended one hand. "It doesn't scratch or bite, does it?"

"I hope not, although it has two hands and a face." She laid the watch upon his open palm.

He was surprised and pleased. "Where did thee find it?"

"I didn't, Pa. J Scudd found it. And, Pa, he left this morning to join his company. They've all gone. I know thee was sorry to have the boy run off, but it's a big relief to have the soldiers leave. Perhaps now our chickens and ducks can settle down to business without danger of interruption."

She saw that he understood, and she turned her attention to Calvin Pancoast.

"Your father has promised to take me to Meeting," he announced, "and I believe that George is glad to have me along, too. Aren't you, George?"

"Indeed I am. If there's a lecture coming my way, I'll be glad to share it with thee."

"I won't mind," answered Calvin. "After living next door to your Aunt Cassandra, I'm accustomed to the ways of Friends, and curious to know just how they will receive a fighting man."

"With love and tenderness," answered William quickly. "We are not in the world to condemn, but to minister with kindness and understanding. When a Friend has disobeyed a commandment, we labor to make him see the light according to Jesus' example. We feel that a man's conscience is his safest guide to right living. Therefore, in silence we meet and open our hearts to receive that Inner Light that will counsel and guide us in the way of God's appointing. In regard to the fighting, I believe J Scudd's parents, crude as they are, had the right idea. They could not settle upon a proper name for the boy, and rather than shed blood over it, they agreed upon a truce and a compromise. Some day the boy will decide upon a name for himself and without the use of an axe."

Leaving her father with Calvin and George, Susan hurried into the house to get her family ready for Meeting. Deborah and Myra had to be dressed in their best frocks, and Frank's cleaning-up, superintended.

She checked with Aunt Henny about the dinner, for the family would come half-starved from the Meeting, and food must be prepared before they returned.

Hetty had disappeared, but with such a man as Calvin available, it wasn't like Hetty to waste an opportunity.

Susan flew about her morning chores and tried to be happy.

George found an opportunity to draw her aside. "Tell me something about this lieutenant. Is Hetty interested in him or in Peter?"

"He's wonderful, George, but he's a fighting lieutenant and is not of our belief. I guess he's not for us."

"For us? Is thee smitten, too?"

Her face flushed crimson. "Goodness, I hope not, although he does have his points. Pa would have a fit."

"Not to mention what Brother Ezra would do. By the way, does Ezra know about me and the uniform?"

"I don't know. We were in town yesterday, but did not have time to stop at Ezra's. Pa was in a dither to get home before thee arrived."

"How's Ezra's wife?"

"Miriam? Oh, she's all right and so are the two children. Thee'll probably get a scolding from Ezra. He's so strict."

George made a little face and smiled sadly.

Finally, the family were settled in the carriage to drive to Meeting. William clucked to the two big horses, and as they drove along, Susan thought sadly of Keziah and the children. Surely, at the Meeting, some Friend would have news of the refugees.

CHAPTER

SIXTEEN

After his disownment, Johns Hopkins no longer attended the Friends Meeting. His place on the front bench remained empty, although Friends prayed for him and vainly hoped that he would some day reform and ban the offensive liquor from his warehouse shelves. Since he did not go to Meeting on the first day of the week, he held early devotionals in a sheltered corner of the wide porch that surrounded his mansion. His only companions were his Bible and the two dogs sleeping at his feet.

Now, as he closed the Book and laid it aside, his thoughts were upon the beauty of his surroundings. He took a cane from the rack, whistled to his dogs and went for a walk. This afternoon he would ride over to Furley and visit with William Coale. With this in mind, he went to the stable and addressed the Negro in charge.

"Nicodemus, how are Celey and Jake getting along?"

"Dey all right, suh. Dat lil cabin you done buy 'em down de road, dat jes' fine. Babies is well an' Celey, she got washings for make a livin' an' de man Jake, he got a job hoein' corn. I'se lookin' after 'em, suh. You ain't got nothin' ter worry 'bout."

"When did thee see them?" inquired Johns.

"Seen 'em yisteddy, and gonna see 'em agin right aftah dinnah, suh."

"Very well, tell them to be very careful and not venture far from home. Free Negroes are not safe any more. All a slaver has to do is establish a claim, and since they're a greedy lot, and not always honest, and the colored people are not allowed to speak in their own behalf, there isn't much chance for justice."

"Yowsuh, I'll keep a eye on 'em, but I wishes dey was yere on our own place. Things is got so bad I'se skeered ter step mah foot tother side de fence."

"Well," said Johns, "I have thy manumission papers along with theirs, and if anything happens to me, they're in my strong-box."

"Yowsuh, thank you, suh."

Johns Hopkins turned from the stable and continued his walk. Talk of the slaves he had rescued reminded him of Susan. She was a lovely radiant creature. How different his life would be if he had a daughter. Once, long ago, he had approached Deborah shyly. That was just after he came to Baltimore from the farm, and he was still conscious of his country manners. She was kind, vivacious and rarely beautiful, and she had completely won his heart. He invited her to attend a quilting party with him, and she turned him down for handsome William Coale.

He never asked her again. He sat near her in the Meeting—that was before he was disowned—and he rejoiced in the privilege of being near her once a week. Because of the bigness of his spirit, he was able to give to William a full measure of friendship. His greatest pleasure was his frequent visits to Furley.

He had now reached the lane that separated Clifton from the adjoining property. A short distance along the road, he could see the stone chimney of a tiny cabin by the roadside. This he had bought for Celey and Jake, and since the day was fine and it still lacked an hour until dinner time, he decided to extend his stroll and investigate their condition for himself.

Accordingly, he motioned the dogs to heel and followed the grassy path beside the dirt road. No smoke came from the chimney, which was not surprising, for this was the Sabbath day, and Celey and Jake would be eating cold victuals.

When he reached the little house, he opened the gate and followed the path to the tiny porch. Lilies bloomed along the fence, the apple tree had been pruned and the grass neatly mowed. Some small garments hung on the clothesline, faded in the hot sunshine, and on the porch a homemade rag doll told of the recent presence of a child. The door stood open. Johns entered and looked about him. The cabin was in perfect order except for an overturned chair and an abandoned cornpone, crisp and black, on the spider in the cold fireplace.

Suddenly Hopkins went cold with dread. Where were they? Had they left in haste? According to the provisions of the Fugitive Slave Law, the master or his agent had simply to present an affidavit before a United States judge or commissioner, whose fee was double if he decided in favor of the claimant. In none of the proceedings could the testimony of the alleged fugitive be admitted. Free Negroes were being picked up everywhere by unscrupulous slavers and false affidavits approved by the courts.

Johns Hopkins' first reaction was a desire to confide his fears to William, who was a conductor on the Underground Railroad. He would know what to do. But no, this was the first day of the week and William would be at the Meeting House. Johns must wait until after dinner.

But the clerk of the court lived only a mile or so away. Perhaps he could throw some light on the Negroes' whereabouts. Back at the stable, Johns called for his horse. While Nicodemus saddled the animal, the merchant indignantly related his experience.

The poor fellow was heartbroken. He had taken a brotherly pride in the improved fortunes of his friends, and his grief was genuine.

Johns proceeded at once to the clerk's home, where his fears were vindicated. The day before, a couple of men had appeared with a pair of Negroes and two babies. The men claimed the Negroes had escaped from a North Carolina master. Their claim was upheld and the Negroes made over to the captors. Now the clerk regretted the mistake, but there was nothing to be done about it. Completely frustrated, Johns returned to Clifton and a lonely dinner.

CHAPTER

SEVENTEEN

As Johns Hopkins had surmised, the Coale family were at Meeting. At a quarter to eleven, they had driven into the brick-walled yard and stopped beside the carriage block. The young men stepped over the rear wheel, leaped to the block, and assisted the ladies and children to alight. Then William handed the team over to Billy, who drove it to the carriage shed and fastened the horses where they could stomp flies and rest from the hot sun.

Before them stood the Meeting House, a substantial affair built of brick and roofed with stout hickory shingles. Severely plain, like the Friends themselves, its hospitable doors stood wide to receive all those who came in the spirit of meekness. The interior of the House was of paneled oak with a partition down the middle so the men and woman might worship on opposite sides. Today there were visiting preachers, and the upper parts of these folding partitions were removed so that both men and women might see the faces of the speakers above the forbidding barriers.

At the door, the Coales separated, the men entering the House on the right and the women on the left. Above the partition Susan could see her father and Frank pass along the aisle with George and Calvin Pancoast close behind them. As the Friends already gathered became conscious of the two uniforms, there was a slight rustling of gray silk, gray-mitted hands surreptitiously poked gray-clad neighbors and gray bonnets dipped in the direction of the two young men. On the men's side of the Meeting, several Friends cleared their throats or coughed nervously, and one removed his spectacles and wiped them carefully on his handkerchief before giving the boys a second glance of disapproval.

If William noticed this little stir, he showed no sign. With his usual calm, he placed his walking stick between his knees, folded his hands over its knob, closed his eyes and bent forward in an attitude of devotion.

Cousin Sarah Scott came in and sat on the bench in front of Susan. She turned and whispered, "If the Coales will be at home this afternoon, Thomas and I propose to call upon you. We have some news."

Susan nodded and Cousin Sarah settled down for the devotional meeting. Susan wondered whether the news was of Keziah, and she prayed that the Negro woman might reach safety. God had delivered Daniel from the cruel lions and He would save Keziah from her oppressors.

Among the last worshippers to arrive were Brother Ezra and his family. His wife, Miriam, and the two little girls occupied the bench behind Susan. Ezra entered the men's side, passed to the front of the room and sat on one of three benches facing the rest of the assembly, for Ezra was an accepted minister, an accustomed preacher invited to sit where he might be better seen.

Susan heard a whisper behind her and a small voice saying, "Mother, look at Uncle George!"

Then she heard a startled "Oh, dear me" from her sister-in-law.

Susan darted a glance above the partition toward Ezra. He had just taken his seat and was removing the tall beaver hat, which he placed under the bench he occupied. This accomplished, he glanced over the House to see that his father and brothers were present and prayerfully occupied. At sight of him, Frankie stopped squirming and sat rigidly on the unyielding oak bench. His feet did not reach the floor and the narrow board cut into his legs. The back of the bench consisted of a single narrow shoulder-high board, but Frank's shoulders did not reach it. It bumped the back of his head when he relaxed, and his body slumped through the opening. He had to be alert and sit up straight all through the hour-long Meeting.

Suddenly Susan saw Ezra's long thin jaw drop wide as his eyes fell upon his brother George and the handsome stranger. A Coale in a soldier's uniform! He closed his mouth and sat with bowed head. Susan's heart beat faster. What would they say to George? And what would Calvin think of Friends?

There was silence for some moments, and then Ezra rose to his feet. He did not look at his brother, but there was a pained expression on his face as he gave his text, "Am I my brother's keeper?" He spoke of one among them who had been brought up to obey the solemn dictates of the Bible and the Discipline, but who through unwatchfulness had been led to assume the outward appearance of a man of violence. He told of that great Quaker, William Penn, and his success with the Indians, among whom he had lived with his peace-loving followers and with never a drop of blood shed in controversy. Finally he solemnly adjured Friends to pray for the erring one and, over and above all else, to be forgiving.

Ezra sat down.

Fearfully, Susan glanced over the partition. Her father's expression had not changed. George had a resigned look, and Calvin had turned his head and was looking out the window at the linden trees that shaded the yard outside. Quickly, as if he felt her gaze, he turned his head and their eyes met. He smiled, and she felt the quick color come to her face. All was well. He had caught the sense of loving interest in his right-doing, and he was free to follow as his conscience directed.

One or two visitors spoke, and then the Meeting was over. Two of the elders shook hands and the Friends left the uncomfortable benches and greeted each other joyfully. Frankie wriggled from among the plain-suited menfolks and waited in the good out-of-doors for Myra.

William was anxious to get home, so without seeming too hasty, he gathered his family together and drove them back to Furley.

Susan bounced over the wheel, descended the carriage block and hurried into the house after her mother and Myra.

Hetty took her time leaving the carriage. She leaned heavily against Calvin Pancoast as he extended a steadying hand. He had not shown her any marked attention this morning, but then perhaps he felt piqued because she wasn't at his beck and call the evening before. She smiled coquettishly at him, and was amazed at the way he looked over her head as though he did not see her. Oh, well, she'd make up with him after dinner. Meanwhile, she helped Aunt Henny and Susan get the terrapin soup, baked chickens, a beautiful spicy ham and a large rib roast of beef on the table.

Hetty, who had set the table, had been careful to seat the guest at her side, and now entertained him in her most charming manner. All through the meal, Susan noticed that he seemed strangely quiet and preoccupied.

After dinner, the men went to the porch while the girls helped Aunt Henny clear the table and wash the dishes. When the last plate was polished and on the shelf, Susan busied herself with plans for supper. The Scotts might stay, so there must be something good.

"Don't you worry, Miss Susan," said Aunt Henny. "I got plenty cold chicken and ham, and I'll mix up some biscuits and mebbe a cake."

"Thee might have some pickled eggs."

The old woman looked exasperated. "No, miss, us ain't got a egg on dis place."

"Why not? Did the soldiers take all our hens?"

"No, miss, dey done took some, but us oughter have plenty eggs, only I hates ter tell you."

"Tell me."

"It's dat ornery Abe. I fetches a egg-basket out ter de hen-house, an' they ain't no eggs. Den I seen ole Abe hot-footin' it down dat road wiv a basket on his arm. Bimeby he come back smellin lak a corn-liquor still. I fetch myself a stick an' basted him good on all sides. Miss Susan, you sho got a bad bargain. He too weak to do work, an' he won't do nothin' but eat. He got holler legs. He never git hisself fill up. I wish you'd git him way from yere afore he drive me crazy. Even dat li'l Jerry he some account, but not dat ole Abe."

Susan was troubled. "I'm glad thee told me," she said. "I'll speak to Pa about him. Pa always says that man is made in the image and likeness of God, and if thee can see that good-ness in Abe, he will try not to disappoint thee."

"Yas, miss. I hopes de Lord shows me some good in dat ornery ole critter. I ain't seen it yit," Henny replied. "But you run along now, honey, and git a good time wid dat young man. My, ain't he nice?"

The sly old puss, thought Susan. She thinks she knows what goes on inside me. Aloud she said, "I believe Hetty doesn't know whether she wants him or the young doctor."

Aunt Henny seized her firmly by the shoulder. "You listen to me," she said. "Dat scatterbrain don't know what she want. Don't you step aside and let her spoil your life. He like you. I kin tell, and furthermo' you likes him. Now run along and git yore rights."

But when she reached the porch, Susan heard Hetty saying, "Come on, Calvin, I've found a spot where wild strawberries grow."

He stood at once. "I'm sorry, Miss Hetty," he said, "but my leave is up this evening and I must return to Washington. I'll be on my way. Thank you for a very happy visit, and please express my gratitude to your dear mother."

He strode across the porch to where Susan stood in the doorway of the house. Taking her hand firmly, he led her down the long hall to the front door.

In an effort to avoid his eyes, she looked past him down the shady driveway. There she saw a well-known gray horse rapidly bearing Johns Hopkins toward the house.

Calvin was saying, "I wanted to see you for a moment alone. Susan, I liked your Quaker Meeting and the fine friendly atmosphere. It gave me strength which I will surely need during the weeks to come. And most of all, dear Susan, I have enjoyed being here with you. To sit across from you at dinner, to ride in the same carriage, to worship under the same roof—it has been a time of great happiness. For a while I must wear my uniform and engage in an undertaking that is against the very foundations of your religion and way of life. Until the day when this struggle is over, and I am free to come to you as you would have me, may I have the privilege of writing to you, and will you promise to answer my letters?"

As he spoke, she felt the blood pounding in her veins. The gray horse stopped at the porch. Johns Hopkins tossed the reins to Toy and said shortly, "Thee need not bother to announce me. I can find my way."

As the old merchant entered the house, Susan heard herself saying, "Cousin Johns Hopkins, has thee met Calvin Pancoast?"

The lieutenant acknowledged the introduction, and to Susan he said, "I'll hope to see you in Washington on Saturday."

Then he went to the hitching-rack for his horse, sprang into the saddle and was gone.

Well, thought Susan, Cousin Johns had certainly come in the nick of time. But in her heart she felt a sense of loss and incompleteness.

She turned to Friend Hopkins. It was obvious that he had

something on his mind. His usual smile was lacking as he linked his arm in Susan's and demanded briskly, "Where is William?"

"He's on the back porch, Cousin Johns. I think thee will find him alone, for the children are playing somewhere, and Hetty just took Mother upstairs for her nap."

"I want to see thee, too, Susan. I've just made an unhappy discovery. Come with me, please."

William recognized the brisk step of his friend and went to greet him.

"I was just settling myself for a period of contemplation," he said. "Come and join me."

"Thank thee," said Johns, taking the proffered seat. "I'm afraid I'm going to unsettle thee. I'm in an unbecoming temper."

"In that case," said William quietly, "we'd better sit in silence for a moment before thee ventures to express thyself."

So they sat until the exasperated guest had conquered his impatience. Then he proceeded to tell about the disappearance of Jake and Celey.

When he had finished, Susan told him about the missing Keziah and her family.

"It's a bad business," said William. "The Fugitive Slave Law is the most inhuman ever passed. I think it possible that a party of slave-snatchers are operating in this neighborhood, and until we've located their nest we've got to be watchful. In a little while, Thomas and Sarah Scott will be coming to spend the afternoon and stay for tea. I'll be pleased to have thee stay, too. Thomas has news relative to certain missing packages, and we may be able to piece the whole business together."

While they discussed these matters, Thomas Scott arrived with Sarah. They had indeed brought news of Keziah. Sarah could hardly wait to confide.

"Not long after the Elkton boat left Joppa, it was boarded

by a searching party and the packages removed. We did not hear of it immediately, and by the time the news reached us, the hawks had probably got their quarry back into Virginia. I have reported the case to our agents, and if the victims are still in this community, we will soon know of it and measures will be taken to rescue them. Meanwhile, the operator of the rescue boat has been taken into custody, and we will all have to put our hands into our pockets to pay his fine."

Johns Hopkins cleared his throat. "As to that," he said, "just let me know the amount needed! I'm very much put out by the activities of this gang of slavers, and I'll be glad to contribute a substantial amount toward frustrating their business."

"Oh, Cousin Johns," exclaimed Susan. "Thank thee so much. I feel so badly about Keziah and I do hope we can help her. Then, too, she was worried about her Jasper."

"Concerning Jasper," said Thomas Scott, "we have a letter from Friend Moore in Virginia which states that the man was so eager to join his family that he would not wait for the usual procedure. He ran away and hid in a swamp the first night, and in the attic of a Meeting House the second night. There he was apprehended and returned to his master. He probably got a good flogging."

"Poor creature," mourned Susan compassionately. "What can we do?"

"Nothing for the present," answered Thomas. "It may take weeks to get Jasper. Two opposing armies crouch between that Virginia plantation and this place. He will almost positively have to be rescued by boat. Then, too, Jasper will be closely watched, and so will our Quaker friends who are always under suspicion."

"I know that," said William. "I think a spy came here last week. He pretended to be a sewing machine agent, but he was very nosy about our colored people."

Sarah Scott said, "We will have to be extra careful. I thought you should be told at once because Friend Moore says Jasper is determined. He has carefully memorized thy name and whereabouts, William. If his family have not been returned to the master, he may try another break, although he has been advised against it."

"If he succeeds in finding me, I will do all in my province to assist him," promised William, "but here comes Mother with Hetty and Myra. We'd best not discuss the matter further."

Sarah Scott had come to this house with the firm purpose of securing William's permission to buy each of the girls a fine new silk dress. She felt that they should be rewarded for the sacrifice they had made in rescuing old Abe, but there was something about William's manner which commanded her respect. She knew that if he said they must abide by their decision, he would not change. Sarah had no daughter of her own, and with all her heart she wanted to buy those dresses, but she would hold her tongue. The reception would take place this week and she would have to postpone her giving until some future time. Before she left, she arranged with William to bring the girls to the Baltimore and Ohio Station on the following Saturday morning, where they would join the Garretts. They would proceed to Washington and stay with Rachel Garrett's brother, who was somebody of importance. That evening they would attend the reception, and the next day they would go to Meeting in Washington and return that same afternoon by train. The Scott carriage would meet them, and Cousin Thomas would see that they got safely home. "And I trust heart-whole and fancy free," added Cousin Sarah.

Susan smiled to herself. Imagine Hetty heart-whole! As for herself, she was proving her iron-clad resistance. No, with men she knew where to stop. She'd have no entanglements.

CHAPTER
EIGHTEEN

❧

Johns Hopkins and the Scotts had completed their mission and gone their respective ways.

Susan sat at her window and thought about old Abe. She had told her father about his shortcomings, and after William had a session with him, the old rascal tearfully promised that he would reform and never steal or drink again. His was a clear case of frustration. Seven times, he told William, he had taken a woman and started a family. Seven times he had been sold away from them.

"Got so's I doan much keer," he lamented.

"Well," answered William kindly, "thee has a good home now, and if thee'll behave thyself thee won't be sold again. Bow thy head and I'll pray for thee."

Aunt Henny was present at the arraignment. She had little faith in Abe's reformation. "He got a powerful thirst fer corn liquor," she confided to Susan. "When it git ter cravin' him, watch out, Mister Eggs."

"Oh, Aunt Henny," mourned Susan. "I've brought this trouble on thee, and I'm so sorry."

"Doan you mind, honey," soothed the old woman. "I'se a puttin' Toy ter watch him. Does he steal any mo', Toy sho' fix him."

So the matter had been dropped, and now the family were safely abed and Susan was about to follow them.

Suddenly she heard the soft whinny of a horse close to the house. Peering from her window, she made out the dim shape of a man fastening the animal to the hitching-rack. Hastily, she ran to call her father, but just as she reached her door, there sounded a loud impatient knocking from below.

William left his room and hastened downstairs. His carpet slippers slapped against the marble tiles in the lower hall.

Susan went to the head of the stairs to listen. The great key turned in the lock and the door creaked open.

"Aquilla Matthews," cried William, in a tone of great surprise. "What brings thee twelve miles from home at this hour?"

Aquilla came to the point. "William, where's Johns Hopkins? I went to his house and his man said I'd find him here."

"He's been gone for some time. Why, man, thee looks wild. What's happened?"

"Enough," said Aquilla indignantly. "Last evening as I was closing my mill for the night a wagon came along the road, and the driver stopped at the millstream to water his horses. Recognizing my neighbor, Nick Gallop, I went over to speak with him about some feed I am grinding for his cows. As he drove away, a black head was poked from the canvas on the back of the wagon, and a voice whispered, 'Please, massa, go tell Massa Johns Hotkim dat Jake done . . .' That's all I heard, for the man was jerked back into the wagon. A woman screamed, and I heard children crying. The matter troubled me, for this fellow Gallop is a dealer in slaves. After attending our Friends Meeting today, I went to see him. He lives about a mile north of my mill. Across the road from his house is his barn, a sturdy affair of stone with a heavy outside bar across the door. Before this door, Nick Junior sat with a gun beside him. It occurred to me that this may be the place we have been looking for where kidnapped freedmen are temporarily kept until they can be resold into slavery. What does thee think of it?"

"I think it more than likely," replied William. "Slave-snatchers have been operating in this community and the people in the wagon were undoubtedly a couple recently manumitted by Friend Hopkins. What did this rascal, Gallop, have to say for himself?"

"He denied having stolen the people. He said they were runaway slaves released to him by the court, and he intended to return them to their master. I asked if I might pray with them but he denied me the privilege, contending that Negroes have no souls anyway, and such a proceeding would only tend to make them dissatisfied with their condition."

"Hm," mused William. "The man lied to thee. Just yesterday he snatched them from their home and probably expects to sell them for farm labor. Wait until I get a horse and I'll return with thee. Thee'd better leave thy weary horse in my stable and take one of mine. We'll have to do something at once."

Susan ran downstairs. "Oh, Pa, can I go with thee?"

"No, thee'd better stay with Mother. This is no business for a woman."

"I could help, Pa," begged Susan.

"No, my dear, that is a mad idea. I will not hear of it," answered William firmly.

"Pa, when you get them away from the barn, the woman Celey may need me," persisted the girl.

Aquilla intervened. "Come, William, if thy daughter feels a call to service, thee should not deny her. Perhaps she could be of help to us."

"Yes, Pa, I feel very strongly that I should go."

Reluctantly, William consented. "All right, Susan, if thee is assured, I'll not prevent thee. But thee has a twelve-mile ride ahead of thee, and the business may be rough."

So, while the men saddled the horses, Susan dressed in her

riding habit, and a little later, the three rescuers were on their way.

The men planned that first they would stop along the way and secure the assistance of several Friends.

It was nearing midnight when they drew rein beside a red brick farmhouse and called to its occupants. A whiskered face appeared at an upper window and a voice called softly, "Is that thee, Aquilla?"

"Yes, Mordecai, we have need of thee and it's urgent. Can thee get the boys awake? We'll need several men with shovels. It's a foundation job."

"We'll be with you directly."

The face withdrew and a few minutes later three men on horseback, each with a shovel, joined the Friends waiting under the trees.

"Here's William Coale and his daughter Susan," Aquilla explained. "A man Jake, wife Celey and two children have been stolen from their home near Johns Hopkins' place. Thee knows neighbor Nick Gallop's stone barn near the top of the long hill. We feel sure the Negroes are confined there. We want you three to go around by the back road, fasten your horses to a fence in the woods above the river. Then take your shovels and creep across the field to the back of the barn. Young Gallop is keeping guard in front, and it will be William's and Susan's job to lure him from his position and keep him occupied until you have dug a hole under the foundation and got the people out. You will then follow inside the fence and lead the Negroes over the crest of the hill where I'll be waiting with a load of hay to carry them to a suitable hiding-place. Does thee understand?"

"I do, and will follow thy directions, but even with three at work, it will take a half hour to get under the foundation and make a place large enough for a man to get through," answered Mordecai.

William said, "I know that, and I'll do my best to delay the guard. I think it only right for thee to know that the man has a gun beside him."

"As to that, my lads are stout-hearted and we have no fear."

"Very well," said Aquilla. "Go ahead and wait behind the barn until you hear William's voice talking to the young man at the barn door. Then wait for a few minutes, give the owl call and start digging."

The three horsemen started forward, and Aquilla went immediately to the mill-house. To Susan he said, "Thee go inside, Susan, and tell my Thirsa to pack a basket of food for the colored people. Thy father and I will hitch the farm horses to a load of hay which stands in my barrack all ready for such an emergency as this. We will be ready directly."

Susan entered the Matthews' kitchen, found a candle and lit it. A stairway twisted behind the chimney and disappeared in the darkness of the upper floor. In response to Susan's call, a woman in crisply starched wrapper and hair plaited in two braids came down the creaking stairs and stood sleepily regarding her visitor.

Before Susan had finished explaining her errand, Thirsa was at work packing loaves of corn bread and a jug of sweet milk, cold from the spring-house.

When the load of hay appeared, the basket of food was stored beside the driver. There were whispered farewells before the wagon creaked down the highway.

Ten minutes later, William and Susan followed on horseback. Before them in the waning moonlight, the wagon rolled forward.

At the barn near the top of the hill, two men challenged Aquilla.

"Stop!" they called. "Who are you and where are you taking the hay at this hour of night?"

"I'm Aquilla Matthews," was the cheery answer, "and I'm delivering this load of hay to Friends in Pennsylvania. Thee didn't know me, did thee, Neighbor Gallop?"

"I know you now and I don't trust you. How many niggers are you hiding in that hay?"

"Now, neighbor, see for thyself if thee doesn't trust me." Aquilla sat back on the seat and waited patiently while the men climbed on the load of hay and hunted through it. Then they jumped to the ground and called, "All right, go ahead, we apologize."

The wagon continued over the brow of the hill and disappeared from view. After a few minutes William and Susan rode from the dark shelter of the locust trees, and walking their horses slowly, continued along the highway.

At the barn, a lantern was flashed upon them and a voice called, "Sorry, but we're checking all travelers in an effort to smash the Underground."

"Quite so," replied William, "and since you are so civil, I wonder if you would do me a great favor, gentlemen?"

The two men came forward.

"We are badly in need of food and a little rest," explained William. "Could we impose upon you for a little while—an hour perhaps? My daughter here would like to walk about and forget the unsteady rocking of her horse, and I'm a bit stiff myself although I'm more accustomed to the saddle. Our horses, too, are thirsty and long for the water trough."

In the dim moonlight, Susan made out the faces of a young man and of a middle-aged man with sideburns and large eyes that seemed able to pierce through the semi-darkness.

"Your daughter, sir?"

"Yes, my daughter Susan."

"Follow me to my house yonder, and I'll be happy to make you comfortable for the night," said the elder Gallop politely.

"Thank thee for thy fine hospitality, but an hour's rest is all we can indulge in before we must be on our way."

William dismounted and lifted Susan to the ground. He tossed the reins to the young man, and walked beside the father toward the house.

"Nick," said the man, "water the horses and tie them at the rack. Then get back to your place."

Susan said, "If there's no objection, I'd like to stay near Firefly. He is difficult to handle when he's with strangers. I'll be with thee directly, Pa."

"Very well, daughter."

Nick Gallop looked at William with surprise. "Aren't you afraid to trust your lovely daughter with a strange young man?"

"Not at all." William laughed genially. "My Susan can take care of herself, and the young man is obviously a gentleman."

Nick Junior bowed politely, and as William and the elder Gallop walked to the porch, the quavering hoot of an owl gave assurance that the rescue work was going forward.

Susan followed the son to the watering trough beside the barn and held the bridle until Firefly had quenched his thirst. Then Susan herself must have a drink at the wooden pump and, finally, she suggested that the saddles be removed and the horses rubbed down a bit.

While he endeavored to please her in the care of the horses, young Gallop thought he had seldom met a creature so vivacious and entertaining as Susan. "Come," he said, "my mother and sisters are asleep, but let's go to the house and raid the pantry."

Susan declared she was about to starve, so pies and cider were brought out and the four had a merry and leisurely party.

126 ·

An hour had passed and William said, "Come, daughter, let us thank our hosts and be on our way."

Nick Gallop held the horses while young Nick assisted them to their saddles.

"You gave to us most generously," said William, "and we are grateful."

"You are more than welcome to all you got," said the elder Gallop cordially. "Stop in to see us again. We'll be glad to welcome you."

William and Susan proceeded silently until they had passed over the brow of the hill.

"Wait until he discovers all we got, and he'll not be so pleasant about it." William chuckled. "Stop thy horse for a moment, Susan, and see if thee can hear the wagon. It must have been gone from here for some time."

They listened at the side road but there was no sound.

As expected, Mordecai and his sons were awaiting them. Eagerly they told of the escape, of how they had crouched at the rear of the barn until the sound of voices had faded into the distance, and had then given the owl signal to tell William they had arrived and were at their task. They shoveled the earth carefully until they had made a hole under the stone foundation, through which after a little whispering Celey and Jake with their two children crawled from the barn.

"Dar's some mo' folks wants to know kin dey come, too," whispered Celey.

"How many?"

"Woman name Keziah got six head of chillen."

"That's a good many."

"Come mawnin', dey gonna take 'em back to Virginny," said Celey, a plea in her voice. "I done hear 'em say so."

So Keziah and her children were pulled, with the others, through the hole. They either walked or were carried behind the fence until they crossed the brow of the hill where, below them, waited the friendly hay wagon. In the darkness and in their excitement, they did not notice that one of their number was missing.

Strong arms lifted them one by one into the wagon. When they were covered with hay, Aquilla shook the reins, and the horses moved briskly forward. Following side roads into Pennsylvania, he hoped to reach the welcoming loft of the Fawn Grove Meeting House before daylight, where he planned to release the Negroes to the temporary care of the Quaker farmers in Pennsylvania.

William and Susan were delighted to hear that Keziah and her children were once more on the road to freedom. But there was no time now to talk about it. They must hurry away before they were discovered. William made a practical suggestion. "When daylight comes and that barn door is opened, there will be a hue and cry," he said. "You three Friends had best be out of sight with those shovels. Aquilla and I will be suspected, but they can't prove a thing against us."

Mordecai and his sons accordingly rode off into the darkness, leaving William and Susan to contrive a safe way home.

"I think we had better not try to return past Gallop's," William said. "We can cut through this pasture and follow the river road back to the mill." He slid from Ginger's back and passed the reins to Susan. "I'll just remove the top rails from the fence."

"Please hurry, Pa," begged Susan nervously.

At the sound of her voice, a dark shape appeared from the elderberry bushes beside the road, and a voice chattering with terror said, "Scuse me, missy, but ain't you dat lady what done help me in dat slabe market?"

Susan was startled. "Jake?" she whispered.

"Yowsum, dat me. I'd of knowed you voice anywheres I done hear it. It alway comes like de soun' ob angel wings.

You don't know where dat wagon at what I'm suppose ter ketch, does you?"

She was horrified. "The wagon has gone, Jake. Why didn't thee go with it?"

"Musta got yere too late," he mourned. "I didn't tell no-body, but I stayed back by de barn and waited twell dat white man toten a gun come back. He done set de gun down, so's he kin git de barn door undid, an I crep' up on him."

"Thee did not kill him, did thee?" asked William, coming from the fence.

"No, suh, I don't reckon so, but I shore busted him up so's he don't find out we gone. I pull he shirt off him, and I use it ter tie him fast to a post in dat barn. Ef'n he do wake up, it gonna take him some li'l time gitten hisself untied. Mistah, what I gonna do?"

"Susan," said William, "we must act quickly. Would thee be afraid to hide here in the bushes until I return? I'll need thy horse."

"Certainly not, Pa. Even if someone should come along the road, they would not see me in this gray habit. I won't budge a step until thee comes back."

He helped her from Firefly, and saw her safely over the fence and hidden among the bushes.

Jake scrambled to the horse's back and called tearfully, "God bless you, Miss Susan. You a good lady."

They cantered into the side road, and soon Susan heard only the faint rhythmic clop of the horses from a distance. She sat very still. In the damp night air, she smelled elderberries and the more pungent scent of crushed mint leaves. It was quiet except for the night sounds: the whinny of a horse in the field behind her and the doleful bellow of a lonely cow from far away. Susan seemed a small part of an immense world. Then close beside her a little fledgling cheeped. There was a flutter of wings, and he was quieted. "He shall cover thee with His feathers and under His wings shalt thou trust." She felt safe and without fear.

In a short while, William returned. "We overtook the wagon," he reported. "Too late, Celey discovered that Jake was not hidden in the hay with the rest of them, but Aquilla was afraid to return for him. The poor woman was in a dither by the time we came alongside and left Jake with them. Poor hunted creatures, they thought we were the slave-catchers. But come, we must hurry and get away from this neighborhood before young Gallop gets himself loose and starts a search."

He led the horses into the pasture, replaced the rails and helped Susan to the saddle. They crossed the pasture to the river road, and a few minutes later arrived at the mill-house.

They reported the success of the night to Cousin Thirsa.

"Susan, does thee think thee is able to stand the long ride back to Furley tonight?" William asked Susan.

"Certainly, Pa, I'm as fresh as a daisy."

But the daisy was feeling very wilted when a little after sunrise Uncle Toy helped her from the horse.

"Aunt Henny," she said, "I'm going to bed and I don't want to get up until suppertime. And, Aunt Henny, I think Keziah and her children are quite safe by now. She promised she would not be afraid, and I believe her faith has been rewarded."

CHAPTER

NINETEEN

"Susan," said William, "I notice that Hetty is in a fine state of nervousness this morning. Isn't she expecting Peter sometime today?"

"Yes, Pa," said Susan, smiling. "She's as jittery as a poplar leaf. He's in love with her, and she thinks she doesn't want him."

"A brisk canter will bring the color to her cheeks and help fill the hours until his arrival. I'll tell Toy to bring our horses."

"Thank thee, Pa. I'll ask Hetty to get herself ready," said Susan.

Because it was a hot summer morning, they chose a bridle-path along the creek for their ride. The way was shaded by gum and tulip trees, and bordered by cool green ferns. Birds sang in the tree tops, a turtle slid from a log and splashed clumsily into the stream, and from somewhere on the branch of a sugar maple, a tree toad croaked its dismal demand for rain.

In a little while, they turned from the path into the open fields of the nursery, planted as far as the eye could see with rows of young fruit trees—apple, peach and plum, cherry, apricot and pear. Farther away, the delicate green deepened to the black-green of hemlock, spruce and fir, which in the fall would be transplanted to neighboring estates.

In a two-acre lot they were passing, the land had been

sown in grass which, now ripened, had been mowed. William's nursery hands were hard at work raking and tossing the hay into mounds ready to be carried to the barns.

While William talked with his foreman, Hetty pointed her riding whip toward an apple tree across the field by the roadside. "Look, Susan," she said, "the Transparents are turning yellow. Let's see if they're ready to eat."

They rode across to the tree, and as they reached into its branches for the golden fruit, Hetty's horse snorted nervously.

"Look at Ginger," said Hetty. "We'd better leave. He probably smells a copperhead."

She was about to return to her father when Susan uttered a sudden cry. "It's a man," she whispered.

From the bushes by the roadside, a colored man, gray with dust, limped toward them. "Scuse me, missys," he panted, "but does you know a man name Mistah William Coale?"

"Yes," replied Susan. "He's our father." She looked sharply at the Negro. "What is your name?" she asked quickly.

"Mah name Jaspah, miss."

"Jasper?" Susan turned and called, "Pa, come quick, please."

As William rode up to them, the poor slave fell on his knees. "Massa," he wept, "please, please won't you he'p me. Dem slave-ketchers, dey right behin' me. I done run till I most spent. Dey ketches me agin, dey sholy kill me. Dey most git me, but I cut inter a field and now dey ridin' round it. Dey be here any minute."

"Pa, it's Jasper, Keziah's husband. See the dust down by the crossroads. The slavers are probably deciding which road to follow. Thee hide Jasper, Pa, and we'll sidetrack them if we can."

"Do the men have hounds?" asked William quickly.

"No, suh. I was all right ontil I stop at a tavern to beg a bite of victuals. Dey seen me an' I start runnin' and dey jump in dey buckboard an' took atter me."

William dismounted quickly and tossed his reins to Susan. Then he led Jasper into the field, covered him with hay, and instructed the Negro hands to go ahead with their work.

A minute later, two men drove up in a buckboard. When they saw the girls gathering apples, they pulled in their horses.

"Miss, you seen a black boy running this way?" one asked sharply.

"A boy?" inquired Hetty innocently.

"A nigger man. Did he pass here?"

Hetty shook her head. "No, indeed," she said positively. "Nobody has passed here. We've been picking apples." Suddenly she lifted her head in an attitude of listening. "No," she said regretfully, "I thought I heard someone calling, but it's only a dog on the other road barking at some stranger."

"Thank you, miss." They turned the buckboard around and were off in the direction of the barking hound.

"That was Sheriff Arnold," whispered Susan, "but the sun was in his eyes and I hope he didn't recognize me."

William wasted no time. He put Jasper before him on the horse, and rode as quickly as possible to Furley.

Peter had arrived during their absence and was waiting to lift Hetty from Ginger. He took her hand and they disappeared immediately.

Susan gave Firefly and Ginger to Uncle Toy and then followed her father to the kitchen door.

"Jasper, thee get inside where thee won't be seen," William said.

"Yassuh, an' thank you, suh."

Old Abe and little Jerry had been shelling peas for Aunt Henny.

"Wisht I could pop 'em out fast as you," said the little boy.

Abe chuckled. "You jest a li'l snapper," he said. "You got

plenty time befo' you. Me, I a ole man, no good to nobody nohow."

"Ain't dat de truf?" agreed Aunt Henny. "Mistah William he say man made in God's image and some day dat likeness mebbe show up in you, but I 'bliged to say I ain't seen no glimmer if it yit."

" 'Oman," answered old Abe, "you got a powerful sharp tongue. Ain't no two-edge sword kin beat it, dat's for sho. Some day I'll mebbe show you dat I got a big heart even ef you already busted it. Ain't dat so, Jerry?"

But Jerry did not hear. His mouth slowly opened and his eyes bulged. He saw his father standing in the doorway, and, without a word, he ran and hurled his little body into the welcoming arms.

"Jerry, Jerry boy, where you mammy at?"

"She ain't here," sobbed the child. "She's goned away an' I been awaitin' so's you would take me to her."

"Yes," said William, much moved, "Keziah and the other children were sent away to the north. We don't know just where they are, but the Friends in Philadelphia know, and they will get you together in God's time."

"Let's go right now an' find her, Pappy," begged Jerry.

"Now take it stiddy, son. Yo' pappy got to git some victuals first," said Jasper, weeping. "Ain't had nothin' ter eat all day 'cept raw turnips."

"Dat a shame," grumbled Aunt Henny. "Set down, man, an' eat yo' fill." She brought out a ham and a loaf of bread and watched with satisfaction while the poor slave wolfed the food with a mug of milk.

"You, Toy," she commanded, "go set whar yo' kin watch dat road jes' like a cat watch fer a mouse, an' don't you close an eye. See somebody comin', tell us fast you kin."

Thus guarded, Jasper was safe to relate his experiences.

"Seen a man takin' watermillions down to de Norfolk boat,"

he said. "Tole me ef I'd help him unload, he'd give me a lift. Us loaded 'em on boat fer Baltimore. Man he go way 'an I tuck mahse'f under a canvas on lifeboat. Boat she dock round sun-up, so I jump overboard, swim to shore an' ask somebody do he know Mistah Willum Coale, de tree man. He say he sho' do, jest keep a movin' north. Bimeby come to a tavern, an' stop ter beg a bite. Dem slave-catchers dey was eatin' dey breakfus an' when dey heard me beggin,' dey start after me. I run. Man, how I run."

"Praise de good Lord fer leadin' you," said Aunt Henny.

"Ain't dat de truf?" agreed Jasper.

At this moment, Toy hobbled into the kitchen. "Men's comin'," he yelled.

Jasper leaped to his feet and stood trembling like a wild animal brought to bay. "Where I gonna hide?" he cried. "What I gonna do?"

"Come quickly, Jasper," called Susan. "Pa will keep them on the front porch for a while and will try to send them away, but they will almost certainly search the place. The attic is no longer safe. I'll hide thee in the cellar chimney."

"You lemme, Miss Susan," begged old Abe. "I ain't done nothin' yit is any good. You lemme hide 'im, please, Miss Susan. You go he'p yore pa. Mebbe you kin handle dem men better nor he can."

Susan hesitated. Then she smiled kindly at the old man. "Very well, Abe. I'll trust Jasper to thee. Put him in the chimney, and be sure thee closes the flue door tight."

She ran to the porch where her father was receiving Sheriff Arnold and his man.

They were stern and uncompromising. "Once before you fooled us, miss, but this time we ain't going to be sidetracked by your pretty ways. Also, Mister Nick Gallop reports he lost eleven slaves, three grown and eight children, and he suspects you of some sort of trickery in connection with their disappearance. This place is getting a good going over right now, and if we find the nigger we're looking for, Mr. Coale, you're certainly going to pay the penalty plus six months in jail."

While William reasoned gently with the slave-catchers, old Abe was hobbling down the cellar steps ahead of the terrified Jasper. Abe pushed aside a barrel that stood before the chimney, opened the rusty door used for cleaning the flue, and wagged a bony finger at Jasper.

"Listen, you Jasper. You kin hide youself, but it ain't gonna do no good. I knows dem men'll git yo' sho'. Ah knows furdermo', dat I ain't got long. Las' night I done heerd angels a callin'. De golden chariot already on de way. An' yo' got a powerful mess ob chillen needin' you. Don't nobody want me. Now you do lak ah say. You crawls high up in de chimbley lak Miss Susan tell you. I humps mahse'f down low umbeneaf yo'. Dem mens looks in chimbley, dey gits me stid ob you."

Through chattering teeth, Jasper asked, "Man, why you do dis? Yo' doan sca'cely know me. Why you gib yo'self place ob me?"

The old man pointed to the open door. The place was just large enough to crawl through.

"Git in dar," he commanded roughly. "Git fast afore I lam you on de haid."

From a peg on the cellar wall, he seized a discarded hat and pulled it low over his gray head. At the same time came the loud voice of the sheriff.

Jasper heard the crunch of heavy boots on the graveled walk as they approached the cellarway. He ceased his arguing, crawled hastily through the opening, climbed the rough bricks inside the chimney and hung like a great bat on the inside. Below him there was a scuffling and the sound of the door stealthily shut. Then silence.

"You down dere, man?" he whispered.

"Shet up, or I pokes a rusty nail in yo'."

There was silence while the men tramped rudely into the cellar. They peered into barrels and overturned boxes. Finally, one of them said, "I guess he ain't in here."

"Wait a minute," said the other. "There's a little heap of soot under that chimney door like it's been opened recently." He swung open the door, reached in and seized Abe by the pants.

"Come out o' there," he called.

Old Abe scrambled out and rolled his eyes at William, who stood speechless with amazement. "You knowed old Jasper, didn't you, massa? All right, I go wid you. Only please sell me ter a good massa. Doan send me back to Virginny no mo', dey beat me sho'."

"Get into the buckboard," commanded the men, hustling him to the door.

William started to intervene. "I'm afraid there's some mistake," he began, but as the significance of the old man's sacrifice dawned upon him, he bowed his head. "May the Lord bless thee and keep thee," he murmured.

The old Negro did not answer. He stepped as briskly as possible, climbed into the vehicle, and lay on the floor, his head on his arm. The men sprang to the seat.

"I don't know whether you knew the man was hiding in your cellar or not," called Arnold savagely, "but you looked so surprised when we found him, I've half a mind to let you off again. I warn you, though, you Quakers had better be more watchful. This week we arrested one of your number for sailing a woman and children up the Chesapeake toward Elkton. He's had a fat fine to pay, and we mean to break this business up. Sooner or later, you'll be brought to justice and your pretty daughter won't be able to help you."

"Sufficient unto the day is the evil thereof," quoted William quietly, "and thank thee for thy kindness."

Sadly the family went about their several duties. At the dinner table there was an attempt at gaiety, but Abe's abduction had cast a gloom over the whole family, and now that the time had come for George and Peter to be on their way, there was tension in the air and tears were near the surface.

Jasper sat in a corner of the kitchen and sniffed audibly. Aunt Henny dropped a plate. She felt badly about Abe.

"I kep' a tellin' him he warn't no good," she wailed. "He knowed it, so he jes' give hisse'f place ob Jasper. Dat Abe a fine man. Wish I could tell him so, Miss Susan."

"Never mind, Aunt Henny," said Susan sadly. "We all hope that Abe comes back some day along with our own boys."

That evening William called two of his most trusted Negro hands from their work in the fields. "I'm going to ask you to dig a deep hole in one corner of the cellar. You can make a little room under the floor and brace the roof with timbers. It must be large enough to hold several persons. I'm trusting you to tell nobody. It may be that some poor body of your own color will need it as a place of refuge. Our attic is no longer a safe hiding place. When you've finished, I'll move a corner cupboard in front of the opening. From the front it will look as though it fills the whole corner, but the back of the cupboard is flat, so there'll be quite an air space between the back of the cupboard and the wall. This will be the entrance to the hiding place. Can I trust you?"

The Negroes grinned with pleasure. "Yassuh," they promised, "us won't tell nobody, not nobody."

They went to work with real vigor, and within a few hours the place was ready for occupancy.

CHAPTER

TWENTY

With the reception to look forward to, the separation from George was a little less mournful for Susan and Hetty than for the other members of the family.

William said little, but he put his hand affectionately on George's shoulder and prayed, "May thy feet be shod with the gospel of peace, thy shield be faith, thy breastplate righteousness, and thy sword the spirit which is the word of God."

There were hasty embraces and the boys were gone, leaving behind them a sense of loss.

Susan walked through the house to the kitchen, and then decided to go outdoors. She discovered Billy sitting disconsolately on a bench by the back door.

"Cheer up," she said. "Thee looks as gloomy as a thundercloud."

"I ought to go along with George," he said. "I could carry a stretcher and do some good."

"Thee'll do nothing of the sort. Pa needs thee here, Billy. He looks pale and shaken, and I noticed tonight that he leaned heavily on his cane. Thee's got to assume more responsibility and relieve him."

"I'll try, Susan, I really will."

She rumpled his hair affectionately and left him to his reflections. She went for a walk to shake off her own sorrow, and to bring into the house again that quiet joy on which the family depended, especially her father.

It was nearly dark when Frankie discovered a carriage coming slowly up the drive. He ran to report it to his father. Toy had already heard it and was on hand to help with the horses.

"Susan," said William, "I presume we're being visited by the Meeting."

She looked worried for a moment and then asked, "About George?"

"Perhaps. We shall soon see. I hope they won't upset Mother. She's had quite enough for one day."

They were surprised to see Ezra with William McKim and Mahala Dewberry at the door. William and Susan ushered them into the parlor where after the usual greetings they seated themselves in a businesslike manner.

Mahala did most of the talking. "At the last business meeting," she reported, "it was brought to the attention of Friends that you have a servant held in bondage."

"The accusation is true." William admitted it frankly, and told the story of old Abe and of the self-sacrificing way in which Abe had given himself in Jasper's place. "My other servants," said William, "are free and I should have manumitted this old fellow, too, but his condition was so frail as to make his life very uncertain from day to day. For this reason, he was only a care to us and we felt he was safer under our protection."

The Friends agreed.

"Now that that concern against thee is removed," Mahala said, "we would like to see George in regard to joining a military company, which is against the principles laid down by the Bible and further set forth in the Friends' Book of Discipline."

"As to that," said William, "it is a matter that has caused me some concern, but I am convinced that George, who has ever been strong for the right, has obeyed the dictates of his conscience, and like the good Samaritan, has gone forth to gather up the wounded and suffering and give them the benefit of his training. My good Friends, George has enlisted as a surgeon."

"But he is in uniform," moaned Ezra.

"Yes, my son," agreed William, "but what matter the outside of the cup or platter if the inside be lacking in brotherly love and understanding?"

After this admonishment, Ezra looked ashamed.

William smiled gently. "Let him that is without sin among you cast the first stone."

"I'm sorry," said Ezra. "I'll try to see my brother's action in a different light. Before we drop the apparent shortcomings of this family, there's one other matter that has not yet come to the attention of the Meeting. I notice that since my last visit, the house of Coale has come into possession of a music box. Is that also in accordance with the dictates of thy conscience?"

"It is. Thy sister Myra seemed heavy-spirited, and I got the piano to occupy her time and thoughts. Her whole appearance has brightened, and I feel the instrument will do much to restore her spirits."

Ezra was unconvinced. "She might get the same result from reading her Bible," he ventured.

William McKim showed interest. "I think thee did right to buy the piano," he said with conviction.

Mahala smiled brightly upon the group. "I believe," she said, with a twinkle in her eye, "that we came to condemn and are ourselves admonished. William, we will report to the Meeting that we have visited here and find all clear. Is that agreeable to the rest of the committee?"

Ezra and William McKim agreed, and, the business being at an end, the Friends departed.

When they were on their way, William said, "I feel a call to move Jasper and little Jerry tonight. Within a few hours, Abe and his abductors will reach Virginia, and Jasper's master will inform them of their mistake. Tell Henny to feed Jasper and get him ready. We'll leave in an hour."

"Pa," gasped Susan, "not tonight, please. Tomorrow will be time enough. Thee must get thy sleep. Thee's had a hard day, with many trials."

"It won't hurt me a bit, Susan. I'll only take them as far as the Meeting House in Gunpowder and hide them in the loft. From there they can be moved to Fawn Grove, and Friends will take them on to Philadelphia tomorrow. Meanwhile we must try to locate Keziah and her brood. It's a beautiful night, and I'll enjoy the drive and be home for breakfast."

Billy spoke up. "Pa," he said eagerly. "I'll go. Please let me. I'm old enough now to take responsibilities, and I want to. Please, Pa."

William looked uncertainly from Billy to Susan.

"Yes, Pa," said Susan. "Billy and I will go together. We'll spend tomorrow with Cousin Thirsa and Cousin Aquilla, and start home in the afternoon. I'll enjoy a little outing. I'll get ready at once."

William reluctantly consented. "You're safe enough," he said, "since Jasper is no longer followed. I guess I'll let you obey your leading. God knoweth best."

Aunt Henny was heartbroken when she heard that Jerry was to be taken from her. She took the little boy in her lap and rocked him. "What I gonna do, you goes off wid yo' pappy? You doesn't want ter leave Aunt Henny, does you, sugarfoot?"

Jerry looked at her with his great dark eyes. "I sho loves you," he admitted, "but I wants my mammy, I does."

"Mornin's I puts you outside dat kitchen door fer to play," mourned the old woman, "an' every time I opens de door, you comes poppin' in jest like a li'l fly. I'll sho miss havin' you buzzin' round. Dat I will."

His lip trembled. "I wants my mammy, I do."

"Well, don't you cry, lambie. Guess you gotta go." She wiped her eyes on a corner of her apron and resigned herself to the inevitable.

By ten o'clock the wagon was ready to start.

"Remember," admonished William, "you are carrying a shipment of nursery stock to Aquilla Matthews. After you leave your packages at the Meeting House, go right to Matthews' and Cousin Thirsa will put you to bed. Aquilla will have the wagon unloaded and the trees planted by the time you're ready to return. Tell him the trees are a gift from me in return for his hospitality. Be sure to start for home early in the afternoon. I want you back by nightfall."

With Jasper, Jerry and the basket of food safely stowed among the trees, Susan and Billy climbed up on the wagon seat and waved good-bye to the family.

It was good to be young and alive on this beautiful August night. The moon rode full and bright across the hills, shedding a misty light on the valleys and meadowlands. Except where the road led through patches of dark woodland, there was no need for artificial light. The horses stepped briskly along, and by midnight, half the distance had been covered.

Susan, tired with the responsibilities of a long day, began to nod. Her head dropped against the high back of the seat. The steady pace of the horses, the gentle rocking of the wagon and the murmuring of a creek beside the road lulled her. Far away, a loon cried mournfully. Gradually she dozed.

But she was soon aroused by a prod from Billy's elbow. "Susan, wake up," he whispered, "listen to all that commotion."

There was a great baying of hounds from a nearby estate. A few minutes more and the dogs would be headed toward them. Billy guided the wagon off the road and stopped under a barrack just as the dogs bounded into the field. A small dark shape streaked in front of the wagon, followed by the dogs yelping with bloodthirsty determination. In another few minutes the sound of the chase came from far away, but Billy waited to be sure that no horsemen were following the hounds. Then he backed the wagon into the road, and they went on without any more frightening experiences.

It was after two and the moon was settling toward the west when they drew up before the Meeting House. Billy held the horses while Susan felt under a shutter and found the key to unlock the door. She waited until Jasper and the boy were safely inside, crouched down behind the Meeting House benches.

"Where my mammy?" asked the child. "Is she yere?"

"No, Jerry," said Susan softly, "but you're going to her and it won't be long now. Thee be a brave boy."

"It powerful dark in yere," Jasper said. "I wonders ef sperits runs round yonder in dat grabeyard."

"No, Jasper." Susan laughed. "The only thing that wanders around in this Meeting House are a few mice, and they won't hurt thee, but they may get into thy basket of food. Lie down on a bench close by Jerry and get some sleep. Tomorrow evening, a Friend will come with a load of hay to carry thee and the boy a little farther toward Keziah. Remember that we will do all we can to find thy two big boys and get you together again. Good-bye, and may thy troubles soon be over."

"Good-bye, missy, and I prays God to bless you. I do dat."

She closed the door, locked it and returned the key to its place under the shutter.

A few minutes later, the wagon turned into Aquilla Matthews' driveway. As it reached the house, Cousin Thirsa poked her head from the second-story window. "Who is it, please?" she called.

"A couple of sleepy Friends," answered Susan, "with packages to be delivered."

"I'll be right down."

A candle was lighted and Cousin Thirsa appeared in her

wrapper, with Cousin Aquilla who was still hitching up his suspenders. After they had told their story, Susan and Billy were sent upstairs to bed, and only after a refreshing sleep and a satisfying dinner at the mill-house, did Susan and Billy prepare to return to Furley.

Before they left, Aquilla promised to take Jasper and little Jerry that very night to the next station along their way.

CHAPTER

TWENTY-ONE

At last the day for the President's reception came. In spite of the fact that Lee's army was too close to Washington for comfort, Lincoln thought it best for the morale of the people to carry through all social arrangements.

Susan and Hetty were in high spirits as they went about their packing. Hetty stopped for a moment.

"I want to tell thee something, Susan, something very special," she said. "Peter wants to marry me, but I don't want him. Calvin is more to my liking, but I'm not sure that he likes me. What shall I do?"

Susan's heart missed a beat. She turned her face away.

"I'd just wait until there isn't any doubt," she said after she had recovered. "A lifetime is a long while to live with a person. Peter is a dear fellow, though, and we all like him so much. Now do let's get our clothes ready for the party."

Hetty became businesslike at once. "While thee was away, Aunt Henny brought the satchels down from the attic and wiped them off. They're ready to be packed."

"Good. We'll put in the silk dresses to wear to the party, and our new slippers, gloves and best shawls. Then we can wear our second-bests on the train. I hear the trip is very sooty, and it takes an hour and a half to go to Washington."

"Think of it," said Hetty. "We'll be whizzing along at twenty-five miles an hour. Did Pa say we could have the flowers?"

"Yes, he was sweet about it. He told the foreman to arrange two bouquets with lace paper and have them ready when we leave for the train. Oh, Hetty, we'll see George and Peter and —and everyone."

At mention of Peter, Hetty lapsed into troubled thought. Susan went on with the packing. She would see Calvin, of that she was certain. He had not written to her, but she felt the sincerity of this great quiet man, and she knew that he would let nothing short of an actual battle stand in the way of his appearance. She finished packing her bag and went to have a visit with her father before it was time to leave.

She found him in the rose gardens superintending the cutting of the flowers. "Pa," she said, "if any green roses are blooming, may I have one, please?"

"Certainly, my dear. I noticed a bud last evening. It should be opening a bit today and may be just right for cutting. I'm glad thee feels a sentiment toward the bush. I have gone to great pains to preserve it." He picked the bud and ordered it placed in her bouquet. Together they returned to the Hall.

"Susan," he said, "I'm very much concerned over thy sister Cornelia."

"Why, Pa, what's wrong with Kippy? Girls have had babies before. I wouldn't worry too much."

"It's not that. Her husband is a hot-tempered fellow and I hear that he sympathizes with the Secessionists. She's not in a condition to bear any mental strain, and I think thee had better go up to Frederick to be with her until after the baby arrives. Then thee can bring her home with thee for a visit."

Susan sparkled. "I'd love to do that, Pa. Could Hetty go with me? I'm sure Myra and Aunt Henny could look after Mother. If thee needed Hetty at any time, thee could send one of those telegrams and she could come home."

"I'll consider it. Now thee run along and get thyself ready for Washington. We'll leave in a half hour."

Aunt Henny appeared at the door. "You clothes is all press," she announced. "I laid 'em on de baid."

"Thank thee. I'll be ready in a jiffy."

She found Hetty dressed and pacing the floor like a cat in a cage.

"I'm worn out," Hetty announced. "I was afraid thee had forgotten about going. Hurry up, Susan."

"I'll be ready," said Susan, laughing. She slipped out of her frock and into the stiff bombazine. With a few deft strokes of the brush, her unruly curls were parted above her forehead and plastered down in the direction of her ears. The curls wouldn't stay in place for long, but at least Susan herself would not see them untidy. The fine white silk kerchief was pinned into place and the strings of her Quaker bonnet tied beneath her chin.

There were quick farewells and the two girls were off with satchels and a covered basket containing the bouquets. William sat on the front seat of the wagon beside Toy, who did the driving.

At four o'clock they reached Camden Station, which was in a commotion. A company of troops, natty in new blue uniforms and carrying guns tipped with shining bayonets, were about to entrain for the camp below Washington. There was a tenseness in the air as officers shouted commands. Mothers clung desperately to their sons, and wives and sweethearts wept for the men they loved.

Into the station crawled the train, its bell ringing, its smokestack belching soot and smoke. The men roared, and with one accord burst into the "Battle Hymn." The train squeaked to a stop, the soldiers climbed noisily aboard and the conductor signaled to the engineer.

From every window, soldiers leaned out for a final handclasp. The train lurched slowly forward. Women ran beside the track, some of them hysterical. Finally, as the train picked up speed, they were forced to release the hands they had clasped so desperately.

Above the rumble and clang of the train came another roar from the men, a roar which made Susan think of some tremendous dragon screaming with blood-lust as it rushed upon its prey. She shivered and found that Hetty was clinging to her arm.

"Come on, Susan," she cried. "The Scotts are here and we're to ride with the president of the railroad in his own private train. See, there's John W. Garrett now."

The girls were presented to Mr. and Mrs. Garrett, who graciously made them welcome.

Johns Hopkins, who was a director of the railroad, was also present to see his friends on their way. He presented each of the girls with a small package.

"Here are two little ivory fans," he said modestly. "They're inlaid with mother-of-pearl, or some such material. One of my ship captains brought them to me from China, and I thought you girls might find some use for them."

They embraced him with such spontaneous affection that he was all but overcome. He removed his beaver hat, flipped a square of linen from his pocket and mopped his perspiring forehead.

The bell on the engine clanged imperiously and the party boarded the car.

"Good-bye, William," called Cousin Sarah. "We'll take good care of thy girls. Good-bye, Johns."

There was a great puffing and tooting as the train moved slowly down the track, carrying Susan and Hetty for their first ride on the steam cars.

"And," whispered Susan, "thee'll faint when I tell thee something. Pa may send us next week out to visit Sister Kippy. Wouldn't it be glorious?"

An hour and a half later they reached Washington, transferred from train to carriage and drove to the elaborate home of Rachel Garrett's brother. Here they were to have dinner, and here, after the reception, they would return for the night.

In honor of her distinguished brother-in-law and his guests, the hostess had brought out her best damask and silver. Hothouse flowers and candles in gleaming holders decorated the dining room.

At home, Cousin Thomas in his quiet way had been a prosperous Friend and kindly neighbor to the girls. Now they were to know him as an official of the railroad. His appearance commanded immediate respect, for, with a war shaking the nation, John Garrett's railroad was of tremendous importance, and Cousin Thomas shared the responsibilities of that railroad and its part in the war.

Much impressed, the girls listened to discussions of the latest war news. There had been a battle at Chantilly and things were not going to please the President. How long would the fighting be likely to continue?

The stimulating conversation prolonged the dinner pleasantly, but the girls, dressed in their best, could not suppress their excitement. Cousin Sarah had presented them each with a pair of stockings, handknitted from the finest silk thread. In these, their new slippers and lace mitts, they felt equal to any social occasion. As the carriage rolled to the door, the maid brought their bouquets and silk shawls. At last, the great moment!

Darkness had scarcely fallen, clear and starlit and lovely, when the carriage arrived at the White House. The President was a man of simple habits and did his receiving as early in the evening as possible. Under the white portico, the girls left the carriage, and gazed about them with wonder.

In the dressing room, Susan gave her shawl to the maid and turned to look at herself in the mirror. Her curls were coming a trifle loose. Beside her, a large billowing lady in evening dress, with jewels flashing on her arms and throat, turned to fasten a sparkling ornament in her hair. The sight of her gave Susan an idea. She drew the green rose from her bouquet and fastened it against her curls.

The stout lady beamed her approval. "It's just the right touch, my dear. You're lovely."

Cousin Sarah called her and she followed along the dignified white corridor to the door of the East Room. Lights gleamed everywhere and sparkled upon the great chandeliers with their thousands of crystal drops. A long line of dignitaries extended across the room, and it was a half hour before the Garretts and their guests reached the receiving line, where they were given an immediate and warm welcome.

"Mr. Garrett," said Mr. Lincoln cordially, "I should like a word with you and Mr. Scott apart. Please wait for me. I'll be free in about an hour."

"With pleasure, Mr. President. We are in no hurry," John Garrett said. "We have two young ladies with us and they won't want to miss the sights."

"Your wards, Mr. Garrett?"

"For this occasion, Mr. President," John Garrett answered, "they have been entrusted to Mr. Scott's care."

Lincoln's tired face lighted with a smile. "I see by your dress, ladies, that you are of Quaker persuasion. Permit me to say I know of no better citizens than your people. You are always welcome at the White House."

They thanked him. He pressed their hands and they followed the crowd into the adjoining rooms.

"Wasn't it exciting?" whispered Hetty.

"Yes, but he looked so sad. He smiled right into my eyes, and I saw pain and terrible suffering. I wanted to cry for him."

"Wait until thee gets home, and don't bawl all over the party," warned Hetty. "I wonder where we'll find the boys. George and Peter promised to be about, and surely James and Calvin are looking for us."

The Scotts and Garretts stood apart while they waited for

the President. People brushed past them, servants brought refreshments on great silver trays, and from somewhere an orchestra played softly. There was an attempt at gaiety, and yet anxious faces and nervous laughter betrayed the high tension of the guests.

A half hour passed uneasily. Then Hetty exclaimed, "I see Brother George. He's coming this way, and yes, Peter's with him."

George was puffing from exertion when he reached them. "I injured several feet on my way over here," he laughed, "but with the aid of a kindly fate, I made it." He spoke to the Scotts and Garretts, presented Peter, and then asked, "May I take my sisters aside for a few minutes of family discussion?"

"Certainly," said Sarah Scott, "but mind thee doesn't lose sight of them."

They found a quiet place and chatted eagerly. "Hetty, I am going to leave thee with Peter for a few minutes," George said. "See that thee doesn't stray away. Come, Susan, I want to see more of the White House." He tactfully led Susan to another room. "We'll be on the march at any moment now," he said. "Lee's planning something, and a big battle is in the offing."

She held him tightly. "Oh, George," she said, "I hate to see thee go."

"Somebody has to do it," he said. "And I'm glad to be on the saving side instead of the killing. That I couldn't do."

"I know," she whispered. Then she added nervously, "George, thee doesn't know anything about our Cousin James, does thee? He was to be here with his friend. I haven't seen them."

He looked at her suddenly and she dropped her eyes. "Oh, so it's Pancoast thee is interested in," he teased. "I thought he was Hetty's choice, although I'd much rather see her marry Peter. No, I haven't seen them tonight, although they're stationed close by. I think they won't be allowed to leave the troops; conditions are too jittery."

She was disappointed but tried not to show it.

"Wait a minute," said George, "thee stay back there out of sight, and I'll make a quick survey. I'll be back in no time." He pushed her behind a curtain and she found herself on a balcony overlooking the grounds. Walking to the railing, she stood looking out upon the starlit garden. Behind her, the music came dreamily, and from a catalpa tree, a little mocking bird trilled sleepily.

Then she heard a high, reedy voice beside her. "Ah, you're one of Mr. Scott's little Quaker girls, are you not?"

She turned quickly to face the President of the United States. "Don't be startled," he said kindly. "I wanted to see you and tell you that you look very beautiful to me in your simple gray. Mrs. Scott has just told us how nobly you and your sister sacrificed your new finery to free an old Negro man from slavery. Heaven will reward you."

"Oh, Mr. Lincoln," gasped Susan, "indeed your approbation is all the reward we would ever want. And old Abe gave himself up to the slave-catchers in place of a younger man. He was very fine about it."

"I'm sure of that. One noble act often inspires another. I wish I could stay here and talk with you, but I've just finished my chat with your friends and now there are others awaiting me. Good-bye, my child. It is such women as you who have made our nation what it is."

He patted her shoulder with a great kindly hand and was gone.

Susan's knees felt weak. What a story she'd have to tell when she reached Furley Hall. Hetty would dramatize it all over the place. Now she wished George would come back. He would never find the other boys in all that mass of people. She drew the curtain to one side and peeped anxiously from her hiding place. At the same moment a strong arm drew her behind the curtain. Startled, she looked up at Calvin Pancoast.

"Susan," he said eagerly. "I've looked everywhere. I finally met George, and he showed me where he had cached you. How lovely you are."

He held her hand and she forgot to take it from him.

"I was so anxious," she admitted. "George was afraid they wouldn't let thee come. Oh, Calvin, is the situation as bad as it sounds? Will there really be another dreadful battle?"

"It seems to be shaping up that way," he admitted. "I wish it weren't so. James and I couldn't leave our company at the same time, and so we drew straws for the honor. This time I was the lucky one."

This was the moment she had dreamed about, and now that it was here, she knew she must put him off. She wanted him, but something within her whispered that she must be loyal to her sister.

Nervously, she clutched her bouquet until the flowers crumpled in her grasp. She told him about her trip on the train, of her presentation to the President, of the surprise interview on the balcony. Finally, she paused for breath and stole a glance at his face.

He was bending over her, eagerly drinking in the sound of her voice, watching the way her curls caressed her lovely face, the kindness in her blue eyes, and when those eyes met his, she saw such sadness and hunger that her heart throbbed and she uttered a little gasp.

Immediately, his arm went about her.

She wanted to push him away, but the woman in her heart was stronger than her will. She dropped the broken flowers to the floor and her arms crept about him. She felt him tremble against her heart, and then the tremendous joy of his love. Nothing mattered now. She forgot all about Hetty and what the Friends would say to her breach of the Discipline. She knew only that she loved him with all her might, and that she would follow him anywhere. He was hers and she was as much his as the very heart that beat in his breast and that, in turn, was hers.

Into their happiness, came the mellow chiming of a clock. He started, and lifted his head to listen.

"My sweet, my little Susan," he whispered, "I love you. I had not meant to tell you until later, when with the fighting over I could come to you as you would want to have me. I have been weak, but I am not sorry. Come what may, you will always know that I love you, and you will be brave. I must leave now—one more kiss."

"No, no, thee can't go. I won't let them take thee away." Tears wet her kerchief as she clung to him desperately. He wiped her grief away with his kisses, and gradually she, too, was filled with his calm resignation.

"Forgive me," she begged. "If I am going to be a soldier's wife, I must be a brave one."

She smiled, and he knew that she would keep her word. Unfastening the green rose from her hair, she kissed it and dropped it in his pocket. "Carry it with thee," she whispered.

"Yes," he promised, "yes, my darling, it's like you, pure at heart, but different from all its kind."

"And 'twill bloom for no one else," she reminded him.

There was a low whistle at the curtain, followed by George's voice announcing, "Come on, Sue, the Scotts have retrieved Hetty and are raising a frightful dust about thy disappearance. Come quickly. I pledged my skin I'd look after thee."

There was no time for even a last embrace. Susan was conscious of a sudden farewell, and of Cousin Sarah saying crisply, "I trusted that brother of thine to look after his sisters. I found Hetty sitting in the corner with some army surgeon, and as for thee with thy rumpled flowers, where has thee been?"

Susan's eyes filled with tears. "Oh, Cousin Sarah," she said, "why did thee ever tell the President about buying the slave? He took my hand and said the sweetest things."

"Hm," said the old lady, peering at Susan over her glasses. "Judging by the disgraceful look of thy hair, I'd say that Abe Lincoln is a big surprise to me."

She led them away from the White House, took them to her brother's home and saw them safely abed.

In the adjoining room they could hear Cousin Thomas laughing softly, and then Cousin Sarah's voice, "I declare, perhaps I've been saved a lot of worry by not having daughters, but weren't they cute about getting rid of me?"

She chuckled to herself and the girls knew they were forgiven.

Tomorrow would be another day. They would have to attend the Washington Meeting in the morning. Then there would be dinner and after that they would be free to return home. Susan wanted to go home. She wanted to tell her father all about Calvin. She needed William's comfort and advice. He would grieve but he would be kind, and he would know what to do about Hetty. In the security and quiet beauty of Furley Hall, she would find peace.

She tossed nervously. Sleep was impossible. How could she tell Hetty? Her own troubles made her wonder about Keziah and Jasper. She believed they were safe by now, but she knew that if the merciless hunters discovered them, they would be sold by their angry master to live the hardest possible life in the cotton fields or the rice swamps. Their problems were greater than hers.

Then she remembered the Psalm, "The Lord shall help them and deliver them, and save them because they trust in Him." He would help them and He would help her, too. She released her burdens, wiped her tears on the pillow and finally slept.

CHAPTER
TWENTY-TWO

They returned to Furley, and Hetty entertained the family with the story of their adventure. Immediately after breakfast, Susan followed her father to his study. She sat on her accustomed stool, and looked anxiously at him.

"Yes, my dear, what troubles thee?"

"Pa, thee won't like it," she whispered.

"No? Will God like it?"

For answer, she dropped her head against his knee and her tears wet the hand that sought to comfort her.

"Now, now, Susan. This is not a bit like my cheerful girl. If Hetty is going to marry Peter, she's not going to destruction. She should be very happy with such a fine Quaker boy. I anticipated this and I've given it some thought. I might even set up an office here for Peter and George and have them form a professional partnership. In that case Hetty won't have to leave us. You can still be together every day. Does that make thee any happier?"

For reply, she clutched his hand a little tighter and her grief came in hard, bitter sobs. He waited quietly until she was controlled.

"Now go and wash thy face and then come and tell me," he said softly.

She did as she was bid and when she returned she went right to the point.

"Pa, it's partly because of Hetty, but she doesn't want to

marry Peter. Thee remembers Calvin Pancoast, James' friend?"

A shadow of alarm flitted across his face, but he only nodded.

"He was stationed near Washington and came to the party."

"To see Hetty?"

She picked nervously at his sleeve. "No, to see me. He says that he fell in love with my picture on Aunt Cassie's parlor table and he asked James to introduce him. Hetty just took possession of him at first, but he finally broke away from her. Pa, I knew that first evening when he came with James. I've fought it all summer but I—I can't any longer. It's got to be faced. If I marry him, Friends will disown me as they disowned Cornelia."

William gazed thoughtfully through the window toward the little summer-house in the grove. Between that and the house stretched his lawn and his rose gardens. He had spent his life perfecting his fruits and his flowers. Now, this fairest of them all was not to bloom as he had planned. She would be different, different from her kind. He had a green rose and he could do nothing to change nature.

His voice shook, but he was very kind. "Has he asked thee yet?"

"No, Pa, not in so many words, but he will ask me just as soon as he's free to come home."

"Then if Divine Love has destined thy course to follow that of Calvin Pancoast, thee will obey thy leading. In the meanwhile, we will make very sure of the Light."

"But, Pa, what of Hetty? She thinks she wants Calvin. She will be so terribly hurt. What shall I do? Peter loves her, but she doesn't seem to care for him."

He considered for a moment in silence. "Suppose we let the situation ride for the present," he advised. "Time is a great solver of such problems. Hetty falls in and out of love very easily. To tell her now might wound her unnecessarily. If

Calvin and Peter were here, the situation would indeed be difficult, but with a battle so imminent, they will not be free to come. A little time and a little love will straighten matters out."

She bowed her head. "But, Pa, I feel so guilty."

"Thee need not. Thee gave her every opportunity and besides"—his eyes twinkled—"Hetty has a pliant heart, but she has never really been in love. When she does fall, she will fall hard and we will know what to do."

William stood up, put an arm about Susan and led her to the porch. "I think I hear Billy coming with the mail," he announced cheerfully, but Susan knew that in his heart, he was grieved. "And, Susan, I hear through Thomas Scott that when the Negro Jasper reached the Central Committee in Philadelphia, he was told that Keziah and the six children had already been forwarded to Canada."

"Oh, Pa, what a disappointment. Poor little Jerry wanted his mammy. From Philadelphia, one group might be sent across New York State, and the other might follow the route west through Ohio and the Great Lakes. It may take months to bring them together."

"Don't cross any bridges until thee comes to them," cautioned William. "The Friends handle these matters very skillfully, and they aren't likely to lose any of their passengers. But here comes Billy with my newspaper."

With his usual clatter, Billy rode Ginger as far as the porch where he brought her up with a flourish. "Watch out for the Pony Express," he yelled. "I brought a letter from Sister Cornelia." He handed the paper and the letter to his father, and rode off to the hitching rack.

"That Billy," exclaimed Susan fondly. "I wonder if he'll ever grow up."

"Suppose we go back to the porch," William said. "The rest

of the family are there, and Billy will fasten his horse and be with us directly. Then I will read the letter aloud."

As soon as they were assembled, he broke the seal on Cornelia's letter. Cornelia was in great distress. She spoke of her helpless condition and the expected child, and she begged William to write to her young husband, Eli, urging him to remain out of the war. "He says nothing," wrote the frightened wife, "but I can see that a desire to join the Confederate forces is eating at his heart. What can I do to stop him? Almost every day someone is here to importune him, to make him act on his conviction about the rights of the States. Only my health and our unborn child holds him back. I fear to let him out of my sight, and the knowledge of this is making him resentful and unhappy. Please advise me, Pa. What shall I do?"

Deborah wept softly, and with one accord, the family looked to the father for counsel. William sat in silence while he sought Guidance. "The way is clear," he finally said. "Susan, thee and Hetty must go at once, and, Billy, thee has shown mature judgment on several occasions of late and I feel minded to send thee along. Perhaps thee can dissuade this young madcap from his views. If, however, he follows his present inclinations, my three girls must not be left without a man in the house. Thee will forget thy unsteady ways and accept thy responsibilities as occasion arises. What does thee say to this?"

Billy hung his head for a moment and moved the toe of his boot across the pattern in the rag rug. Then he lifted his eyes.

"Yes, Pa, thee can trust me," he said. "Nobody ever put much faith in me before. Now I'll not disappoint thee."

William extended his hand and the two shook hands solemnly. There was a gladness in the boy's face that went to Susan's heart.

"Billy," she said admiringly, "thee was magnificent. I'm so glad thee's going with us. And, Billy, there's a leftover piece of pie in the kitchen safe. Thee might eat it and save it from spoiling."

Having made up his mind, William was quick to act. He went to the City Hall to secure three passes, for since the first of August, no one had been allowed to leave the city without permission. His three children prepared themselves for the journey, and bright and early the following day they were off to Frederick. Toy stowed their luggage under the carriage seats, and Henny staggered from the kitchen with a hamper full of ham and chicken sandwiches, deviled eggs, cake, a jug of cold cider and great bunches of luscious grapes, white, blue and purple.

"Dat's a long trip," she explained, "and I doan want no skelekoms to fetch up at Miss Kippy's. Look to her lak you been starve at home."

They laughed and hugged her. "Dear Aunt Henny," said Susan, "nobody will ever starve around thee."

"Go way, Miss Susan," chuckled the old woman. "Git out o' yere. You all done muss up my bandanner, an' look what you done to you kercher."

She straightened the kerchief across Susan's shoulders and gave a few last-minute instructions to Toy. It was Saturday, and on this day of the week the old man literally let his hair down. Aunt Henny unraveled the two plaits of wool that clung to his pate, combed them carefully, replaited them, and after winding them about his head, fastened them securely with a piece of twine. This ordeal over, Toy was in an unhappy state of mind, and could hardly restrain his resentment.

" 'Oman," he muttered, "some day I gonna git mahse'f shore lak a sheep, an' you ain't layin' a hand on me atterwards." He worked off his spleen on the horses. "Giddap, you ole coupla polecats," he complained. At his familiar voice, the horses trotted forward.

At Camden Station, Billy bought the tickets and found a

boy to help carry the baggage. He presented the passes to the officer in charge at the gate in plenty of time before the train came puffing into the station. There was the hubbub of getting aboard and finding seats, and a violent lurch as the train started.

They passed slowly through the city into the bright country beyond. It was the first of September and the cornfields stood waiting for the harvest. The train rumbled across a bridge over a stream where a group of boys dived from the bank into a swimming hole.

"I'd like to be with them," cried Billy. Then remembering his new dignity, he added, "That is, if I hadn't anything better to do. Susan, is it time to eat?"

"No, it certainly is not. Thee just had thy breakfast, and thee'll have to wait until noon." Then seeing his disappointment, she added, "At least, until eleven o'clock."

So by noon the luncheon was eaten, and the three sat close to the windows to watch the mountains. At first, from the valley they appeared as a blue shadow in the west, but now as the train began the tortuous ascent, the mountain slopes were covered with a concealing green. Beside a little mountain pool, a young deer stood for a moment, wide-eyed and fearful, until with a bob of his tail, he turned and fled into the woods.

"Wish I could see a bear," said Billy excitedly, but try as he might, he had no glimpse of one. Finally, however, the train stopped at a station, and there, chained to a post in front of the local emporium, were a pair of beautiful cubs. While the train took on water, both Billy and the girls walked about and looked at the animals. Here from the mountain's summit they were able to look out over the vast expanse of country. An eagle left a tall pine and swooped out over the plain they had just crossed. How easy it looked and how immense the world they lived in.

Overawed, they crept back into the coach and dozed and talked. Toward the end of a long afternoon they reached Frederick, where there were several carriages at the station for hire. These were operated by Negroes who darted up to the passengers, seized their baggage, crying, "Dis way, lady," or, "Right yere, mistah." The passengers were expected to follow their bags. In this way, the three pieces of Coale luggage were in three carriages, and there was a violent argument as to which driver should have the passengers. While they were quarreling, Billy secured two of the bags, put them with the third, helped his sisters in and took the reins in his hands. At once the grinning driver sprang into the seat, yelled to the horses and they were off on a run leaving the disappointed rivals gaping after them. They reached the neat town house of Eliakim and Cornelia Sprague, a bit of a place set even with the stone sidewalk. Inside, there was a tiny parlor, a small dining room, a bright kitchen and two bedrooms upstairs. Billy would have to sleep on the parlor sofa, but Billy was partial to sleep and could make himself comfortable anywhere.

Cornelia was overjoyed to see her guests. She laughed and cried all in the same breath. The baby would arrive almost any time now, and she was relieved to have some of her family near her to share the ordeal. Eliakim welcomed them gladly. His relief was so obvious that Billy whispered, "Susan, perhaps we did wrong to come. Now that we're here to assume the responsibility, he may take a notion to cut loose and join the Confederates."

"Hush, Billy, Eli is very emotional, but I don't think he'll lose his head. Try to keep near him if thee can," cautioned Susan.

That evening Eliakim took Susan aside, and confided news which gave him very evident satisfaction. General Jackson had appeared very suddenly at Manassas, where a large Union supply station was located. After appropriating such of the supplies as he could use or carry away, he applied the torch to the remainder. On August 26th, the Northern commander learned of the sudden appearance of Jackson and gave orders for a concentration of his troops against the Southerner. The armies met for a two-day battle at Bull Run. Fourteen thousand Union soldiers and nine thousand Confederates had been lost in the campaign. The Union army had been forced to seek shelter in the fortifications around Washington.

"I wonder what Lee will do next," Eli mused. "After eighteen months of war, Virginia is practically a desert. She can't maintain an army of one hundred thousand men, so Lee is almost forced to turn to Maryland and Pennsylvania for subsistence. Don't tell Kippy about this. It might upset her."

There was no need to swear Susan to secrecy. She spent a restless night of worry. Where would Lee go? In the morning she heard Cornelia stirring about in the kitchen where Susan joined her. Hetty soon followed, and cheered by the presence of her own relatives, Cornelia was more like her usual gay self. To keep her in this mood, Hetty told her merry tales of their experiences in Washington. Susan was silent. Thoughts of Washington brought to her heart a fierce sorrow and a sense of guilt.

Billy concentrated his attention on Eli and persuaded him to go fishing. The girls packed a lunch for them and they departed for the river. It would be a relief to Kippy to know that her husband was a safe distance from the Southern recruiting officers who did their work secretly but efficiently, and the three girls spent a happy day together, all unmindful of the gathering battle clouds.

In the late afternoon the fishermen returned with a good catch. Eli was in excellent spirits, and after a fine supper of baked fish, corn bread and lima beans, the little family sat out in the garden and watched the sun set below the rim of the mountains.

"In the newspaper today," said Hetty, "I read such a fine poem by John Whittier about how nature goes right on producing in spite of silly wars. He says,

> " 'And still she walks in golden hours
> Through harvest-happy farms,
> And still she wears her fruits and flowers
> Like jewels on her arms.
> She knows the seed lies safe below
> The fires that blast and burn;
> For all the tears of blood we sow
> She waits the rich return.'

He wrote a lot more, but I haven't had time to learn it."

"It's a grand poem," agreed Cornelia.

But Eli said nothing. He got up suddenly and complained of fatigue. The mood of contentment was gone and the little family separated for the night.

Susan, after an exhausting day, welcomed the comfortable bed and sleep.

CHAPTER
TWENTY-THREE

The sun was just rising above the edge of the mountains when a wild clatter of hooves beat along the street. Susan jumped from her bed and ran to the window in time to see a horseman gallop by. He wore a Federal uniform, its blue now tarnished with dust. Flecks of foam blew from the horse's mouth as it tore past the Sprague house and turned toward the Federal camp. A moment later the air was filled with the sound of bugles. From the adjoining room, Susan heard Eli clomp one foot into a boot and then the startled pleading of Cornelia. "Darling, thee won't go out without thy breakfast. Please, please, Eliakim."

"I'll be back in a moment, sweetheart. Don't worry about me. It was just somebody bringing news, probably from Virginia. I'll find out what's going on and I'll be right back."

He ran past Susan and clattered downstairs to the street.

Thus awakened, Billy reached for his boots and trousers, and was half dressed by the time Hetty called to him. "Oh, run, Billy. Don't let Eli go without thee. Something must have happened."

The front door slammed behind Billy, and Susan returned to the window. Beyond Frederick, she could see the mountains, green with their oak and chestnut; between Frederick and the mountains stretched orchards of apples and peaches heavy with ripe fruit, cornfields with fat, golden ears ready for gathering. Over all this peace and plenty the rising sun shed an aura of rosy light and war seemed completely remote. Only the stars and stripes floating from a few houses along the street gave any indication of political feeling. People rushed from the houses to peer after the horseman. There was a twitter of tongues which made Susan think of a hive of bees suddenly disturbed. From a small house directly opposite, a frail old lady stood in the doorway shading her eyes with her hand.

"What's the disturbance?" she called.

A small boy padding barefoot along the dirt street paused for a moment to yell, "The Johnnies is comin', Missus Frietchie—Lee's whole army. We gonna git kilt." As he vanished around the corner, the old lady re-entered her house, and Susan hurried to her sister.

Kippy was sitting on the side of her bed, her eyes wide with fear.

"Susan," she cried, "help me get dressed. I'm going after Eli. Did thee hear what that boy said? Lee's army's coming."

"Kippy," said Susan firmly, "think of thy child. Thee must be quiet. Pa would tell thee that God can take care of Eli without thy help." She sat beside her sister and tried to comfort her. If Kippy would only cry. Instead she just sat, wide-eyed and terrified.

Hetty brought hot tea, but until Eli returned, Kippy would take nothing. He finally came in, smiling at her fear. No, he had not enlisted, and he expected to stay with her all day. Lee's army was crossing the Potomac at the Point of Rocks, and there would be no violence. The Confederate officers were gentlemen. They paid for what they took, and they demanded only what they needed to live. Cornelia's relief was so great that she ate her breakfast with Eli and then they sat with Susan, Hetty and Billy to watch the evacuation of Frederick.

All day long a stream of carriages and wagons filed past the house, carrying frightened inhabitants who took with them what property they could. Many less fortunate people left on foot, and it was reported that the roads leading to Baltimore and Pennsylvania were jammed with fugitives.

Eli laid in a good supply of smoked meat, potatoes and flour from the store. The army would leave little food, and because of Cornelia's expected confinement, flight was impossible.

"Eli, will there be any fighting?" asked Hetty nervously. "If Kippy is having a baby, it won't be good for her."

Eliakim grinned. "If they want to fight, they won't stop on account of Cornelia," he said. "But comfort yourselves, for there's only one Union company stationed here. The officer in command is loading all available wagons with his stores and they will leave before nightfall. I understand that six hundred wounded men will have to be left behind."

"Perhaps we can help them," said Hetty.

Susan spoke quickly. "Unless I'm mistaken, thee'll have thy hands full right here. Kippy is as white as a sheet and I'm afraid she's beginning her ordeal. Before Lee's army arrives, I'll send Billy to the telegraph office to inform Pa that we're safe."

"I'll go right now," offered Billy, who was glad of an excuse to get away.

He left at once, and was gone only a few minutes before he returned, much excited.

"General Stonewall Jackson has broken up the Baltimore and Ohio Railroad," he announced, "and cut off all telegraphic and other connection between Harper's Ferry and Washington. That means we're isolated."

Susan was silent for a moment. "Don't worry, Billy," she said. "We always have been cared for, and I know that if Pa has heard the news, he's sitting calmly in his study, knowing the truth that we are always in our right place in God's plan, and have only to look for the good, lovingly and trustingly, and all must be well."

"Yes," he said, "I know thee's right, Sue, and say, does thee remember all those flags that were floating from the houses yesterday, they've all disappeared."

She glanced up and down the street. "That's true," she said, "all but one. I notice the old lady across the street is hanging hers back again. She has spunk, hasn't she?"

Cornelia had come onto the porch behind them. She smiled faintly. "Good old Mrs. Frietchie," she said. "She's a good friend and neighbor, and she'll be loyal to that flag if they kill her for it. Susan, I wish thee would help me to bed. I feel very sick, and the pain is getting more than I can bear."

The doctor was summoned, but it would be several hours before the baby arrived. He would look in from time to time during the evening, and at midnight he would stay.

To Susan, the next few hours were endless. Eli sat beside the bed and held his young wife in his arms during her periodic pains which at first were a half hour apart; then they came more often and with greater violence. Eli's mind was no longer on the Confederacy. He gave all his attention to helping Cornelia in her time of trial. Finally, toward midnight, when it seemed to Susan that there was scarcely a minute between Kippy's frantic pleas for help, there was a quick knock at the door. As she opened it for the doctor, Susan was shocked by the red flame which cast a fiendish glow over the town and its fleeing inhabitants.

"Oh, Doctor," she whispered, "I'm so glad thee's come, for I think my sister is dying. Whatever is that unearthly light?"

"It does look rather hellish, doesn't it?" he admitted. "The captain learned that the Confederates were only three or four miles away. He couldn't get all his supplies out, so he set fire to the rest—all, that is, except some for the hospital."

The doctor went to Cornelia and gave Susan and Eli instructions. When they had brought clean towels and hot water, he went to work.

"Now, little lady," he comforted, "we'll have this baby in no time at all. You're spunky to take your suffering so quietly. Take your husband's hand in one of yours and your sister's in the other, and pull with all your strength."

A half hour passed wretchedly.

Susan could hear Hetty and Billy talking excitedly from the room below as they watched the fire and the fleeing people. Susan's arm ached from Cornelia's frantic pulling. She saw the sweat stream from Eli's face and drop unheeded against his ruffled shirt. Finally, the ordeal was over. Eli was exhausted. Susan took the baby, like a bundle of flannel on her arm, to Hetty.

"Here, Hetty, take thy little nephew and bathe him. Isn't he a dandy?"

Billy wiped his face on his sleeve and grinned. "What makes him so unhappy?" he asked.

"He's not unhappy. He's just celebrating his birthday with a good yell. I've got to go back to the doctor. He says Kippy's all right. Our family must be tough, for I never thought she'd live through it."

Susan went back to the doctor and helped him make her sister comfortable. Billy had taken Eli outdoors to get some air and walk off his nervousness. When they returned, the doctor had left, and a new serenity settled over the house. Hetty, Billy, Cornelia and Eli fell asleep without any trouble. Only for Susan was there no rest. Fourteen thousand lost—fourteen thousand men. Where was Calvin? She crept from her bed and leaned her elbows on the casement sill to stare out into the night. A man-child had just been born into the world and fourteen thousand Yankees and nine thousand Johnnies were gone in just one campaign. No wonder Pa hated war. He would let them kill him but he'd never fight back. Calvin would fight. Either Pa or Calvin was wrong. Which one? What was it the President had said? "In great contests, each party claims to act in accordance with the will of God. Both may be, and one must be, wrong. God cannot be for and against the same thing at the same time."

Lincoln was right about that. Suddenly, in her wretchedness and confusion of thought, she remembered William, calm and resourceful. He had a way of putting himself outside his problems and leaving the solution to a higher Power. That thought brought peace to Susan's heart. She looked out toward the towering mountains. Somewhere beyond them she felt assured Calvin both lived for her and loved her.

The infant wailed and she went to him. How sweet he was. His tiny hands clutched at her finger and she felt a tenderness and pride in her family. Now she could rest for a few hours before the dawn.

CHAPTER

TWENTY-FOUR

❧ ───────────────────────────────

Susan awoke to the sound of drums. She heard the baby crying and Hetty's voice attempting to soothe him. For a moment she lay in a daze, trying to orient herself. Then she remembered: the Southern army was entering Frederick. She sat up and steadied her aching head. If God gave her work to do, He would also give her the strength to do it. She dressed and went downstairs where all but Cornelia were assembled. Eli had lighted a fire in the kitchen stove and Susan made a pot of tea.

Billy and Eli were at the front door, drawn irresistibly by the sound of marching soldiers and the insistent roll of drums.

"Come quick, girls," called Billy. "Here comes General Stonewall Jackson."

With a shaking hand, Susan set her cup of tea on the kitchen table. From the door she peered over Hetty's shoulder at the approaching column. Confederate sympathizers crowded the sidewalks and cheered wildly. Like startled ants, frantic women ran up and down searching the lines for their sons or husbands.

Susan could not fail to admire Jackson, who rode quietly and unassumingly at the head of his ragged army. There was a dignity in his bearing which substantiated all that she had heard of him: his sense of order, his love of justice, his temperance in all things, his kindness to his slaves and, above all, a crystal clarity of soul. He once said that his faith taught him to feel as safe in battle as in bed.

His goodness of heart was soon proved, for, as he came opposite the Frietchie house, he saw the Union flag flying from the window. As his soldiers were about to destroy it, the old woman ran to the gate and berated them soundly. The tumult of voices, the rumble of wagons, the rattling of artillery and the heavy tramp of infantry drowned out her words, but her distress was obvious. Jackson issued a quick command and his men returned to their places. The flag remained where it hung.

As they filed past, it was plain to see that the troops were in great want. They were not only dirty, but wretchedly clothed and shod. Thousands were without shoes and went either barefoot or with their feet tied up in bloody rags. The wagons were empty except for ammunition.

After watching for a few minutes, their suffering made Susan sick with sympathy. She was about to re-enter the house when a passing drummer-boy suddenly stopped his rat-a-tat and cried, "Howdy, Miss Susan."

Hetty exclaimed, "Well, if it isn't J Scudd!"

Susan walked swiftly to the edge of the sidewalk, and with unbelieving eyes stared at J. His thin face was pinched with hunger and suffering. The uniform that had been his pride was torn and frayed, but he walked jauntily and with determination.

"J!" she cried. "Thee poor boy. I'm glad to see thee." She ran along the street beside him. "Has thee ever seen thy father and brothers?"

"Yep. Seen my brother Zeb and Jim at Manassas. They done tole me Paw got kilt. Looked for Zeb and Jim after the fitten was done, but never found 'em. Don't clearly know ef they's livin' or not. There's a powerful lot got kilt."

"Where's Captain Carter?"

J looked away. "I'm powerful sorry, miss. A sniper got him

yestiddy. I knows you was sweet on him and I done what I could."

Susan did not answer. She returned slowly to the house. Gaunt-eyed men looked hungrily at her as she walked slowly with averted eyes. She entered the cottage quietly, wiped away her tears and went to Cornelia.

All day long the Confederate troops tramped by the house, but Susan did not look again. Her heart was heavy. Where was the Northern army? Where was Calvin? And what of George and Peter, for wherever the army went, hospital wagons would follow close behind.

In the city, martial law was proclaimed, with Colonel Bradley Johnson, a native of the place, in command. There was neither disorder, violence nor incivility. From the surrounding country the commissaries brought in supplies of provisions which were paid for in either Confederate or Federal money.

With the Confederate wounded added to the six hundred Yankee patients already in the Frederick hospital, the cots overflowed and men lay side by side in rows on the floor.

Immediately the women of the town offered themselves for service. Linens were brought out and cut up for bandages, nourishing soup was prepared in huge kettles and served to the hungry sufferers. Nurses kneeled beside the men, dressing their wounds and relieving their thirst. Ministers passed in and out, bringing comfort to the hopeless. A Catholic priest administered last rites, and an old woman with paper and pencil wrote down messages for homefolk.

Hetty and Susan took turns with the others. It was necessary for one of them to stay with Cornelia and the baby, but whenever Susan could spare a few hours, she was at the hospital. Her gray frock and smiling face were a welcome sight to the wounded men. To Susan, accustomed as she was to the sheltered sweetness of her father's gardens, the odors were stifling, but she gradually forced herself to accept them.

Recognizing her dependability, the doctor invited her to take charge of one of the officer's wards. "These men," he said, "are in cots, and you won't have to crawl on the floor to care for them. Carry on, and I'll be here to help when you need me."

She nodded. She was not here to choose, and she did as she was asked. There were fifty men in the room, and it was hard to know which one needed her most. She started at the first bed, rebandaged a wounded leg, and went to the next patient who had a head wound and was delirious. She gave him water and pushed him back against the pillow.

As she moved to the third cot, she saw a small figure in a ragged uniform come into the ward, search anxiously up and down the rows of cots, and then, having found the object of his search, go quickly to the side of a bed and peer into the face of the patient.

It was J Scudd, and she went to him at once. She touched him on the shoulder. He looked at her with dumb anguish in his eyes as he pointed to a broad-shouldered man lying before him. For a brief moment, Susan stared at the face of the unconscious captain. Sorrowfully, she brushed the long hair back from his forehead.

"Randolph Carter," she whispered.

At the touch of her hand, Carter's eyes slowly opened and a faint smile flitted across his grimy face.

"Susan, dear girl," he whispered faintly.

She brought a basin of water and washed his face and hands. Then impulsively she stooped and kissed his forehead. A light shone for a moment in his eyes and then the labored breathing ceased. Susan folded his hands, felt in his pockets and removed his few possessions.

J had dropped to his knees beside the bed and was sobbing without restraint.

"Come, J," said Susan quietly. "I have taken his things to

send home to his mother, but his watch, I am sure, she would want thee to have. See, I am going to give it to thee to cherish all thy life. Now at last thee'll have a watch all thy own."

J clutched the watch and cried all the harder.

"He was sech a good feller," he sobbed. "After we left yore place he took a likin' to me and kep' me by him. When the fitten was hard, he'd send me on errands, so's I wouldn't git kilt. He was awful sweet on you, Miss Susan, and account of you, he didn't want nothin' to happen to me. I could tell it."

He paused long enough to wipe his dirty face on his sleeve. "Crossin' the river jest below yere, he got it. A sniper hit him right in the belly. I hopes that man goes . . ."

"Hush, J."

" 'Scuse me, miss. Captain said I shouldn't cuss so much, so he let me use one cuss-word a day, and that's for today."

"J," said Susan, "I'm about ready to leave. Could thee go home with me and take a bath in Carroll Creek while I wash thy clothes and get them mended?"

"Yes, miss, I got the afternoon off—only you needn't bother. My clothes do stink powerful bad. I've wore 'em now sence I left you all."

"Then come quickly," said Susan.

She led the way to her sister's house, and while J went for a swim, she washed his uniform and dried it in the hot September breeze. A neighbor contributed some clean underwear, and when J was ready to leave, he said gratefully, "Thank you, Miss Susan. Will you please keep my watch for me? Sometime I'll come and git it. Now it ain't fittin' I be kerryin' it account it might git lost."

"I'll take good care of it, J, and when thee wants it, thee'll find it at Furley Hall in my father's strong box."

He took a generous slice of gingerbread with him and set out for camp. She walked with him across the bridge over the creek.

"Thank you, Miss Susan, fer all what you done fer me and . . . fer him," he said shyly.

She patted his shoulder, and sick at heart hurried home to Cornelia. These wonderful men, so young and strong. Her thoughts turned from the dead to the living. She must hear soon from Calvin. A sob caught in her throat as she clutched the doorknob and practically fell into Hetty's arms.

"Susan, whatever is the matter? Here, sit down and let me get thee some hot tea. Thee should have let me go to the hospital," scolded Hetty. "Thee takes all the responsibilities, and I'm younger and can stand more."

In spite of herself, Susan smiled faintly. "I know I'm nearly twenty," she admitted, "but I've still a good bit of life in me."

Susan accepted the tea gratefully, and together the girls awaited the return of Billy and Eli who had gone to a farm for provisions. It was late when they returned. They brought a pail of milk, but the soldiers had foraged the countryside, and there was not an egg, an ear of corn, or a pat of butter to be had. They would have to content themselves with ham and potatoes. Well, they would be grateful for what they had.

"And," said Cornelia, glancing nervously at her husband, "when the meat and potatoes are gone, we can be thankful that we are still together."

CHAPTER
TWENTY-FIVE

Sunday dawned as beautiful and cloudless as only a Maryland day can be in early September. Susan, looking from the window, saw small groups of people on their way to church. It was rumored that General Jackson expected to attend the Presbyterian service, and encouraged by the atmosphere of quiet and order, the few people still in town ventured to attend the church of their choice. The officers and many of the enlisted men followed the general's example, so that the churches of Frederick were crammed with worshipers.

Because Cornelia could not leave her bed, the Spragues decided to have their morning worship at home. Eliakim read a chapter from the Bible and Hetty offered a poem. Cornelia prayed with deep emotion, expressing gratitude for her young son and for the protection of her husband. Eli was deeply touched by her words, and unashamed, brushed tears from his eyes.

Susan felt relieved. At last Eli knew that he must stay and care for his little family. He would not worry Kippy again. Susan looked into his eyes and the smile died from her face. He wore an expression of great anguish, not at all like that of a man who has found peace and a sense of what he must do. Could it be that he still intended to join the army as soon as Cornelia felt stronger? Then she realized that if his mind was made up, there was nothing she could do about it. Somehow, events would work out for the best. That she must not forget.

The worship hour at an end, Susan busied herself with dinner. The Spragues could not afford a maid, and Hetty remarked upon the joys of having Aunt Henny at home to prepare the savory meals that had been so much taken for granted. When they returned to Furley, they would appreciate Aunt Henny.

"I've got a ham baking in the oven. Call Billy, please, and ask him to lift it out for me," Susan said.

Billy did not have to be called. When it was time to eat, he was always on hand. He lifted the spicy ham to the table and sniffed the delicious odor of the meat, crunchy with its topping of brown sugar, vinegar and spices.

Susan carried a tray to Cornelia and the others gathered around the table for their Sunday dinner. They were young and they were hungry, and for the moment, there was nothing to cause alarm. Frederick seemed more like the scene of a Fourth of July festival than a gathering of armed invaders.

When his appetite was satisfied, Eli said, "If you don't mind, I'd like to go to church this evening. I hear the Reverend Daniel Zacharias has vowed that he will pray for the success of the Union troops. I don't believe he will have the courage to try it. If he does, with all the Southern soldiers sitting there, you may be sure he'll be quieted in a hurry. I don't want to miss the fun."

The girls were alarmed. "Thee doesn't think they would harm him, does thee?" asked Hetty.

"They won't be too gentle with him. After all, this is war."

"I'll go with thee," offered Billy. "I'd like to see the scrap."

"Billy," chided Susan, "thee ought to be ashamed of thyself. It is almost as bad to watch as to fight. Anyway, we need a man here."

"Yes," said Eli with dignity. He lowered his voice so that Kippy could not hear. "I know why Billy follows me like a bloodhound. He wants to keep me from joining up. But he might as well stop guarding me, for if I have refrained from doing this thing, it is not because I've been watched but because I could not bear to offend Cornelia. It's a problem I've got to face and solve alone. Nobody has a right to hinder me. In your Quaker belief, you say that each must obey his own conscience, and when the time comes for me to make up my mind, that's exactly what I'm going to do. Nothing can stop me."

He got up from the table, took his hat and strode out the front door.

Billy whistled softly. "Now you know," he said; "looks like I've lost my job."

Susan did not answer. She was deeply affected and left Hetty and Billy to do the dishes while she went to sit with her sister. The baby cried. When it had been fed, Susan sat in a low rocker and held it in her arms.

"Has thee decided on a name for thy baby?" she asked.

"Eli wants it named for himself, so I guess that will be it," said Kippy. "Eliakim seems like a long name for such a mite, but Eli wants a son to carry on for him."

There she was, always fearing what would happen to Eli. Susan must change those thoughts to something more cheerful, so she talked about Myra, the new piano and of the visit of the Friends to reprimand them on their way of life. She told how their father had pleaded his case so skillfully as to win them over completely. Dear Pa, thought Susan. She wished he could be with them now. She knew that late of a Sabbath afternoon, he would be walking in his rose garden, and his thoughts would be of his children safe in the Secret Place of the Most High.

Finally Kippy fell asleep. Susan put the baby in his cradle

and tiptoed from the room. She went noiselessly downstairs and stepped to the porch. Across Patrick Street she could see Dame Frietchie's flag still fluttering daringly in the afternoon breeze. On the left side of the Sprague house, a little garden sloped down to the edge of Carroll Creek. A flock of ducks swam by, cackling and gossiping, and some small boys were paddling a homemade raft, trying to gig bullfrogs. It looked peaceful enough.

She sat in the parlor and watched for Eli through the half-opened blinds. She heard the church organ very faintly as it led the congregation in the closing hymn. Eli would have only two blocks to walk home, down Market Street and into Patrick. She went to the porch again and peered anxiously into the distance. He was coming now. He walked as usual, not with the haste of a person leaving a scene of violence.

As Eli came onto the porch she inquired, "How was the service?"

"Quite as usual." He grinned. "Jackson is a stickler for order. He said there was to be no violence in the town and he meant it. When he heard about the preacher's vow, he decided to attend the service himself, so there he sat and not a man dared lift a finger."

"Good for him," breathed Susan, much relieved. "He must be a grand person, Eli."

"I think so. His men all admire and respect him."

"Did Daniel Zacharias keep his word and pray for the Union forces?"

"He did that very thing. I looked at the general and he was sound asleep and never heard a word of it."

"I guess he was just exhausted," said Susan. "Poor man, he's had so much to trouble him, and in the quiet of the church he relaxed and found peace."

Eli grinned. "Perhaps so," he answered, "or maybe he

• *181*

thought he could save his face by pretending to be asleep. Jackson is a smart man, Susan."

Later, as they were preparing for bed, Hetty said, "To-morrow I'll go to the hospital and thee stay with Kippy."

Susan was too exhausted to argue. Perhaps she should not allow Hetty to go, but then she could send Billy along. Yes, that was it. She would send them both. Eli had dismissed Billy and Billy must be of service. He was strong, willing and badly needed. Some day she would tell Hetty about Randolph Carter, but not now. She was too tired to speak of him. Some day she must know the truth about Calvin, too.

Susan untied her petticoats, and Hetty gathered them up and hung them in the wardrobe. Good little Hetty. She had changed since the night when Peter came to Furley Hall. There was no more play acting. Life at the moment was too grim, too tragic, with all her hopes depending upon the vague unknown of an immense battlefield.

CHAPTER
TWENTY-SIX

Hetty and Billy had an early Monday breakfast and prepared to leave for the hospital.

"Before you go," said Susan, "I'd like to have Billy carry the basket to the store for me. I feel safe enough, but there are so many soldiers standing about, and I dislike the way they stare."

"I don't believe thee'll find much food left in the stores," said Billy, "but we can try anyway. I'll get the basket."

Susan took out her purse and put on her bonnet. It covered her curls and partly shielded her face from the eager eyes of the soldiers. The Quakers were well known for their kindness and Christian charity, and in her plain gray, she moved with the perfect respect of the men.

They crossed the Patrick Street bridge and approached their usual provision store. Before the door a sentinel stood forbiddingly.

"Sorry, miss," he said, with a soft Georgia drawl, "but the stores are all closed. General Jackson's orders, miss, to keep hoarders from grabbing up everything in sight."

Susan smiled brightly. "And very wise of him, I think. Does thee think I could get a little cornmeal somewhere? My sister has a new baby boy, and we can't let her go hungry when the baby's life depends upon her strength."

The guard jerked his thumb toward the rear. "Go around back, miss," he whispered, "and tell the guard that Fred sent you to him."

She nodded gratefully, and they passed through an opening in the arborvitae hedge and so to the back door.

The sentry lowered his gun, blocking their entrance. "Fred sent us to thee," said Susan. "We have a new baby boy, and I must have food for the little mother."

The man was interested. "How's she doing, ma'am?" he inquired.

"Quite well, thanks to the quiet way in which your splendid men have conducted themselves."

"Thank you, ma'am, we're here to liberate you, not to destroy. Go right in, ma'am, and get whatever you need." He added wistfully, "My wife has a new baby and I'd give something pretty to see it. Good luck to you and yours." A sudden brightness appeared in his eyes as he stepped aside and allowed them to enter.

The shelves were all but swept clean of provisions, but Susan was able to purchase meal and some dried vegetables. The butcher who had served Cornelia for a long while gave Susan a fine beef bone with bits of meat clinging to it. She had enough ingredients for a generous pot of soup, and she returned home in better spirits.

As soon as Hetty saw her, she said, "Thee stay with Kippy and get a little rest. I'm ready to go with Billy to the hospital. I ought to have a little experience in hospital work, and this will be good for me."

"No, Hetty, it won't be good for thee. The odors are horrible. The men haven't had baths or clean clothes for weeks and the weather has been very hot. Then there are the wounds, which smell dreadfully, and swarms of blue-bottle flies crawling everywhere. The groans and misery are very depressing. I hate to have thee go, but I promised, and thee go ahead. But if thee gets very sick, come on home."

"I'll come," promised Hetty, "but my stomach's as good as thine. Come on, Billy."

Susan watched them down the street. When they were out

of sight she prepared her soup pot and left it simmering on the stove while she went to care for Cornelia and the baby. She brought a kettle of warm water and filled the bowl on the wash stand. Then she undressed the baby and gave him his bath. He was handsome and healthy, and Susan rejoiced in him.

"I wish Ma could see him," said Cornelia proudly. "She loves babies so much and I don't believe Ezra's wife has encouraged their children to visit Furley Hall very often."

"No," agreed Susan. "Now that Myra has a piano, I guess Ezra will never let them suffer the sin of looking at it."

"Perhaps," said Cornelia wistfully, "my husband will take the baby and me home for a little visit. I love Eli very much, Susan, but sometimes I get homesick for all of you. We had such fun."

"Wouldn't it be grand if we could all go home together?" Susan said enthusiastically as she went about her task.

Slowly the morning wore to a close. Hetty returned from the hospital and after a few minutes went wearily upstairs and fell across the bed. She moaned softly, "Billy said the soup was good, Susan, but I couldn't eat. I tried to drink some tea, but it choked me. If I live to be a thousand, I'll never forget that hospital. Susan, our stables at home are not as filthy as the straw some of those boys are lying on—and the smell and the flies, and even—rats."

Susan sat down on the side of the bed. "I should not have let thee go," she mourned. "How did Billy get along?"

"He was amazing. At first he turned green, and lost his breakfast. Then he seemed to find himself and worked like a beaver. I'm tired, Susan. I think I could sleep. Here are some papers I brought thee to read, but don't let Kippy see them."

She felt in the pocket of her petticoat and brought out the papers. Susan carried them to her room and read the first, which was a Proclamation by the provost-marshal:

To the people of Maryland:

The Government of the Confederate states is pledged by the unanimous vote of the Congress, by the distinct declaration of its President, the soldier and statesman, Davis, never to cease this war until Maryland has the opportunity to decide for herself her own fate, untrammelled and free from Federal bayonets.

You must now do your part. We have the arms here for you. I am authorized immediately to muster in for the war companies and regiments, the companies of one hundred men each, the regiments of ten companies. Come all who wish to strike for their liberties and homes. Let each man provide himself with a stout pair of shoes, a good blanket and a tin cup. Jackson's men have no baggage. Rise at once!

Remember the cells of Fort McHenry. Remember the dungeons of Fort Lafayette and Fort Warren; the insults to your wives and daughters, the arrests, the midnight searches of your houses!

Remember these, your wrongs, and rise at once in arms and strike for liberty and right!

Bradley T. Johnson, Colonel C.S.A.

September 8, 1862

Susan laid the paper aside and took up the second one. It read:

Although thousands of soldiers are now roaming through the town, there has not been a solitary instance of misdemeanor. All visitors are required to have passes and the only persons arrested are those who are here without leave. None of the Unionists have been interfered with. It is not the policy of the commander to retaliate. He pays for everything, the farmers being compensated for any damage done to crops, fences, etc.

Recruiting here goes on rapidly. Within two days five companies have been formed. Pennsylvania has sent nearly a hundred recruits who prefer voluntary enlistment with the Confederate army to being drafted into that of the North.

Susan put both papers in her bureau drawer. When she returned to Furley, she would take them along for William to read. She went to the parlor, closed the blinds and waited for Billy and Eli. She was knitting a sacque for the baby and her steel needles clicked steadily for an hour or so. Billy returned alone. His old carefree attitude was gone as he walked into the parlor and sat down heavily on a chair. In his hand was another proclamation.

"Here, Suz," he said, and settled himself to listen while she read:

Headquarters Army N. Va.

Near Fredericktown, Sept. 8th, 1862

To the people of Maryland:

Within the limits of this army at least, Marylanders shall once more enjoy their ancient freedom of thought and speech.

We know no enemies among you, and will protect all of every opinion.

It is for you to decide your destiny, freely and without constraint.

This army will respect your choice whatever it may be, and while the Southern people will rejoice to welcome you to your natural position among them, they will only welcome you when you come of your own free will.

General R. E. Lee

"He must be a very fine person," said Susan. "I'll save the paper for Pa. Did thee hear any other news?"

"No," said Billy, "except that the cavalry and artillery are nearly all barefooted. I don't see how the army can go ahead in its present pitiful state. More than two hundred men marched past the hospital, and I counted forty-nine without shoes. Some of the lucky ones still had them, but their toes were poking through the holes."

"Poor fellows," mourned Susan, "what they are doing seems very wrong, yet they do it so valiantly."

"I hope they'll put out of here," said Billy, "before McClellan arrives. I hear that he's leaving only enough men to defend Washington and is coming after Lee with a force of eighty thousand. That means George and Peter will be with the army. They've been on their way for three days, and thee mark my words, we're going to see some lively scrapping. If I had a carriage and a pair of horses, I'd move you girls away from here. I guess you couldn't walk?"

"That's impossible," said Susan. "Kippy couldn't stand it, so we're stuck, and we'll have to make the best of it. Somehow we'll be cared for, and I'm not afraid."

Her heart beat madly. Calvin would be with McClellan. What would she do about Hetty?

She went slowly to the kitchen. Eli had not come home. What could be keeping him? A husband, she reflected, could develop into a staggering problem.

While she waited, she wrote a long letter to her father, telling him all that had occurred. It was said that the Union army would be along in a couple of days, that then the railroad would be put back in working order—at least the part between Frederick and Baltimore—and in a few days they would be able to start for home, but before that, she hoped to see Brother George and would bring news of him.

It was late when Eliakim returned. There had been speeches in the town hall and he had stayed to listen. He was in a lighter mood than usual and after supper went immediately to Cornelia. For a long while he sat beside her holding his young son in his arms. Finally, night drew a soft curtain upon the town, and the only sounds were the gentle murmur of the creek, the occasional measured tread of a sentry and the heavy breathing of tired young bodies.

Susan went to the window to say her prayers. This close contact with the outer world seemed to help tie Calvin in with her declaration of faith. She was governed only by the law of God, and as He planned the orbit of the stars, so He would order her own pathway. Comforted, she went to bed.

CHAPTER
TWENTY-SEVEN

The next day was marked by the hurried preparation of Lee's army for departure. There was a growing tenseness in the air, but the little family on Patrick Street carried on with their duties as usual. Eli went out in the morning and did not return until suppertime. He ate in silence and then sat with Cornelia and the baby.

"You had better get to bed early," he advised his guests. "Before daylight, Lee's troops will start marching, and it's not likely you'll be able to sleep after they begin to roll. They'll be coming right along this street."

Before they followed this advice, Susan and Hetty sat for a few minutes on the porch while they discussed plans for the next day. Carroll's Creek had the busy murmur of a stream generously fed by mountain springs. Frogs croaked and gossiped along its bank and fireflies danced upon the lawn. A group of soldiers came along the street and stopped on the bridge. One of them drew a flute from his pocket and played softly while his companions sang:

> How can I bear to leave thee
> One parting kiss I give thee
> And then whate'er befalls me
> I go where honor calls me.
> Farewell, farewell, my own true love
> Farewell, farewell, my own true love.

Saddened by the pathos of the song, Susan seized Hetty by the hand and drew her into the house. She quietly slipped the bolt into place, shutting out the outside world with all its disquiet.

"Come," said Susan firmly, "it's nine o'clock, and we had better follow Eli's suggestion and try to get a little sleep."

Silence fell on the house. Susan felt more relaxed than she had been for a week. The men were going out and there would be no battle sounds in their ears. If McClellan caught up with Lee, it would have to be outside of Frederick. In the pantry, Susan still had half the ham, the sack of cornmeal and a bushel or so of potatoes. They could get along for several days, and by that time the farms would produce more butter and eggs. Cornelia would be able to leave her bed by tomorrow, the baby was thriving, and they had two men to care for them. Best of all, Calvin was on his way. Slowly she stopped thinking and drifted off to sleep.

Then from the hall, a stealthy creak sounded. Someone was going downstairs. Perhaps Kippy wanted a drink of water and Eli was going to fetch it. Eli! A sudden terror seized her. He was sneaking out in the night. He was afraid to tell them. Susan seized her wrapper and wrapped it about her as she followed him to the lower hall. The front door was open, and silhouetted against the night, she could see Eli slipping into a uniform. She went to him swiftly and laid her hand on his shoulder.

"Susan," he whispered hoarsely, "it had to be this way. I couldn't tell her."

"It's all right, Eli. I want thee to know it will be all right. Kippy would not want thee to stay if it be against thy Inner Light."

"I know, Susan, and thank you for just being you. As soon as you can get my little family through the Union lines, take them to Furley and keep them close. I hope I'll be coming soon to bring them back again." He turned to the door and was about to go when he thought of one thing more. "If I don't come back, give this to my son, and tell him to carry on." He put a soft package in her hands.

She nodded. "I'll take good care of it," she promised. He stooped quickly and kissed her forehead.

She listened to the quick tap of his heels fading into the distance. Then, with beating heart, she crept back to her room and put the package along with the papers in her bureau drawer.

Shivering with nervousness she crept to the window and sat in her rocker, tense and apprehensive. Then, unbidden, a verse from her testament came to her: "I will both lay me down in peace and sleep, for thou, Lord, only makest me to dwell in safety." She must not forget that. McClellan's army would inevitably meet Lee's not too far from Frederick, but she had nothing to fear.

From far down the valley, a cock warned of approaching dawn. Faint streaks of light crept over the eastern horizon and reflected rosily against the mountains in the west. A bugle close by sounded a sharp call. It was followed by the tramp of marching feet, the jangling and clatter of harness and wagons, the thud of cavalry hooves. A regiment of Confederate infantry came swinging by, new men who walked briskly with unfestered feet. She saw a face lifted for a moment toward the window and she waved her hand. The regiment tramped on and on, like the waves of the sea, on and away, and she sat staring, fascinated.

The rising sun cast a glow over the marching host, gleamed upon their polished bayonets and the tin cups dangling from their belts. The men took the brightness of dawn as a favorable omen, and suddenly burst into song.

> For Dixie land, I'll take my stand
> To live or die for Dixie.

There was a sharp roll of the drums and she heard a familiar voice above the din say, "Good-bye, Miss Susan."

"Good-bye, J." She waved her hand to the boy and a cheer went up from the company and was carried down the line.

From behind Susan a weak voice spoke. "Susan, Eli has gone."

Susan led Cornelia back to her room. "Kippy, thee must be brave. Don't pretend it's any shock. We all knew it would come. If thee gives way to grief, thy milk will grow feverish and will poison the baby. Thee must keep thy thoughts upon the little one and keep calm."

"Yes, Susan." Kippy nodded. "When last night came, I thought the danger was over. I'm glad it was this way. I could not have said farewell."

"That's just what Eli said, and, Kippy, Eli wants me to take thee and the baby home to Furley Hall until he's free to come for you."

Cornelia was silent. She did not cry. Susan wished she would.

Hetty was indignant. "I think the men are all crazy," she confided to Susan. "They just stand there stupidly and mow each other down."

"Think of the widows there will be," grieved Susan.

"Think of the old maids," answered Hetty impatiently. "As for Kippy, I just hope we won't have a broken-hearted sister to stare into the night. I couldn't stand her grief."

Susan smiled. There was one thing certain: Hetty would never stare into the night for any man. She would get her beauty sleep and then prospect for another beau.

Susan sent Hetty to sit with Cornelia and keep her courage from sinking. Meanwhile she sought to comfort Billy who was disconsolate.

"Pa trusted me," he mourned. "He thought I could keep

Eli from joining up. I tried to, but he wouldn't let me stay with him."

"I know, Billy. Thee's been wonderful. I'll explain everything to Pa and he'll understand. Come now, and try to be gay for Kippy's sake. Tomorrow is another day."

And another army, she thought.

CHAPTER
TWENTY-EIGHT

The advance guard of the Northern army reached Frederick on September twelfth. Their cavalry entered with a great clatter as the first company took possession of the city.

The President had long been impatient with his general for hesitancy in coming to grips with the Confederate forces. He had ordered McClellan to go after Lee and get him, and it seemed that the general was going to do something about it.

As the guard filed past the little house on Patrick Street, the girls peered anxiously through the blinds to watch them. To Susan, and Hetty, it meant the possibility of seeing Calvin again, and perhaps James and Peter and George, but poor Cornelia felt only dread and despair.

"I'm glad we have a little food left," said Hetty. "The countryside has been scraped pretty bare, and another army will just about lap up the last morsels."

"Don't worry too much," comforted Billy. "I hear that the railroad is being repaired, and if Cornelia is ready to travel, we should be able to leave here in a day or two. I'll go out and scout around for news."

"Thee'll do nothing of the sort," answered Susan. "Next thing they'll clap thee into a uniform. Thee keep thyself out of sight."

Billy laughed. "They could clap me, but it wouldn't do them much good. I'd make a poor soldier."

Susan looked at him searchingly. "What did thee ever do with that gun thee had?"

Billy wrinkled his nose. "That gun is a little joke between Pa and me," he said, "only we have never mentioned it."

"Tell me," commanded Susan.

"Well, the other fellows all talked so much about the rabbits and squirrels they killed, I thought I ought to do the same. I went to Pa and asked him for a gun." He paused reminiscently.

"What did he say?" she asked.

"He didn't say anything. He just sat down and thought for a few minutes. Still he said nothing, but finally he went to town and bought me a gun. The next day I took a lunch and went to the woods. I took my time. Squirrels came from the trees as they always had, to beg a bit of bread."

Susan smiled. "What happened?"

"Nothing. When I got home, Pa was sitting on the porch reading. He just looked up and said, 'Well, Billy, how are things in the woods?' 'All doing well, Pa,' I said. I put that gun away and I haven't touched it since."

Billy hesitated and grew thoughtful. "As for all this fighting," he said finally, "I'll be glad to get back home again where everything is quiet and peaceful."

Susan was surprised. Billy usually had a fondness for excitement. "War is an evil, Billy, and we can't run away from it. If we sincerely believe in the goodness of all God's children, there will be nothing to run from. Nevertheless, Pa will be glad to see us home again."

For herself, she could not be dragged away from Frederick and the possibility of seeing Calvin, but she would be glad to have Cornelia, Hetty and Billy safe under her father's roof.

After McClellan's Union cavalry had entered Frederick, silence of a sort fell upon the town. There was a nervous expectancy in the air while they waited for the arrival of the main army. A few Union sympathizers drifted back to their homes, but for the greater part of the day the street was practically deserted. The sun set below the western mountains and left a curious afterglow which only increased the general sense of apprehension.

Finally, darkness descended on the town. Cornelia and the baby were asleep, and the others were sitting in the little parlor discussing the chances of seeing their brother George. The hospital equipment would surely follow the main army, which was expected on the following day.

Suddenly, there was a quick insistent tap at the window. Billy peered into the darkness and then drew the bar from the door. He was immediately pushed aside as J Scudd shoved his way into the house, slammed the door behind him and fell on the floor, panting for breath.

"Here, Miss Susan," he gasped. "Take these here papers and don't let nobody git them."

Then he fainted dead away. Billy lifted him to the couch and made an effort to revive him. Hetty brought cold water to bathe his head, and Susan hurried with the papers to her room where she put them in her bureau drawer with the package and the proclamations. If people continued to entrust things to her, she would soon need a strongbox.

As she came downstairs, she heard Hetty again at the door.

A Union sergeant was saying, "Excuse me, miss, but I'll have to search your house. A rebel spy was seen sneaking in here, and with so many Southern sympathizers about, we can't take no chances."

As Susan stepped from the stairs, four soldiers entered the house. J was regaining consciousness. They shook him roughly, and as soon as he was able to talk he asked weakly, "You done what I ast you, Miss Susan?"

"Yes, J," she said, "but I wish I understood."

Two of the men walked him toward the door.

"Where is thee taking this boy?" said Hetty angrily. "He's just a youngster and should be sent to his mother."

"Yes," pleaded Susan. "Please let him go. He's no spy. He was just homesick and wanted to see us."

"Kinfolk of yours?"

"No, but we're fond of him, and we wouldn't want anything to happen to him."

"Well, we've been chasing him all afternoon. The little weasel ducked in and out of blackberry patches and elderberry bushes and near about give us the slip. Could have shot him, but we wanted him for questioning. If, as you say, miss, he's just homesick and run away from the army, the colonel will decide what to do with him." They led him away with them.

The sergeant looked with admiration at Susan. "I hope what you're sayin' is the truth, miss. I wouldn't want to see you in trouble. I'll have to search the house."

"Can't thee see that we're quiet Quaker people?" asked Hetty sweetly. "Quakers don't take sides with either North or South, but," she added smiling, "our sympathy is with the North."

"Sorry, miss, we'll just give the place a quick going-over. We can't afford to take no risks."

Hetty went up to sit with Cornelia, who was wide-awake in a moment. "Don't be frightened, Kippy. These are good Union soldiers and they just want to know that they're on neutral ground. I'll stay with thee until they're gone."

"Yes, ma'am," agreed the sergeant, "I won't take a minute." He walked to the cradle and smiled at the sleeping baby. "My, but ain't he cute?" he said. Then he jerked open a few drawers and glanced through the wardrobe.

"Ain't nothin' suspicious here, ma'am," he said politely. "I ask your pardon." He went out, closed the door and joined his companion in the front bedroom.

"Look what I found," the man said brusquely. "Here's

copies of proclamations by the Southern Generals Lee and Johnson, a bunch of papers in an envelope addressed to General D. H. Hill, and a package of some sort. A nice kind of Quakers these are, and harboring a Confederate spy at that. Perhaps that boy delivered Hill's papers here."

The sergeant looked over the contents of the drawer, then searched the room carefully. When he returned to the first floor he was grinning triumphantly.

"Whose room is that up front?" he asked.

"Mine," answered Susan saucily, "and I wish thee would keep out of it."

"You will have to come with me, miss."

"Why?"

"You'll tell that to the colonel in command, miss. It's too much of a problem for me."

"Thee can't take my sister tonight," said Billy stoutly. "She's a lady and she's done no wrong."

"Suppose you come, too."

"All right," agreed Billy. He brought Susan's bonnet and shawl from the hall cupboard and slipped into a warmer coat. The nights were growing chilly and they shivered as they stepped out-of-doors.

"Does thee think we should tell Kippy and Hetty?" asked Billy.

"No, it would only alarm them, and as soon as we see the officer in charge, I'm sure all will be well. Thee knows Pa has taught us, The Lord is our fortress, our refuge and our strength. He will not suffer our feet to be moved."

"I wish Pa could be with us."

"He's with us in his prayers, Billy, so don't look scared. They'll know that we're harmless."

At headquarters the sergeant saluted, stepped forward and laid a bundle on the colonel's desk. "I sent the spy ahead," he reported, "and searched the house where we caught up with him. I arrested the lady because I found those papers in her room."

The Yankee colonel glanced at the envelope. Suddenly his eyes brightened. To an aide he said, "Carry these papers at once to General McClellan."

While he waited, he looked over the proclamations. The aide returned immediately with the announcement that the general wished to see the young lady.

Susan rose to follow the aide. "Don't come, Billy," she said. "I can handle this situation better alone. If they question thee, tell the truth and only the truth and don't let them confuse thee into contradictions. I'll be back directly." She smiled as unconcernedly as she could. Billy looked so wretched that she tried to restore his assurance. Her family believed in her, and she must be strong.

The general and his aides were seated about a table, examining the contents of the envelope. The soldier saluted. "General McClellan, sir, the young lady."

They glanced up quickly and immediately rose to their feet. The general waved her into a chair. "Have a seat, miss. I'm afraid you're in a pretty bad situation. You must tell us the truth at once. Where did you get the envelope?"

"What envelope?"

"This one. It was found in your bureau drawer."

"Oh—oh, thee mustn't touch that, really." Her eyes grew wide with consternation. "I'm keeping it for someone and he told me not—" She stopped suddenly.

"You're keeping it for the Confederate spy who was caught in your house?"

"Really, General McClellan, that is a good lad. He came to our home near Baltimore and was in such a pitiful condition that we took him in and nursed him. We are Quakers and we know no enemies."

"If your home is near Baltimore, why are you here where the Confederate army has just been camped?"

"My father sent us here to care for my sister who has just had a baby and to bring her home again as soon as the railroad is in working order."

"Where is her husband?"

Susan's throat went suddenly dry. "I don't know where he is," she said weakly.

"Is he in the army?"

"Yes."

"Which army?"

"The Southern army, General McClellan. Eli is not a Quaker like the rest of us. My sister Cornelia was disowned from the Friends Meeting for marrying him. His Southern sympathies have distressed her greatly. He only waited for the baby to come, and then he went away with Jackson's army. We hoped that when thee came, we could all go back to Baltimore."

"How did this spy happen to come to you?"

"Let him answer for himself. I don't know. We were sitting in our parlor when we heard a tap at the window and there was J. He asked me to keep the envelope for him and then he fainted."

"Young lady, this envelope contains a copy of Lee's orders to General D. H. Hill disclosing the movements of the Confederate army. It appears that Lee intends to capture the garrison at Harper's Ferry. We'll just send some men to interrupt his plans. Now what's in this package?"

"I don't know, but I hope you'll give it back to me. It's something I cherish."

"You don't know what it is, but you cherish it. Open it, Sergeant."

The wrapping was ripped from Eli's little bundle and the sergeant shook out the contents. It was a Confederate flag.

Susan gave a little cry, and covered her face with her hands. A tense silence filled the room. She felt that they were smirking at her. One of the men said softly, "That's a pity."

The door opened, and she heard somebody enter the room. Then the general said, "Did you question the boy, Major?"

"I did, sir, and I don't think he's a spy. He was selected because of his small size and hillbilly training to carry a letter through to General Hill. He must have taken the wrong fork and fallen into the hands of our outposts."

"See that he's kept under guard—what's the matter with you?"

Susan had dropped her hands from her face. As she rose to her feet, Calvin stared at her with unbelieving eyes. With a little cry, she ran toward him, and he took her in his arms joyously. "Susan darling!"

For a moment he held her against his heart. "Excuse me, gentlemen," he murmured, and led Susan, sobbing, from the room.

"Well," said the general mildly, "while my officer is busy with the witness, suppose we get after the rebels. Lee orders Hill to hold Crampton's Gap controlling the road to Harper's Ferry. Longstreet is ordered from Hagerstown to support him. General Reno, you will advance upon Crampton's Gap and chase Hill out before Longstreet arrives. Be prepared to leave tomorrow as soon as our main army catches up with us. We will follow you immediately and close with the enemy."

Susan heard no more, for Calvin had closed the door and shut them away from the prelude to battle.

CHAPTER

TWENTY-NINE

Stepping into a room set apart for his conferences, the major addressed his orderly. "I have instructions to question this prisoner," he said. "See that there are no interruptions."

The man glanced admiringly at Susan's flushed but joyous face, lifted his eyebrows, saluted respectfully and stood outside the door.

The major's reserve dropped from him like a cloak. "Susan, my precious girl," he cried, drawing her to him. "Never mind how you came to be here. Oh, Susan darling, how I've longed for you."

She sensed the hunger in his eyes, his voice, his hands. Nothing mattered now but his happiness and hers. Her eager arms crept about him as she felt the tightness of his clasp that held her so very close. Finally, he drew her to a bench and sat beside her with her warm curls against his throat.

"Now tell me," he commanded, "and don't let any more tears dim the blueness of your eyes."

Eagerly, she related the story of her adventures. "We wanted to go home," she said, "but we have no conveyance, and we were told there's no train service. Now I'm glad that we couldn't get away. Oh, it would have been dreadful if we'd gone."

He kissed her forehead.

"The railroad officials have thrown every available workman into the task of repairing the tracks," he said. "By Monday at the latest, we should be able to get you through to Baltimore. I'll give you the necessary passes for your family. Don't worry. All will go well."

She clutched at him in alarm. "I will not leave while thee is within calling distance."

"That cannot be for long, my sweetheart. Come now, we'll go back to the council. Take my arm, and don't be afraid."

She followed his bidding, and as they entered the staff room, the officers rose.

With a twinkle in his eyes, the general said, "Well, Major Pancoast, do you have a satisfactory report to make on your prisoner?"

"Quite, sir. She has promised to be my wife. I find her entirely clear of any guilt, you may take my word. She is one of a family of devoted Quakers, and out of the kindness of a big heart she has followed the manner of Friends and cared for a poor suffering boy. That is all, sir."

"And the flag?"

Susan spoke. "The flag was a complete surprise to me, General McClellan. When my brother-in-law went off with Jackson's army, he left that package with me for his baby son. I had no idea of its contents."

"Your explanation is acceptable. I'll return it to you. Some day the boy will look at it and wonder."

"Yes," said Susan. " 'No fountain can send forth both sweet water and bitter.' One or the other must be stopped. I pray God that it will be stopped quickly."

"May your prayers be answered, ma'am. And now, Major Pancoast, you may have leave until midnight. Tomorrow when the main body of the army arrives you will be very much needed."

The major expressed his gratitude, and after a few instructions to his staff, he hurried Susan away.

"Goodness," said Susan, "I'd forgotten all about Billy. He must be frantic about me."

Coming into the room where they had parted, she found him tipped back against the wall sound asleep. She laughed and gave him a little shake.

"Billy," she said, "I was afraid thee'd be worried."

"Me? No. Thee told me thee'd be all right, didn't thee?"

Together they walked the short distance to Patrick Street. As they went, Susan told the story of old Barbara Frietchie and the flag.

"There it hangs," she said. "It's a bit the worse for wear, but it's still waving, even in the dark."

Cornelia was introduced along with little Eliakim. Hetty, she said, had gone across the street to sit with old Dame Frietchie.

"Tell me," she begged, "when will Brother George arrive?"

"They should be in tomorrow early," answered Calvin. "They followed us directly from Washington, so they'll arrive with wagons empty of wounded, and they'll be able to spend all of tomorrow with you. I won't be so fortunate, for I'll have to attend to my duties and I won't be free until nightfall. I'll just have time enough to say good-bye."

"What about our Cousin James?" asked Cornelia. "He might leave camp long enough to have tea with us."

They all looked at the major, who was suddenly startled into silence.

"Did I say something wrong?" asked Cornelia.

"I'm afraid you haven't heard," he answered in a strange voice.

"Heard what?" they chorused.

"James fell at Manassas." His lips twitched as he said it. "He went nobly and you may well be proud of him."

They sat in silence, and then Cornelia spoke. "Aunt Cassandra will die of heartbreak," she said softly.

"She'll do nothing of the kind," answered Susan stoutly. "Aunt Cassie has too much sense to take that attitude. She'll live for her life and his, too. She'll carry on for both of them. It's a great pity, but there's nothing we can do about it now. Come, Calvin, let's go to the kitchen while I cut a slice of apple pie for thee. It won't be as good as Aunt Henny's, but it will taste all right after army rations."

But it is doubtful whether the big major knew what he was eating, for he was conscious only of smiles and the sparkle of blue eyes.

"Tell me," she said, "how thee came to be a major."

"Automatically, I took James' place as captain and then, after the battle, I was promoted."

"I suspect that James was not the only valiant one," she answered.

A shadow of sadness flitted momentarily into his eyes. He gave her arm a little squeeze and did not answer.

When they returned to the parlor, Cornelia had disappeared and Billy was asleep on the sofa. They tiptoed past him and out to a corner of the darkened porch. There he caught her to his heart.

"My sweet, my precious Susan," he murmured hungrily, as he kissed her eyes, her hair, her mouth.

She caressed the back of his head with her shaking hands, and yielded to the joy of his nearness. He was hers, and his arms were so tight about her that she hurt from his embrace, and yet she exulted in the pain. She knew that nothing, not even death itself, could separate their love.

Finally, a clock chimed a quarter of twelve, and he must leave her.

"Good-bye, sweetheart. If I come through, and something tells me that I will, 'good-bye' is a word that we will never speak again. Do you think the Friends will ever accept an old army veteran?"

She considered. "Perhaps not at first, but they will welcome thee in the Meeting, and in time, as thee proves thy sincerity, they will probably accept thee as a member."

"I'm glad I asked," he said. "Ever since that day when I sat in the Meeting in Baltimore, I have thought about that verse, 'Blessed are the peacemakers for they shall be called the children of God.' I knew that your meditative way of worship is what I have wanted and needed. Some day I'll come back to it—and to my Susan. Then, and only then, will my heart find peace."

From her pocket, Susan took a piece of paper and slipped it into his breast pocket.

"A note?" he asked.

"No, it's the ninety-first Psalm. I tore it from my Bible to guard thee from harm."

"I shall treasure it," he whispered, "and commit it to memory so that it will always be with me."

He kissed her once more, promised to be with her the next evening and was gone into the night.

She stood on the porch until he had passed from sight, and she could no longer hear the tap of his boots against the cobbled street.

Suddenly she thought of Hetty. Guiltily, she rememberd that her sister had not returned from Dame Frietchie's. She glanced across the street and saw that a light still burned in the old lady's parlor. Perhaps someone was ill. Susan crossed the street and knocked softly.

The door opened. There were Hetty and a young officer.

"Oh, Susan," Hetty exclaimed contritely. "Please don't scold me. I know it's late, but Mrs. Frietchie has the most entertaining guest. Do come in. This is Lieutenant Horatio Higginbottom, my sister Susan."

The lieutenant bowed.

"He's been telling me all about winter time in Vermont,

Susan. It's the most fascinating story, really. I heard thee go out with Billy and I didn't mean to stay away from Kippy for so long, but I forgot."

Susan smiled. "It's quite all right," she said, "but now it's really dreadfully late, and we must get some rest. Good night, Lieutenant."

Lieutenant Higginbottom escorted them across the street and promised to see Hetty again.

When he had left, Hetty exclaimed, "Isn't he wonderful, Susan?"

Susan nodded wearily. "Another string to thy beau? What will thee do with him tomorrow if Peter comes?"

Hetty paused at the stairway. "Peter?" she said. "Dear Peter. I think he needs me, Susan. I've thought about him so much, especially since we've been working with the wounded. I like Calvin only when I'm with Calvin, but I think of Peter always when I'm by myself. Thee doesn't think I'm in love with Peter, does thee?"

Quick tears came to Susan's eyes. She turned away and busied herself with the blinds. "I hope so, Hetty dear," she said. "I hope so with all my might."

CHAPTER

THIRTY

Before daylight, Susan awoke again to the jarring tumult of an army on the march. She ran to her window and looked down on the long line of Union cavalry coming out of the darkness. She heard a quick command, and the voice which gave it made her heart throb. From the head of the line, a form emerged out of the morning mist, a face uplifted toward her window and a hand was raised in salute. The horses tramped on, carrying their riders into the fog.

There was a knock at the door and Billy appeared with a note. "A soldier left it for thee," he explained.

Susan lighted the lamp and tore open the message. Calvin wouldn't be able to keep his appointment with her for that evening. He had been sent forward with General Burnside to drive the Confederates from Middletown, only eight miles distant. Later in the day, the main body of the Union army would follow them. If there was no resistance, he might be able to return that evening for a few minutes. He would do his best. Her heart felt like a lump of lead, but she knew she must keep up her courage for the sake of Cornelia and the baby.

The sun rose blood-red and reflected across the town and beyond it on the towering slopes of Catoctin. Through a pass south of this mountain, Calvin would be following the Frederick to Hagerstown turnpike west toward the range known as South Mountain. Between Catoctin and South Mountain, the soldiers would cross a gentle valley drained by the Catoctin

Creek. Below South Mountain the road led through Turner's Gap, and before they reached it, they must first dislodge the Confederates from Middletown and then capture the Gap itself. Thus, they planned to close the road and shut off Longstreet's Confederates who were stationed at Hagerstown.

Billy explained the tactics to his sisters by laying two parallel sticks on the floor. "Those are the two ranges," he said. "The road to Hagerstown goes past the end of first one and then the other. Middletown lies between. A soldier told me the town should not be hard to capture, but the mountain pass will be another story. To the south of the next mountain, the Confederates have fortified Crampton's Gap, which leads to Harper's Ferry. All along the east slope of these mountains the Confederate army is dug in and waiting. It's going to be a fearful battle."

Cornelia covered her face and wept. "I wish I didn't know about it," she confided to Susan. "Have the soldiers all gone? It seems so quiet."

It was quiet, quiet with the stillness of an early autumn morning.

"Yes, Cornelia," said Susan, "the advance cavalry has gone. They came in yesterday ahead of the main army, spent the night and have gone ahead into the west. Soon the main army will arrive and the din will start again."

They walked out to the garden and gathered some late flowers, a rose or two and some gentians.

"It reminds me of the silence before a rainstorm in the garden at Furley," said Hetty. "The birds stop their chatter and everything is hushed, waiting for the storm to break."

"I'm glad that the cloud won't burst right here in Frederick," said Cornelia. "I don't want to hear the thunder of the guns."

As they turned toward the shelter of the house, Susan paused to listen. From far down the street she was conscious of a confusion of sounds. As the sounds grew louder she could distinguish the beating of drums, the steady pounding of human feet on the road, the neighing of horses, the rumble of wagons, and above all, the sound of men's voices singing "Onward, Christian Soldiers." Soon the main body of the Union army entered the little town, passed through it and rolled on into the west. But all day long rear troops marched along the street; all day their voices shouted the daring chant, "Forward into battle, see our banners go."

Susan leaned wearily against the window frame. It was all so wrong, she felt, so sickeningly wrong. Some day when it was over she would hold Calvin in her arms, and they would talk about it. They would decide whether war was ever justifiable. She wondered, too, whether her father would keep his calm if cannibals appeared at the door of Furley and demanded a young Coale for the soup pot. In that case, Susan felt the savages would be softened by the love and kindliness in William's hospitality and the guests would be willing to settle for a pig or a sheep.

Now as she watched, she hoped the endless lines of fighting men would soon give way to the hospital equipment bringing George and Peter. Finally, toward night, they came—the canvas-covered wagons for ambulance service.

One wagon detached itself from the train, and pulled into the side yard. George sprang eagerly out of it, to be welcomed by his family. He was not surprised to find his sisters and Billy, for his father had written him that they were with Cornelia. He was relieved to know that they were safe but he was distressed to learn of Eli's enlistment. With pride, his sisters exhibited young Eli, and George was generous in his admiration.

"I can't stay," he said, "but Peter will be somewhere along the line. Our wagons got separated. He knows you're here, and as soon as we make camp, you'll more than likely see him."

He sprang back into the covered wagon, the driver yanked

at the tired horses and the ambulance fell back into line.

In vain, Hetty's eyes searched each passing vehicle. There was no evidence of Peter. When the last wagon had rumbled by, the girls went indoors and made some pretense of eating supper.

Shortly after dark, a horse galloped down the street, and stopped before the house. It was Peter. Susan, Billy and Cornelia tactfully withdrew to the second floor, leaving Hetty to find her happiness.

Peter had taken time to shave, but his face was gaunt and haggard. He reached out to Hetty with all the hunger of a starved heart.

"Is thee—is thee just a little glad to see me?" he whispered. "I'm not much of a man, but all that I am is thine. I've thought of thee constantly and only the hope of seeing thee has made life bearable in spite of the work and exhaustion."

"And I've thought of thee, too, dear Peter. I didn't know how much I cared until thee went away into the battle area. Working here among the wounded, it came to me just how fortunate I am to have such a man as thee."

They were happy in their love until it was time for Peter to leave.

At daybreak, the Union army would advance to the attack. A pitiful five thousand gallant Confederates had been left to guard the mountain pass after they had marched all the way from Richmond with a deficient commissariat, inadequate clothing and courageous but untrained officers. The battle was imminent, and George and Peter with the hospital wagons containing first-aid equipment must therefore stay behind the Federal line ready for the tireless action that would be required of them.

After Peter had gone, Billy went downstairs to the sofa, and soon slept serenely. Susan sat at the front windows watching the mountains, blue-black against the starry sky. Somewhere not far away, a tall major would be at his task. He had not come to her, and Susan knew that he could not leave his men. Perhaps his hand sometimes strayed to the bit of paper folded over his heart, a bit of paper and the dry bud of a green rose.

"He shall cover me with His feathers, and under His wings shall I trust. His truth shall be my shield and buckler."

In the back room, a bed creaked as Cornelia tossed restlessly beside her baby.

There was a light step in the room, and Hetty came slowly to the window to sit beside Susan.

"Darling Susan, I have something wonderful to tell thee," she whispered.

"Peter?"

"Yes, Susan, I'm going to marry Peter."

For answer, Susan laid her head against the window sill and wept softly.

Hetty touched her gently. "Isn't thee glad, Susan?"

"Yes, dear, I can't tell thee how happy I am."

Hetty reached out and took Susan's hand in hers. It was icy-cold. "Is thee crying for our boys out there beyond the mountain? George and Peter will be fairly safe behind the lines." She waited a moment and then said, "Susan dear, I'm going to get thee some hot tea. Thee isn't thinking of that handsome Captain Carter, is thee?"

Susan shook her head. "No, Hetty, I didn't tell thee. He's dead."

"Dead? No, Susan," Hetty moaned softly. "And James is dead, too. I heard about it from Billy. Was thee thinking about someone else?"

"Yes, Hetty." Now that the time was right, the confession came easily, just as William had predicted. "It's—it's Calvin. I've loved him ever since that first evening when he came with James."

"Susan!" Hetty was shocked. "Why didn't thee tell me?"

"I didn't know what to do. When we came home from Washington, I told Pa all about it and he wanted me to wait. We all felt that Peter was so right for thee, and we wanted thee to find it out all by thyself. It is better this way."

"Does—does Calvin know?"

"Yes, dear. He was here last evening and we will be married as soon as possible."

Hetty was silent for a moment. Then she said in a subdued voice, "What must he think of me?"

Susan gave her a gentle hug. "He thinks thee is going to be the best little sister a man could possibly have. But now I suppose we really should be in bed. We may be needed tomorrow," answered Susan.

"I'm sure of that—but, Susan?"

"Yes?"

"Didn't the major say we were to go home on the evening train day after tomorrow?"

Susan turned from the window and looked at Hetty seriously. "We can send Cornelia and the baby. I think the rest of us should stay to help with the wounded. Thee can go with Cornelia if thee likes. I'll keep Billy here for a day or two."

"Thee knows I won't go without thee."

"Thank thee, Hetty. In a sense we ought to go. Calvin said so and I know Pa wouldn't want us to send Cornelia alone. He's probably wondering about us right now." She stood for a moment looking toward the mountain. Then she said quickly, "I just can't go and leave—leave him out there in all that horror and wretchedness. I'm a little closer to him here."

"I know, Susan. Let's stick together. Billy will stay with us. I know he will. He isn't exactly the valiant type, but he could carry a stretcher."

So they whispered together as the night wore away.

CHAPTER

THIRTY-ONE

A hush lay upon the valley. The mournful song of the whippoorwill was stilled. A faint breeze fanned the folds of Dame Frietchie's flag, and from afar a rooster crowed lustily and was answered by crowing cocks from all over town. The first faint streaks of light appeared above the rooftops. From somewhere down the street a door banged.

Hetty shivered. She still sat huddled against Susan at the window.

"Is thee cold?" asked Susan in a flat voice.

"No, I have no feeling. I was just thinking of them. Wouldn't it be horrible if Eli and Calvin—"

Susan caught her breath sharply. "I've thought of that, too. They've never met, so they wouldn't know each other, and Eli doesn't know about Calvin. Among so many, though, it's hardly possible."

"It's getting lighter. I can see the mountain top standing out of the mist."

Even as Hetty spoke, a muffled roar reverberated among the peaks. A horse whinnied in a nearby stall, while in the adjoining room, little Eli set up a wail, and with trembling voice, his young mother sought to comfort him as she fed him.

Nervously, the family went about their work. At nine, Susan, Billy and Hetty went to the hospital to help. The casualties were beginning to arrive. By noon, the churches were filled with long rows of suffering victims, but still the guns roared and the butchery continued.

"There's no sense bringing any more poor maimed creatures in here," said Hetty indignantly. "Every inch of space in this town is already full: the schools, the churches and private homes. They say that all the surrounding towns are just as crowded. I've lifted, fed and poured water until if it were not for Peter I think I couldn't stand another minute of it."

With an armful of bandages, Hetty walked down the aisle to help Susan lift a groaning man. Suddenly, she heard a little cry from the floor beside her. There was a familiar ring to it, and she stooped quickly to look at the powder-blackened face.

"Susan," she cried, "come here."

"Howdy, Miss Susan," the boy said weakly.

"J! J Scudd, how did thee get here? I thought thee was a prisoner," said Susan, greatly surprised.

"I done got away, miss. You hear them Yankees call me a weasel? I busted loose jest afore sun-up, and I got ahead of them. Couldn't find my captain, but I hole in with some other fellers. They done give me a gun."

"Where is thee wounded?"

"My shoulder. I'd thank you kindly to git a letter to my mother, miss. It's Miz Elvira Scudd, Scudd's Mountain, Maryland. Tell her I got my dozen Yankees."

Susan felt a wave of nausea. The sweat streaming down the boy's face made little rivulets in the dirt. She took a damp cloth and wiped his mouth and eyes. She helped Hetty remove his coat and waited while a surgeon relieved him of the offending bullet. J would be all right. She gave him a drink of water, promised to write the letter and went to the next sufferer.

As six o'clock, Billy arrived with a pot of steaming tea and some food for his sisters. He had carried a stretcher all day, but hunger had finally driven him home for a bite to eat. Cornelia

216 ·

had sent him off with refreshment for Susan and Hetty. Gratefully, they sat down on the pulpit steps and consumed the food. The tea revived them. It was nearly dark and soon the fighting must cease, although the wagons would continue rolling in with the wounded. Perhaps Calvin would come to Susan.

George arrived with a badly injured man whose uniform Susan helped George remove. She laid it on the altar steps, bandaged the wounds, wrapped the soldier in a blanket, and went on to the next patient.

George took her arm. "Susan, I've bad news for thee. This afternoon, among the Confederate dead, I found Eli. I think we had better not tell Cornelia now. Let her go home tomorrow with the baby, and Pa can tell her. I'll write him a letter as soon as I can."

A sudden weakness gripped Susan's knees and she sat down hard on the edge of a chair. "Poor Kippy," she murmured, "poor thing. She loved him so terribly, George. She has given up so much for that love. All her Quaker principles were set aside for his way of life, a way of life she forced herself to accept."

"I know. Perhaps that's why she loved him. It was because she sacrificed so much for him."

"Thee may be right in that, but I must tell her, George. She must know the truth."

George was firm. "No, she would naturally be upset and that would be bad for the baby. Let Pa take care of it. She'll feel secure with him, and it will be easier for her."

"I don't like it," objected Susan, "but if the baby's life is at stake I guess thee knows best."

"And, Susan—" He looked at her anxiously.

"Yes, George?"

"One thing more and thee had better be prepared. This

battle was no picnic in the woods. The casualties were high on both sides."

What was he trying to tell her? She clutched the altar rail until her knuckles hurt.

"General Reno was killed, and I hear that Pancoast's cavalry got hit pretty hard. I don't know about Calvin. Take it with spunk, Sue. I'm going back there as soon as I get something to eat, and I'll try to locate him."

He patted her shoulder and strode away. Dear George, he was so kind. Hetty and Billy were working at the far end of the church. She sat down again on the altar steps and prayed. God was able to help her, but what was this fear that clutched her heart? Surely, as her father had taught her, God was able to care for his own. The wounded soldier's coat and trousers still lay on the altar steps beside her. She gathered them over her arm and prepared to take them out of the way. Then, suddenly, she knew why the clothes were there.

Some time later George returned from his hurried meal and went to the ambulance wagon which stood waiting to return to the battleground. He carried a lighted lantern. A soldier sat on the wagon seat, reins in hand ready to start. George climbed in and said, "Go ahead. I'll lie down in the back of the wagon and rest until we get out there. Go through Middletown and keep straight to the foot of South Mountain. Then wake me up. The Confederate forces have withdrawn to the south. Longstreet got to their relief at Crampton's Gap and they held out against the whole Yankee army until every wagon load of their supplies and ammunition got safely away from us. It seems incredible."

The soldier slapped the horses' flanks sharply with the ends of the reins, and they started forward on the trot. Two hours later they passed through Middletown, and advanced toward the towering tree-clad slope of the mountain. Finally, they were brought to a halt.

A voice from the driver's seat called, "George, wake up. We're there."

George sat up in the darkness. For a moment he thought he had fallen asleep on the porch at Furley. "Is that thee, Susan?"

"Yes, wake up."

"Where are we?" he asked.

"We're at the mountain, George. Thee told me to awaken thee."

George seized the lantern and looked her over. "Susan," he said in a horrified voice. "What is thee up to?"

"George, forgive me," she begged, "but I had to help look for Calvin. I borrowed the clothes from someone who will not need them again, and I knew thee would be too tired to recognize me. Let's tie the horses here, and start our search."

He was exasperated, but he admired her pluck. Climbing out, he tied the horses to a tree, took the lantern from the wagon and handed her a supply of splints and bandages. Then, taking his instrument case, he led the way.

"Follow me," he said, "and try not to fall."

They stepped into the narrow mountain road, avoiding the dead. Beside every heap of rocks or jutting boulders lay a heap of twisted bodies. It was as though some had died while seeking protection behind their dead comrades, or in their peril had simply huddled together behind some small rock.

At every sentinel, George paused to ask where Pancoast's company had been located. Finally, they found a man who had seen them.

"Early this afternoon, they were up among them rocks at the top of the ridge," he said, pointing upward. "They charged straight up, with Johnnies popping at them from all sides, went right through the rebel lines and broke it. Most of them is waiting for the burial squad."

Susan glanced upward at the steep side of the mountain,

• *219*

dark with evergreen and oak. Beneath their branches was a mass of great rocks, oddly sustaining an undergrowth of sassafras, chinquepin and blackberry. Above the treetops, a few stars shone like tiny tapers against a blue-black sky.

If her major could climb this precipice in the face of merciless fire, she should be able to do it with George to help her. But no, George's hands were occupied with lantern and instruments, and she would have to depend upon herself. She was grateful for the absence of petticoats.

Step by step, they felt their way among the treacherous rocks. George paused only long enough to flash the lantern on the still body of some fallen man or to warn Susan of a jutting boulder. Briars tore at her ankles, mosquitoes nipped her throat, and a branch cut across her face and raised a stinging welt. There was a rushing of wings beside her, and a flock of huge birds rose from the trunk of a dead tree and flapped away into the darkness.

Buzzards! A dreadful nausea and a dizziness gripped her. She couldn't play the weakling now. She brushed her hand across her face and looked up for a moment at the stars. She must not think of the gloom, only of the stars. She stepped on something soft, tripped and sprawled full length on the ground. A deep groan sounded beneath her. George dragged her to a sitting position and handed her the lantern.

With deft fingers he pulled the man's shirt aside.

"Steady now," he said. "You have a bad wound. I'll pack it to stop the bleeding, and then I'll send a stretcher for you." He whistled three times, and two men came clambering to his aid.

"It's hard to tell the wounded from the dead in this thick bush, sir, and so dark, too," said the aide.

The wounded soldier whispered gratefully, "Thank you, Doctor. I'd just about give up hope."

George took his hand. "You'll soon be in a comfortable

place," he said. "Can you tell me anything about Major Pancoast?"

"Yes, sir, and a fine man he was, too. He lies over there at the foot of a big poplar tree. His horse was killed and fell on top of him. We lifted the animal off of him, but I guess it was too late."

Something inside Susan went cold. Her feet felt like leaden weights. She lifted the lantern and looked beyond them. From the foot of a giant rock came a whirring sound. A brown heap lay coiled a few feet away from them. The aide fired at it with his revolver, and it leaped into the air, hissed, squirmed and lay still.

"That's what I'm skeered of," said the man quietly. "Them diamondbacks is plentiful and more treacherous than the Johnnies."

The sickness lifted from Susan. She was not afraid. She had felt no fear of the rattler; she need have no fear of anything. She handed the lantern back to George, and her feet were firm as she followed where he led.

Over boulders, over the dead, over fallen trees—and finally George halted before the body of a great bay horse. He stepped across it and knelt on the ground, handing the lantern to Susan. She saw the light shining on the major's face. George laid a hand upon the pulse, then quickly felt around the body.

"He's alive," said George, "and soaked with sweat. He has a deep bayonet scratch on his left arm, but he hasn't lost too much blood." He straightened out the legs. "Ah, here's the trouble. He has a broken thigh, probably where the horse fell on him, and he's fainted." He whistled again for a stretcher.

Skillfully, he slit open the trousers and splinted the leg.

Calvin groaned miserably as he regained consciousness.

"Never mind, darling," encouraged Susan. "Everything will be all right." She felt the faint pressure of his hand in hers and she knew that he was comforted.

In another twenty minutes, they were in the ambulance and headed for Middletown. Here they stopped long enough to set the leg correctly and pick up other wounded. Then, with George driving and Susan supporting Calvin in her arms, they returned to Frederick.

It was midnight when they arrived. Billy was sitting on the steps, and for once he was worried.

"I looked for thee everywhere," he said to Susan. "I went around to all the places where they had wounded men, but nobody knew where thee had gone. Hetty wasn't worried. She said thee could take care of thyself. If she had gone off in soldier's clothes, nobody would be surprised, but *thee* . . . !"

"Well, we're all safely home now, and, Billy, will thee give up the sofa to Calvin, please, and sleep on the floor?"

"I certainly will, Susan. I could sleep on a rock pile, I'm that tired."

He helped carry Calvin into the house and get him comfortable.

"And now," said George, "I'll have a bite to eat if you can spare it. Then I must get back to my ambulance and to the army, which by now is pursuing Lee into Virginia."

"Because I robbed thee of thy driver," Susan said, "thee'll not be able to lie in the wagon and rest. I'm sorry, George. I gave the soldier a dollar to go away and let me be alone with thee for an hour. Then I put on the uniform and waited for thee."

"Let me go with thee, please, George," cried Billy eagerly. "I can drive, can't I, Susan?"

"No, Billy," said Susan. "Thee cannot go. With Ezra and George both away, we need thee at home."

George ruffled the boy's hair and patted his shoulder. "Do as Susan says, Billy," he said, "but I appreciate thy offer anyway."

After many instructions to Susan about the care of the

patient, George left. At the door, he held her for a moment in his arms. "Susan," he said, "I'll never forget to be proud of thee."

Susan closed the door on George. She saw Billy rolled up in a blanket, but the most grateful sight was Calvin asleep, relieved after his long hours of suffering.

She tiptoed to the kitchen and found a kettle of water still hot on the stove. After removing the blood-stiffened uniform, she took a bath and put on clean clothing, and then went to sit beside Calvin.

He was out of the fighting, but that was beside the point. He must know that bloodshed was not according to the pattern of conduct set by the Sermon on the Mount. The battle sounds were gone and the night was peaceful. For this she felt grateful, and it made her remember one of William's favorite quotations, "The Lord is in His holy temple, let all the earth keep silence before Him."

She sat on the floor beside the sofa, rested her head gently against Calvin, and slept.

CHAPTER

THIRTY-TWO

The Battle of South Mountain occurred on Sunday. By Monday morning more than four thousand wounded had been carried into Frederick. Indeed, the entire countryside had become a vast hospital with every available building packed to the limit. Federal and Confederate sufferers lay side by side, receiving equal attention. Wagons from the surrounding farms poured into the towns, bringing volunteer nurses, bandages and food.

In this labor of love, Quaker and Mennonite worked together, bound by a common desire to give to those less fortunate. Many of them brought Negro servants to help lift and bathe the patients, or change the straw on which they lay.

Cornelia, who wanted to help, contributed all her muslins for bandages. She even presented Susan with a pair of hand-woven linen sheets. "These are all I have left," she said. "Thee take them for Calvin."

For a moment Susan was shocked. "Kippy, I couldn't cut up Grandma's sheets. They mean too much to all of us."

"Thy happiness is more important than Grandma's handwork," answered Cornelia resolutely. She seized a pair of scissors and slashed the sheets into strips. "Grandma would want me to do it," she said.

Dear Kippy. She would never need the sheets for Eli. Much moved, Susan accepted the sacrifice.

At noon, Hetty and Billy returned from relief work. Hetty sank into the nearest chair and called weakly, "Susan, come here. Thee'd never guess who I saw just now."

"I wish it had been Pa. Tell me."

"Not Pa, but thee will be happy to hear the good news."

Hetty launched into an account of the morning's experiences. She had finished helping a suffering man, in time to get to her feet to see a country Friend clothed in plain bonnet, gray frock and white apron enter the church. The woman carried a steaming cook-pot, and behind her came a colored woman bearing such a mound of snowy muslin sheets that her face was hidden. Suddenly the bedding fell to the floor. The Negro woman recognized Hetty and cried out tearfully, "Oh, missy, missy. Oh, where my Jasper at? Where my li'l Jerry?"

Hetty stared with unbelieving eyes. "Is it really thee, Keziah? I thought thee was in Canada. Where'd thee ever come from, and what's thee doing here?"

But Keziah had turned to her benefactor. "Dis yere am one dem ladies what he'p me ter git 'way from dem slave-grabbers. Ask her do she know where Jasper at?"

The Friend set her kettle of stew on a bench and answered Hetty's questions. "Keziah and her six children were passed to us along the Underground on the way to Ohio and the Lakes. Because there were so many children, we decided not to send them immediately to Canada but to keep them on our farm which is a long way from the public road. This is the first time Keziah has left the house, but I felt there would be no slave-catchers in this town today, so I brought her along to help."

Hetty nodded. "I understand," she said kindly, "and, Keziah, I wish I could give thee news of Jasper and Jerry. All I know is that they were sent ahead to Canada. Be patient and as soon as it's safe, we'll see that you're together again. What became of Celey and Jake?"

"Dey workin' on farm few mile away. Dey all right, miss." She was drying her eyes on her apron.

Hetty wrote down the Friend's address and promised to tell Susan about Keziah.

Now, as she related the incident to her family, she felt in her pocket and produced the slip of paper.

"Well," exclaimed Susan, "I wish I'd been there to see Keziah, but I'm happy to know she's safe and well cared for. What did thee do with Billy?"

"Here I am, on the porch," called Billy. "I can see smoke, and I hear a train creeping up the valley. The Confederates blew up the iron bridge at the Junction, and it'll take a while to get that fixed, but that's only a short distance away. Now we'll be getting a letter from home. Hooray."

An hour passed, and then a livery carriage stopped before the house. The driver set a leather satchel and a large hamper on the porch, and William stepped to the ground.

Billy, who was dozing on the porch, was the first to be aware of his father's presence. He leaped over the railing and greeted William effusively. Hetty and Susan came running from the house, and Cornelia stood in the doorway, tears of joy dropping unheeded upon the infant in her arms. Together they hustled William, the satchel and the hamper of food into the house.

"Pa," said Susan, "here is Calvin Pancoast. He was wounded in yesterday's battle. George and I found him and brought him here, and Cornelia has been kind enough to welcome him into her home."

"And, Pa," exclaimed Cornelia, "do sit down and hold little Eli. I want thee to see how handsome he is."

"Pa, thee should have been here day before yesterday," said Hetty. "Peter was here, but he could only stay for a little while. He had to keep with the army."

"And, Pa," Billy added, "Brother George stopped to see us. He has an ambulance wagon and I wanted to go with him and carry a stretcher, but he said I wasn't old enough. I am old enough, aren't I, Pa? Susan wouldn't let me go with George."

William sat down and received his grandson. "With all of

226 •

you talking at once," he laughed, "I'm beginning to feel very much at home. What a splendid baby, Cornelia. I'm proud of thee, my dear. No, Billy, thee can't go with George, but I'm sorry to have missed him. Hetty, I'm glad thee had a chance to see Peter. . . . And, Susan, tell me about Calvin. Is he badly hurt? And, Susan, thee'd better unpack the basket. We heard that two armies had been through here and we figured there wouldn't be much left to eat. The basket's got a baked ham in it, and cakes and pies and dear knows what else Henny packed. I told her to put in eggs and butter, and if you have a cool place to keep them . . ."

"Yes, Pa," interrupted Susan. "Oh, it's so good to see thee."

Billy lugged the heavy basket to the kitchen, and sniffed approvingly as its contents went on the empty pantry shelves.

"Just in case I don't live until dinnertime," he suggested hungrily.

"Thee will live," laughed Susan, "with all that to live for." But she relented and gave him a handful of cookies. "That may hold thee with us for another ten minutes, and I'll have lunch as soon as I can get it on the table."

Never had a father been more welcomed by his children. He had received Susan's letter about Eliakim's enlistment, and tactfully refrained from mentioning it. Instead, he was warm in his enthusiasm over the baby. When Susan had a chance, she took him aside and confided the bad news about Eli. She also told him of Calvin's plan to send them all home on the first train.

"Things always come out for the best," said William. "I'll send Cornelia home along with Hetty and Billy, according to the plan worked out by Calvin. They have their passes and I'll see them on this afternoon's train. Thee and I will stay here until Calvin can be moved. Then we'll return to Furley, and if thee is still of the same mind, we can have thy wedding there."

"Hetty was going to stay here with me," said Susan regretfully, "but now that Peter and George have gone on with the troops, I know she won't mind leaving."

"About Eli," said William thoughtfully, "while thee helps her pack, tell Hetty not to tell anyone at home about his death. I'll warn Billy. That will give Cornelia a little while to accustom herself to living without him. The baby will keep her amused. When we come home, we can tell her, and I'll be there to help steady her."

So it was agreed, and at five that afternoon William drove Billy, Hetty, Cornelia and the baby to the train.

"Thee must be just as tired as I am, Susan. I hate to leave thee, but Pa says I must. I haven't much choice," Hetty said before they left.

"My bones could ache if my heart were not so relieved," answered Susan brightly. "Go on and take a good rest when thee gets home, and do remember to write often."

She stood in the doorway and waved her handkerchief after the retreating carriage. Then she closed the door and returned to Calvin.

He smiled at her weakly as she knelt beside the sofa and slipped her arms about him, snuggling her face in the warmth of his throat.

"At last we're alone," he whispered. "I thought they'd never go." His good arm went about her, and with a great sigh of relaxation she lay against his heart.

"Promise me," she said, "that thee'll never leave me again."

"I promise," he said, "as long as we both shall live."

An hour passed before they heard William's step on the pavement. Susan hastily rose from her knees and went to greet him. If her hair was in an unusually mussed state, he didn't notice it.

William sat down wearily. "This has been a trying ordeal for Cornelia," he said. "She looks twenty years older."

"Yes," answered Susan, "but Hetty's always good company

and they can keep up each other's spirits. Hetty has changed, too, Pa. This last week she has given up play acting for real life. She'll feel brighter after she gets rested, but she'll never be quite the same carefree child she was. As soon as the war's over, Hetty and Peter will be married."

"I'm rejoiced to hear that," answered William. "Peter's a fine young man, and they'll be very happy together."

"Father Coale," asked Calvin, "if I tried pretty hard, do you think I could learn to be a Quaker?"

William smiled with happiness. "Now as to that," he said, "I'd not be surprised at all. If thy heart is set on it, I'll help thee to study the queries in the Discipline. We'll have plenty of time for it while we wait for thy leg to mend sufficiently for thee to take the trip home. Then, if thy mind is clear, we can present the matter to the Meeting. Dear me, Susan, this is a relief to me. I'd not want thee to be disowned from membership as a Friend because of marriage with a man who is not of our body."

"It's not just for love of Susan," said Calvin, "although there's nothing I wouldn't do to make her happy. When I was a boy and went to James' house for tea with his mother, I felt it then—something different about his home, a sort of quietude and joy. Later, I felt the same thing at Furley, and then when I went to the Meeting with you, I knew I'd found what I'd always wanted. I felt a great joy and a sense of peace. My father and mother both passed away the year I was twenty, and since then I've had to live with my married sister. Conditions were none too pleasant, for they were always bickering, and I've spent most of my leisure hours with James. We were closer than brothers."

"I understand," said William gently, "and I rejoice that thee has found peace. Now go to sleep and have no fear for the morrow."

CHAPTER
THIRTY-THREE

On a crisp morning in late September, William came from the post office with a letter from George. He read it aloud to Susan and Calvin:

> Peter and I are well except for exhaustion, but our condition is so much more comfortable than that of the fighting men that we can hardly complain.
>
> From the newspapers, thee probably knows that at Antietam there has been another frightful slaughter. In this single battle there were over twenty-three thousand casualties, and neither side can claim a victory. We are now camped on the north side of the Potomac River and the Southern forces are on the lower side, both armies crouched like gigantic beasts ready to spring. We will keep on slashing at each other until one side is too weak to stand, and then there will be peace—peace founded upon force. I often think of Shakespeare's words—
>
> This might have been prevented and made whole
> With very easy arguments of love!
>
> Please tell Hetty that I'm taking good care of Peter. I could hardly get along without him. Doubtless she feels the same way.
>
> Affec., George

William folded the letter and tucked it into his pocket. "I'll send it right away to Mother," he said.

A little later, he called to Susan. "I'm taking the letter to the post office and I want to get a newspaper. Abraham Lincoln has only waited for the right moment to present complete emancipation. Now that the Southern army has retired across the Potomac, he may consider this a favorable time."

After William had left, Calvin gave his opinion. "Complete emancipation will cause dissatisfaction," he predicted. "Many of our boys will desert. They enlisted to preserve the Union, not to rid the country of slavery, however wrong that institution may be."

Susan was troubled. She knew that her father would rejoice over so bold a stroke on the part of the President, even though such an action would not be honored in the South.

A little later, William returned with a copy of a Baltimore paper. As he had anticipated, it contained a proclamation by the President which read:

By virtue of the power in me vested as commander-in-chief of the army and the navy of the United States, in time of actual armed rebellion against the authority and government of the United States, and as a fit and necessary war measure for suppressing said rebellion, on January 1, 1863, all persons held as slaves within any State, or designated part of a State, the people whereof shall be in rebellion against the United States, shall be then, thenceforward, and forever free.

When he had finished reading it, he said, "I forgot to tell thee, Susan, that Keziah's two boys, the two sold at Richmond, have been located. They were sent to a plantation somewhere in the Carolinas. One died of a fever, but the other is alive and anxious to join his family."

"How does thee know this?"

"An agent of the Central Committee in Philadelphia was

sent to hunt for them. I hope that by the time we reach Furley, the boy will be on his way to his family."

"Won't Jasper and Keziah be happy to get their family together again!" said Susan gratefully.

Her father looked pleased. "And won't Deborah and William be happy to get their family under their roof once more!"

Calvin grew restless. "Couldn't I be moved now?" he asked. "I feel badly to keep you here on my account."

"Not at all, my son," said William comfortingly. "When Susan's happiness is at stake, it becomes my pleasure to be patient. I've had a letter from John W. Garrett, who evidently heard of thy condition either through Johns Hopkins or my scheming daughter, Hetty. He's promised to get us home as soon as possible, and he won't forget. We can only be patient and wait, since every available space is needed for hauling troops."

Eventually, however, on the fourth of October, William came in with a telegram. "Get thy things packed, Susan. We're leaving. I've talked with the doctor. He assures me that Calvin may be moved. He'll have a wagon here this afternoon at one o'clock to take him to the train."

Susan read the message aloud to the major: "Am bringing the President to visit scene of recent battles at South Mountain. Will pick you up October fourth at two in afternoon at Frederick Junction. John W. Garrett."

They would see Abraham Lincoln again. Susan's eyes sparkled with excitement as she flew about her packing.

Luncheon was over by twelve-thirty, and when the wagon arrived, Calvin, on a litter, was lifted gently aboard, and the horses went at a slow walk toward the Junction. As they passed the Town Hall, they were stopped by a huge crowd who were hoping to see the President on his way back from the battlefields.

He had arrived at the Junction on October first, gone to South Mountain and Sharpsburg, and spent several days visiting other prominent points of historical interest. It had been announced that he would drive through Frederick in time to reach the Junction by two o'clock, where a private train would carry him back to Washington.

The air on this October day was crisp and cool, with more than a tinge of autumn. Oaks, maples and chestnuts were at their most brilliant crimson, orange and yellow. It was as though all nature had hung out her banners in honor of the great Emancipator.

While there were many women lining the streets, some with little children, and a fringe of convalescent soldiers still wearing splints and bandages, the men had turned out in force.

As usual, Lincoln was prompt. A round of cheers greeted him and a speech was called for. But Lincoln answered simply and in a few words, as was his custom.

I return thanks, not only to the soldiers, but to the good citizens of Frederick and to the good men, women and children in this land of ours, for their devotion in this glorious cause, and I say this with no malice in my heart towards those who have done otherwise. Now, my friends, soldiers and citizens, I can only say once more—farewell.

The people applauded vigorously and the carriage moved on toward the Junction.

Promptly at two, the train arrived. The President and his party went aboard, and the major was carefully lifted onto the train after them. William and Susan followed. The train whistle shrieked importantly, and Susan found herself once more face to face with Abraham Lincoln.

He extended a cordial hand and then said kindly, "Mr. Garrett informs me that you are the same little Quaker girl who sacrificed her party frock for the sake of an aged Negro. I had not forgotten it. Now I see that you're in the company of one of my gallant officers. I trust he's worthy of you and I take pleasure in wishing you every happiness."

"Thank thee, Mr. Lincoln." Susan blushed. "I'd be a poor body indeed, if I did not find happiness with so wonderful a man. I only hope I can keep him content."

The President patted her arm and turned to the young officer lying on a couch with a board strapped to his side.

"It's very kind of you, sir, to make room for a broken soldier," said Calvin gratefully.

"Be at ease," said Lincoln kindly. "You and your fellow soldiers did a magnificent piece of work, and you have earned the respect and gratitude of your fellow countrymen. You seem to be in competent care." He smiled and went back to his conference.

All along the way to Washington, people stood by the track to wave a greeting.

"Pa, we will never have such a journey again," Susan said. "It's enough to turn our heads, traveling with the President and getting such a reception along the way."

Their conversation was interrupted by a sudden demand from the President. "Mr. Coale," he called, "won't you join us at the conference table? We're discussing, in a very informal way, certain matters that will be of vital interest to your people."

What did Lincoln want with Pa? wondered Susan. She watched William take his place beside John Garrett, and she noticed with approval the calm expression on the President's face. Perhaps he had that quiet look and manner because he, too, sometimes sat apart and asked for Guidance before he acted. Susan had heard his advisory body referred to as "Lincoln's Quaker Cabinet."

There was that about him which one could feel rather than define. To be sure, his great-grandfather, Mordecai Lincoln, had been a Pennsylvania Quaker, and Abraham's own grandfather, son of Mordecai, had been disowned from Friends

Meeting for "marrying out" to a woman who was not of the Friendly faith. Well, Friends could disown the Lincolns, but they would never stop the Inner Light from shining in his great heart. Now he spoke again:

"It seems necessary that some means be resorted to for further enlarging our army. We have continually urged our men to volunteer, and many have obeyed the call, but casualties are of a staggering proportion, and we must secure replacements. For this reason we are considering a plan for drafting a new army of three hundred thousand militia in the early spring.

"Your people, the Friends, have had, and are having, a very great trial. On principle and faith, as opposed to both war and oppression, they can only practically oppose oppression by war. In this hard dilemma, some have chosen one horn, and some the other. For those appealing to me on conscientious grounds, I have done, and shall do, the best I could and can, in my own conscience, under my oath to the laws. On the whole, my cabinet are sympathetic with your position. They are willing that your Quakers be exempt from armed service upon the payment of a certain sum of money. Three hundred dollars per person has been suggested. What are your feelings in this matter, Mr. Coale?"

There was silence while William reflected. Susan remembered how her father had read to his children about speaking in the Friends Meeting. God had said to Moses, "I will be with thy mouth, and teach thee what to say."

Now William spoke. "Friends will refuse to pay such a fine," he warned. "We will not pay out money to be used for the support of a war. Such a measure would attack the very fundamentals of our religion. When thee suggests such an alternative, thee but beats the devil around the bush. Whether we are asked to fight with weapons or dollars, we will prefer prison and a clear conscience."

The President rubbed his great hands through his hair, and

considered. "I had anticipated that reply," he said. "You will please consider my position in the matter. I want to help you, but I must be fair. There are those who condemn your Quakers for first having done all in their power to encourage and further anti-slavery measures, and then refused to fight for them."

William nodded. "I know this is hard for thee," he said. "We appreciate thy difficulties, but not one of us has ever wanted to settle the condition by violent means. Our only desire was to bring the evil to an end by gentle arbitration. Our Friend, John Woolman, went about the work very quietly. He visited the slave owners. He did not strike them; he reasoned with them and secured their promises to manumit the Negroes. Many Friends followed his example, traveling from plantation to plantation in the interests of emancipation. Given a little more time, we hoped to gain our ends by peaceful means."

There was no answer as the President sat staring thoughtfully through the window at the passing view. They were nearing the city, and the crowds along the tracks were cheering a welcome. He stood for a moment to wave to a group of school children. Then he turned to William.

"If you have my word that the money will only be used for hospitals, educational and other non-military purposes, will that be acceptable to you?"

William was deeply moved by this generous compromise. "Because I appreciate the awkward position thee is in, and because I do not want to be unreasonable, I shall accept thy alternative. I cannot answer for other Friends. Each will do as his own conscience directs. There will be some who will prefer martyrdom, but I believe that most of us will be willing to pay such a fine if it be used according to thy promise."

"Thank you, Mr. Coale. Your understanding is deeply appreciated. I see that we are entering Washington and in a few minutes I will be leaving you." He shook hands with them warmly.

John Garrett accompanied him to his waiting carriage and immediately gave orders to the trainmen to proceed to Baltimore.

It was quite dark when they arrived, but nothing mattered now that they were nearing home. Calvin was lifted gently from the train into the ambulance that awaited him. Johns Hopkins had arranged for it, and Johns was present to welcome them home.

"It's about time thee returned," he said teasingly to Susan. "Furley is not the same without thee."

He helped her into the back of the ambulance where she could sit beside Calvin. As soon as William was seated beside the driver, the horses started forward. In a short while the chimneys of Furley rose above the blackness of the trees surrounding it. Welcoming lights shone from the windows, for Aunt Henny had lighted every lamp in the house and had a roaring blaze in the fireplace.

Tears of happiness dimmed her eyes as Susan saw her family rush from the house to embrace them—Deborah, Hetty, Cornelia and Billy, Frank and Myra. Waddling from her stand at the kitchen door came Aunt Henny. Uncle Toy, of course, was on hand to hold the horses.

It was good to be home again, good to smell the old familiar garden scents, good to hear the night sounds from meadow and creek, good to feel the security of a beloved home.

A temporary bed had been set up in the parlor for Calvin, so that he would not have to use the stairs. He was soon fed and tucked away for the night, with Billy asleep near him.

With a sigh of contentment, Susan crept into her bed beside Hetty. At last she could relax and sleep with an easy mind.

CHAPTER
THIRTY-FOUR

Two days later, Billy brought a letter from Friend Moore in Virginia which advised William that a box containing certain goods would arrive by boat at Light Street wharf.

With Toy to help him, William proceeded immediately to the wharf. When the boat arrived, the box was lifted carefully into the wagon. While Toy drove, William climbed into the back of the wagon and loosened one of the boards on top of the box containing one of Keziah's long lost sons.

The terrified Negro boy peered from the opening. "You Mistah Coale?" he asked.

"Yes, lie still and we'll soon have thee in a safe spot. In three months' time, there'll no longer be any slaves, but we must be careful now."

"I so glad you get me. It powerful hot in dis box, but I get my nose ginst a knothole an' dat way I git air."

William took the boy home and saw that he was fed. Then he drove him to Aquilla Matthews', who promised to carry him on the next leg of his journey.

Had the Coale family been present at the reunion of Keziah's family, they would have rejoiced indeed. It happened on an October evening at a Pennsylvania farmhouse. Two of the children were at the woodpile filling a basket with chips for the morning's fire when they were startled by the appearance of a farm wagon carrying a Quaker man and a half-grown Negro boy.

The children scampered to the kitchen door, calling, "Mammy, comp'ny here."

Keziah went to the door and shaded her eyes against the setting sun. A white man climbed from a wagon, and a colored boy sprang quickly after him. She wiped her hands on her apron.

"Does you want t'see somebody, mister?" she asked respectfully.

"Is thee named Keziah?"

"Yowsuh."

"Does thee know this young man?"

There was an instant's silence while the lad bashfully met her unbelieving stare. Then she quietly held out her arms. In patient silence she had suffered, and in silence she rejoiced. The Friend tactfully withdrew and left the boy to reacquaint himself with his brothers and sisters.

A week later, Jasper was united with them. Through the Underground station in Canada he was told the whereabouts of his family. "Your wife," said the Canadian Friend, "and your seven children were sent by another route, and are being cared for on a farm in Pennsylvania. We're sending you to them."

"How come seben?"

"We found one of your lost boys in Carolina and we've returned him to his mother. The other boy died in the rice swamps."

Jasper bowed his head. "Dat's a big pity," he mourned, "but he wid de angels now. I glad I got seben left. I sho thanks yo'."

Keziah was in the garden when Jasper arrived. She had filled her apron with ears of late corn, and followed by her brood, was about to find her way home. Suddenly, she was startled by a familiar whistle and looked toward the house in time to see Jasper leap the fence and run to meet her. Her hands which were so strong for toil grew too weak to hold her apron. She dropped its corners and the ears fell to the ground. The children, awed by the sight of the father they had not seen for so long, clustered about her, clinging to her skirt. She swayed and would have fallen but he caught her in his arms. "Praise de Lord," he sobbed.

The children, anxious to comfort him, swarmed over him like ants while Keziah laughed and cried all at once.

Suddenly she missed one child. "Where my li'l Jerry?" she asked anxiously. "Where he at?"

Jasper shook his head sorrowfully. "Dat just warn't ter be," he said. "He want he mammy too powerful bad. Ebery day he ask, 'Gonna see my mammy today, Pappy? Ebery day I says, 'Wait a bit, son. It ain't time yit.' He git peaketer an' peaketer, an' won't eat nuthin. He ain't had starch enough ter hold him. I done all I kin."

She sobbed into her apron.

"I knowed it," she mourned. "Knowed when I done left him I warn't never gonna git him agin. Seems like black folks is got a powerful lot ob sufferin."

"Dat right, honey, but us got de good Lord ter brace us an' seben fine head ob chillen lef' to us, an' dat's more'n some's got."

With her accustomed patience, Keziah sought to be resigned. "Yes," she sniffed, "us got good friends, too."

"Come de end ob dis fitten," promised Jasper, "I aims to git mysef a li'l bitty ground somewhere, an' a nice mule, an' I gonna build you a cabin, an' furdermo', I gonna take keer ob you good, honey."

"Dat'll be fine, Jasper." She smiled through her tears. "Come on now, all you chillen, us got a mess ob hard work ahead. Pick up dat corn an' start toten."

CHAPTER
THIRTY-FIVE

Indian summer crept tranquilly into the valleys of Maryland. October days had been crisp and cold, October dawns hoary with white frost, and then in early November came a morning as warm and balmy as a day in June.

At Furley Hall, colts frisked in the meadow, and hounds, lazy in the grateful warmth, stretched beside the kitchen door and slept in a patch of sunshine that found its way through the trees. Maples along the driveway made a last stand against approaching winter as they flaunted their red and gold against the sombre background of green hemlocks.

As usual, Hetty woke up, rubbed her eyes and then turned quickly to gaze at her sleeping sister. She did not bestow the usual prod. Tomorrow morning there would be no Susan beside her, and the realization brought a lump into Hetty's throat. What would she ever do without her sister? To be sure, Pa had given Susan and Calvin a house all to themselves and only far enough away so that her family could not, to quote Aunt Henny, "smell ginger cakes burning." There were acres enough, William had said, to provide for all his children. Then, too, he was getting along in years and the nursery business was in need of a steady hand to guide its course. Billy could attend to the growing of the trees, but an administrator was needed. Until Calvin was able to walk about he could sit in the office to look after the books and correspondence, which grew increasingly heavy. So after all, Susan would not be leaving them.

Besides, Hetty thought, Peter will be home some day, and there'll be another wedding, not a simple affair in the Meeting House, such as Susan had chosen. Oh, no, Hetty would be married in her own parlor with flowers banked everywhere, wearing a white gown with a veil ten feet long! For once, she would get away from plain gray silk. She lifted a long thin arm to hold her bouquet of white roses so that she could whiff their fragrance.

This gesture woke Susan who opened one eye. "What's thee acting, Hetty?"

"Nothing."

"Oh, yes, thee was. I saw thee wave one arm toward thy head and I know thee was playing something."

Hetty stalled. " 'To be or not to be, that is the question.' "

"Well, if I am to be the wife of Calvin Pancoast, I'd better get up." Susan laughed. "What a sublime day, Hetty. It was made just for my wedding. Come on." She threw aside the covers and stepped down from the high poster to the rag rug on the floor. The wedding would not be until four in the afternoon, so she would have time to pack her clothes in the carriage and get Pa to drive her over to the new house with them. Everything else was in place. Aunt Henny had scoured the cottage from floor to ceiling, and besides furnishing it in a comfortable manner, William had landscaped the grounds and even laid off a bit of formal garden for annuals.

"I'll plant anything that thee wants," said William, "anything but the green rose. That cannot be moved from its present location. There's a bit of thyself in that rosebush."

"Yes," Susan said, "that's just what Calvin told me. He called me his green rose. It's a good thing for me that we are staying at the nursery, for perhaps I'd not thrive if transplanted."

242 •

"I'd not want thee to go too far from me, Susan," William said softly. "Thee has been my right hand ever since Mother's health failed. Now that Cornelia is with us, she'll take over the household cares. She was very fine about Eliakim, but I can see that her heart is breaking."

"Yes," said Susan, "but little Eli will be a great comfort to all of us."

"I'm sure of it," said William. "And by the way, I've had a letter from Friend Levi Coffin, who is sometimes called the President of the Underground Railroad because he has helped organize the road to freedom. He wishes to thank us for the part we took in getting Keziah's family together. And, Susan," he added, "Mother had a letter from Aunt Cassandra saying that she'll be down for the wedding. She's staying with the Scotts. She said there'd be too much excitement here at Furley, and she wanted to be with Cousin Sarah. She wrote Mother that Calvin was all she had left now, and she'd not miss seeing him married."

"Good for Aunt Cassie," said Susan. "I said she'd take her sorrow nobly, and she has."

At first, Friends had not been too pleased to learn that Susan was to marry the tall young officer who had come among them. To be sure, he had laid aside his military uniform and now went to Meeting in a plain gray suit and white stock with severe black tie. Cornelia had married an Episcopalian and she had been disowned for it. Now she was back again, and sad enough for all her sweet patience. She would be forgiven and reinstated as a member, but as for allowing Calvin to join Friends, the matter would have to rest for a while. Meanwhile he limped into the Meetings with the aid of his crutch, and sat in the quiet with such a look of peace and happiness that it gave the Friends a sense of inner joy to have him.

All through the month of October, the dressmaker and

Aunt Henny had been at work, so that Susan had a fine assortment of stiffly starched muslin undergarments. The sheets and towels were hemmed by hand and embroidered with fine lettering. William had carried some wool to the mill to be woven into blankets and the women of the Meeting had met at Furley to sew a pair of quilts, a lightweight one of cotton for summer use, and one padded with wool for winter.

There were gifts of linens and furniture. The Scotts had sent a case of flat silver and Johns Hopkins, a silver tray and service. No girl could have a better husband or a finer home, thought Susan joyously as the hour for her wedding drew near. Hetty helped her into the starched underwear, and the fine new silk of her dress rustled delightfully as she crossed the floor.

After the wedding there would be a feast. Aunt Henny had polished the silver and mahogany until they gleamed. When the table was ready, Aunt Henny went to work on Uncle Toy with equal vigor. His skin felt raw, but his spirit was untrammeled by the ordeal.

As she paused before her mirror to pat a final curl into place, Susan was conscious of the delightful odors of spicy ham, roasting turkey and fresh baked sweet rolls, and she knew that salads were crisping in the icehouse. Susan wanted Aunt Henny to attend the wedding, but the old woman was horrified at the idea of leaving the food to hands other than her own.

"You ain't hiring any no'count in my kitchen," she grudged. "When dem folks comes hongry, dey don't want no burned cake and dried-up meat." So she remained at her post.

Susan heard Calvin at the front door with Billy, who was to drive him to the Meeting House. The one crutch with which he walked would soon be laid aside.

Susan went down to the carriage and sat with her mother

and Hetty. Her father would drive them, and Uncle Toy would follow with the rest of the family.

The horses trotted briskly along the drive. Susan held her mother's hand very tightly. Once Deborah had taken just such a ride to another Meeting House, and after the service she had come away on a pillion, seated behind her new husband. Deborah had been very happy with William, but who wouldn't be happy with so thoughtful and devoted a man?

They arrived at the Meeting House and the children were escorted to their proper benches. William handed a bouquet of white roses to Susan and another of pale pink to Hetty. Then, on Calvin's coat, he pinned a single green rose. He gave the young bridegroom a loving pat, kissed Susan, and taking Deborah by the arm, followed his children to the front benches.

Hetty and Billy walked up the aisle and stood facing the Meeting. Susan tucked her arm through Calvin's and they followed Billy and Hetty to the front where four chairs faced the Meeting. Billy disposed of Calvin's crutch and they were all seated.

The room was very still. Susan thought of all the hours she had spent here in quiet devotion among the people she loved. "He maketh me to lie down in green pastures; He leadeth me beside still waters." Now she was about to take a man's happiness into her keeping. God would make her faithful to her trust.

She looked at Calvin and smiled, and at once he took her hand in his and they stood together. She handed her flowers to Hetty, and with her right hand firmly in his, she heard him take his vow:

"In the presence of God and before these our Friends, I, Calvin Pancoast, take thee, Susan Coale, to be my wife, promising with Divine assistance to be unto thee a loving and faithful husband so long as we both shall live."

It was very still in the large room. Then Susan spoke:

"In the presence of God and before these our Friends, I, Susan Coale, take thee, Calvin Pancoast, to be my husband, promising with Divine assistance to be unto thee a loving and faithful wife so long as we both shall live."

They sat down again and a marriage contract was brought for them to sign. It stated simply that whereas Susan and Calvin had expressed a desire to unite in holy matrimony, and a committee from the Meeting had waited upon them and found the marriage suitable, they had met together on this 5th day of November, 1862, and in the presence of God and before the undersigned Friends had taken their vows.

They signed it.

Calvin Pancoast
Susan Pancoast

The contract was handed to the clerk of the Meeting. Later, the Friends present would sign it as witnesses, and then it would be copied into the record book.

Silence settled upon the Meeting once more. Finally, a Friend spoke, giving words of advice. Another prayed for the success and happiness of the young people. The Friends turned to one another and started to shake hands. The wedding was over.

Billy handed the crutch to Calvin and Susan took her flowers from Hetty, and together they walked down the aisle and out into the late autumn sunshine.

Old Toy waited with the carriage. "Mistah Willum," he had said, "you kin take Miss Susan to de Meetin' House but please, suh, let me fetch her home."

So they drove home alone except for Toy who sat chuckling on the front seat. A soft Indian summer haze purpled the horizon and all about them crimson and gold leaves fluttered down, carpeting the roadway in splendor.

"God has been good to us," she whispered.

He held her hand quietly in his. "Yes, my sweetheart. 'Surely goodness and mercy shall follow us all the days of our lives.'"